ATHENA

Parthenos / Promachus

Huck Fairman

Copyright © 2014 by Huck Fairman.

Library of Congress Control Number: 2014914945
ISBN: Hardcover 978-1-4990-6493-3
Softcover 978-1-4990-6492-6
eBook 978-1-4990-6491-9

All rights reserved. No part of this book may be reproduced or transmitted in any form or by any means, electronic or mechanical, including photocopying, recording, or by any information storage and retrieval system, without permission in writing from the copyright owner.

This is a work of fiction. Names, characters, places and incidents either are the product of the author's imagination or are used fictitiously, and any resemblance to any actual persons, living or dead, events, or locales is entirely coincidental.

Any people depicted in stock imagery provided by Thinkstock are models, and such images are being used for illustrative purposes only.
Certain stock imagery © Thinkstock.

Print information available on the last page.

Rev. date: 02/09/2016

To order additional copies of this book, contact:
Xlibris
1-888-795-4274
www.Xlibris.com
Orders@Xlibris.com
665675

My deep appreciation to Ellie Whitney

For her editing and friendship.

I.

Morning mist obscures the rising plain as clouds of white haze sweep over the ground-hugging fog blown in from the sea by the blustering, whistling wind. The sun begins burning through the layers as we march, calling the moisture back up to the heavens, to be inhaled by the Gods. And now, through the last wisps, we see something massive, the color of bleached bone, blotting out the sky, filling us with awe, the ancient walls calling us back to the past. We knew they were there but were not prepared.

Glancing at each other, we find only resignation at the prospect of our ignominious defeat. No glints remain of the camaraderie we shared on the wooden decks, crossing the white-waved Aegean. Our eyes ... our saddened eyes stare unblinking like sculpted Athena or Odysseus, before our attention is drawn back to the daunting citadel. Despite the distance, it pulses in the brightening sun; infused with Apollo's light, it seems to edge our way, the glare blinding us as if Achaeans landed on the burning shores of Troy. How to avoid the paths of our predecessors, their roads to ruin? Peering through the slanted shafts of sunlight dancing on the columns, can we not discern the cracks and flaws, or detect flashes from the spearheads winking at our folly? The Scaean gate slowly opens, its creaks and groans echoing in the wind, unleashing figures from that storied past. Their rumble shudders through the soil of my soul. The growing clamor soon to envelop us is the clatter of countless chariots and stamping hooves, the tramp and cries of spearmen massed square upon square, history's hoplites, armored in antagonism, surging down upon us.

At my side walks flashing-eyed Athena, my secret name for my gray-eyed wife, the architect of our trip, although Hera might be more apt, if a heresy. Yet either name better suits her than her given name, Belle, chosen by her mother, though kind and smart, misjudged her daughter, kindred, I feel, to Athena Promachus, the battle-goddess, presiding over Athens, ready to hurl her spears or fierce invectives upon all who would threaten. And yet Athena has another side, clear-eyed and kind Parthenos, as wise Odysseus was to learn. But whichever incarnation, she was a striking figure, as is my wife, although her fair features are too easily striped by the strident anger of an immortal crossed in purpose. Indeed how human were all those Gods, conceived by man and yet somehow transcendent ... with whom we yearn to speak, flawed though they were – before they were swept into history by their successor.

What now can they teach us? As we climb the winding road, my Athena shows no interest in those ancient personages, save for her gray-eyed mentor, casting her inquiring gaze ahead to that deity's temple. For it is toward that monument we hike this morning. Her whispers awakened us early, to break our fast and ascend her heights, before the armies of tourists, our modern mercenaries, rush forward cameras at the ready. This day marks the beginning of the second week of our anniversary trip, but things between us have not gone well, have indeed plummeted further into grim Hephaestus's world of fires. I could list the causes, but now is not propitious.

He follows behind at several paces, though out of contrition or preoccupation, I cannot tell. Whatever the cause, it brings me little relief. We'd hoped this trip would resurrect our marriage, reawaken our conversation, but all continues only to wear away.

In the beginning we were a resplendent couple, our luminescence lasting a decade and more. But what then happened, and how to understand? This revisiting circles endlessly through my mind; the disappointments expand, straining seams. He's hardly the man I married, whose name, Wren, I thought honored the great architect, or suggested architectural innovation.

At least here the weather's cleared, the fog's blown off. The sun shines on the great white rocks that gleam around its base, appearing to mesmerize him, conjuring some dream, I suppose. He is, I've come to see, a man of dreams.

We've made our way up from the agora, to the ancient entrance, in among the scant remains of small temples, to the magnificent Parthenon, which I have not visited since I was a little girl. The awe I felt at being in her presence sweeps back, despite cables and cranes draping the site with crawling renovation, clawing back portions of its magnificence, which summons those few enlightened, miraculous, centuries I've studied, when wisdom, language, and reason leapt to new heights, before the city succumbed, sadly, as do most civilizations put to the sword.

It is thus on a double anniversary that I return ... to look anew at those ancient triumphs and failures, and our own. How uplifting was the rise of thought, science, and democratic Athens led by Solon, Pisistratus, Cleisthenes, and crowned perhaps by great Pericles, our seminal statesmen, visionary yet flawed, whose policies accelerated her ascendancy and her decline. Where are their successors today? Indeed, down through history, how few have approached their statesmanship and enlightened vision. Sometimes I dream our current leader could take us there, but he is opposed at every step by the small minded and unappreciated by great swaths of our largely uninformed population, nor has he exhibited the audacity he proclaimed.

I cast a glance back at my husband as he trudges along eyes on the ruins. One can understand an architect's interest, but I suspect he hides in this preoccupation, avoiding our issues and his own. This trip was to grant us time to talk, but we have found no way back, remaining locked in old contention. He still imagines great projects, innovative designs, but where are they? Temples or monuments to mankind (that most ironic of terms) and man's spirit? Where are the manifestations of his vision? I understand that most clients herd after one another, but there must be a few who are willing to reach beyond. Yet he has not found them, and cannot even claim a good income from his slumbering career – which he shares too generously with his young assistant, and confidant. He denies all, but I know men's proclivities, the chief markets of their time, and little have they changed. The tomes of my field detail an abject story. Too often I see that men's focus is wielding power, collecting gold and maidens. Seldom do the good ones rise to the top, as swords or guns dominate in the boardrooms or on the bloodied plain. How few have learned from wise Athena, or much of anything these days.

I watch her as she strides steadfastly toward the temple, barely bestowing a sideways glance at the entrance columns of the Propylea or the low remains of smaller structures. I follow with more interest in these remnants and foundations, having studied them huddled at Promachus's feet and having seen the music in their patterns. But my Athena scorns this idolatry, theirs and mine. Neither suits her modern sensibility, certainly not that which placed that grand statue above democratic Athens. But was it any different than the great cathedrals or corporate towers, temples to one power or another? From the function flows the form – Nature's designing principle. And today, while our designs have grown more elaborate and imaginative, none have exceeded that ancient beauty.

Ahead, she strides on seeking a sign from her namesake, to petition some relief, as I might too, if I had belief. What kindness informed that ancient goddess? – she who rescued cast-away, confined, and out-numbered Odysseus? Other tales recount her forgiveness, but also her lashing out, her revenge or retribution wiping out whole fleets, cities, or civilizations. Today people shake their heads at those superstitious times, but I wonder, agnostic though I am, if those deities are now exacting, at long last, their revenge.

As I pick my way through granite block and tumbled column, staring at the outlines of modest foundations, I am at a loss to understand what happened to our marriage, how our ability to talk fell like these pillars. I know I am the culprit in her eyes, as she thinks Margaux is my consort. But that is far off the mark. If I have sought companionship with her, my lone assistant, it is because I have so little from Belle or elsewhere. As Flaubert lamented, we are alone with our creations. My chilly wife disdains my art and wraps herself in Promachus's mantle of infallibility.

Gazing about, I attempt to imagine those ancient craftsmen shaping statues and temples, in contrast to my mostly prosaic projects – perhaps each symbolic of our worlds. I wonder what lives those ancient Greeks might have lived, down on the plain. To what could he, or she, aspire or hope to gain? Were their marriages as fragile? ... Today, without the Gods, and increasingly without their successor, have we in any significant ways lifted our lives? What have I done with the lessons of the centuries? What great love have I embraced? ... My work? ... My marriage? ... We had it, I thought, for a decade or so, and then it tumbled down, as communication and integrity were cast aside. As I peer back through the heavy smoke of our funeral pyre, I can just make out the outlines of our beginnings. But she sees them not at all, and neither of us can recall the feel of connection, nor the sounds and touch of love. Have we become, then, so much matter living out its cycles, reaching for nothing more elevated? Our deep joys and meaningful endeavors too often put aside as we pursue material comfort? What do I extract from my work? Money to pay the bills, but little more. Is this my inadequacy, or my fate? Have I not sacrificed sufficiently to stern Athena or temperate Apollo? ... While I know *my* Athena's answer, I need to somehow reach the deity for discussion and rebirth.

Ahead, the Caryatids, six marble maidens, each individual in her dress and shape, and yet whose gentle necks together sustain the weight of the entablature and porch roof. Their physiques are ideal, perhaps the most sensual of ancient women, and their architecture is perfect for its purpose: structural support in the form of rounded, aesthetic life, beauty and sensuality suggesting goodness, kindness – Nature inspiring and adapted by man. The ancient Athenians sought to balance these things, reaching in all directions, speaking deeply to each other, while today, too often, we shrink our lives. Wealth, we think will expand and free us, and to an extent it does, but we forget the core of things cannot be bought. This they knew, in their simple life, and in the study of their times we may come upon it once again.

I don't know where he went, as I stand at the edge of the great columns. Here we might've spoken of our issues, inspired by the goddess in her temple. Instead he's wandered off. And so I entertain myself by imagining other visitors over time ... armies from all the eras in their vastly different uniforms, camping upon the interior floor. Standing close to where they did, how can I not compare our lives? Today history places us on a rising trend; since World War II, life has improved for many, and the pace of change is accelerating. But this comes with costs, to the land, and to our understanding of each other. Democracy blossomed in this city, but withered too, and the many digressions it has taken elsewhere are bewildering. Men are ingenious in their circumventing, and eschewing responsibility. Like contemporary Greeks, my husband and his clan deny all culpability. Indeed today's Greeks have raised this to an art, avoiding taxes and effective government. Like children, they flee all calls to order, while in our country, the top cry out for lower taxes while their wealth compounds and the middle class declines – an unsustainable trend, leading at some point to outcry or upheaval. Good governance, like marriage, they say, requires ceaseless rebalancing, away from lurching toward extremes. But too few read history's accounts or comprehend its lessons.

But ohh ... tonight ... I'd nearly forgotten – a party! To which we've been invited, outside the city, east along the coast. Some friend of a colleague has a house on the shore. I want to go and suppose Wren will too. I cannot fairly dissuade him, as we are both hungry for conversation. I assume there will be a mix of our countrymen, Europeans, and Greeks. Sadly I've not yet met one modern Pericles or Odysseus. Where do they hide? Their society, like ours, has spent too much gold and now must retrench – a tricky balance in recession, as too many have forgotten Keynes's key. And more broadly the history I have studied these many years has left me with one lesson: that men mostly go too far and change only when skewered by defeat or devastation. Would women govern more wisely? Is it perhaps that our time has come? ... Why did the learned Athenians choose Athena for their god? They must have seen the wisdom and justice she proclaimed. But while I believe improvement would result from female direction and harmony, I know too well that power corrupts and absolute ... absolutely. And if a woman avoided that, still she must work in the main with men.

Yet somehow I feel my life has been a preparation for these coming years. But what form will it take? At the moment I am but a tourist in a stumbling marriage. But as a student of the past, what lessons should I draw upon? Few women are recorded from those ancient times. Cleopatra, Clytemnestra ... Athena ... What need had they of husbands? ... Yet at home, where we raise our boys, I am not free ... But soon. Even Wren shares that dream I think. What I have is this opportunity to appeal to wise Athena in preparation for stepping out on the tightrope, more audaciously, than I have before.

I see her now, standing by the entrance, dwarfed by its scale, and yet as straight and still. At this distance, she is a handsome woman, determined, well-preserved, something I wish excited me more now than it does, but too much acrimony has flowed between us. We have lost our sharing, our common goals and ideals, and any sense of the good, or God-like, in the other. This trip was to bring us back, to our beginning, and our civilization's. We will see if the two of us can learn and start anew.

At home, I search our two boys for psychic wounds, but they hide them well, though some must be there. Sometimes I try to compensate them for these unhappy parents they've inherited; I try to give them love, as she does too, but I fear they see my stratagem. I wish the two could be here with us, but they opted for camp, and maybe a real vacation from us. Alexander sometimes exhibits, I think, more maturity than his years. I hope he finds joy with his peers. And sweet Patrick – Patroclus to his brother's Achilles – is adaptable and ever his older brother's champion. Perhaps they see that other families struggle with their issues. It is for them, in part, that I hold out hope for us. I wish I could give them a hug here and show them this exalted place, but they will have to discover it on their own, and learn to appreciate its wonders, that men could envision and construct this, amid their clashing lives. What a mixed proposition has human existence long been.

These thoughts raise questions around what we should seek from each other, imperfect as we are. Divided in our views by gender, fate, power, culture and cognition, we wander solitarily, occasionally coming together for some joint purpose, procreation, or other primal function, but then drawing apart. I cannot help but wonder if love these days, in our grinding world, is even possible ... Peering at this sad story, from my alloyed, common cast, I understand why the Gods were born.

II.

Under a pink and yellow sky, a taxi hurries them out of the city to the party by the sea. In the late afternoon, white buildings blur in the sun's heat, which burns through the windows into their bare arms, until they shift them into shadow. The steady hum and rushing air detach them from the present, sending them back to the ancient city, which seems, in some ways, preferable, with Socrates and the playwrights wandering the neighborhoods, raising essential questions.

She watches the gliding landscapes, imagining life long ago in the streets and roads and in the modest homes or huts. She pictures the agora filled with farmers selling olives, wine, and cheese, or artisans displaying pottery, cookware, or sculpture. She cannot help but contrast this with our modern life, rushing here and there until we hardly know why, leaving less time to read and think. Even her husband acknowledges as much, if languidly from his office stool.

Her professorship at the state university suffers from this modern expansion, reaching for productivity quite beyond teaching and writing, into administrative tasks, committees, department politics, preserving and expanding turf. Where are the hours in which to analyze and synthesize? – explorations she'd hoped would be central to her confronting history. Where is the time necessary to weigh origins and influence? Instead, the daily details overwhelm the rest, seldom leaving time to reflect.

Likewise with her two sons: what time has she for them, as they face their teenage years? She worries that Alexander and Patrick are becoming independent without profound and nurturing family interaction ... Indeed it sometimes seems they all share very little now. Is this her fault, in not making time? ... And yet there is love between them, the boys and her. Their gender, she knows, is less likely to show attachment, and their parents' differences are likely only to increase that hesitation.

Wrenching her mind away, she sends her attention back to the streaming suburbs. How different life must have been twenty-five hundred years ago, along this then dusty road. How much slower, except perhaps for wars, marching through to a steady drum. At least now, in some of our cultures, many are finally and slowly moving away from violence, from combative competition for land, treasure, and mates. Have we learned enough, possibly from the Cold War brink, or will it take another? ... There are hopeful signs, but also worrisome ones in the changing Earth. How will all be resolved? Does any god attend?

And yet in truth, she reflects, those long-ago centuries offered no books, little history or science, nor any great schools to guide them. What would she have done? Hoed, weeded, seeded a garden and her womb. Yet Socrates wandered questioning life, reaching to its core, and Plato had his academy and ideals to proclaim, though she does not subscribe to all ... Yes, a different world then. Many of today's ideas are much to be preferred, but too many citizens thrash around in ignorance. There is something to Plato's rule by the brightest, but how would he have reacted to women's growing role?

Wren too reflects upon the past as their taxi rushes east. The early residents walking such a road would have stopped and called hello, knowing each other's names. We, in contrast, fly along in a sealed car, speaking to no one, not to the driver, not to each other.

To share his lamentation, he reaches for a schoolboy poem:

A statue stood in a garden, one day as I passed by,
some Grecian goddess in old white stone ...

Gazing from of the speeding cab, each hopes that the party will engage, uplift, introduce them to guests from across the western world, who may bring news of political change in Arab lands and financial crises in Western ones. She pictures the guests as exotic ambassadors without portfolio, and looks forward to encounters with those from unfamiliar cultures, offering tastes of the Earth's variety that she misses at home. Antaeus, their host, has promised excitement and conversation, for which she's hungry.

He shares this yearning, for seldom now do the two of them discuss, or even talk. He sends his mind ahead, to the host's home, about which he's heard. Intimate, of modest size, its curving, concentric walls are those of a sea shell, lying in the sand, Nature's perfect, portable domicile, whose open side faces the windy Aegean, daring it to hurl its storms and waves ... He's eager to explore, excited to encounter the new and novel, bringing life, for he's found that creation bequeaths deep fulfillment.

Leaving the suburbs, they pass small hills, walled residences, and groves of twisting trunks. He glimpses a band of helots marching to Thermopylae, until turning around, he sees, in the dying light, four young men armed only with bottles, blankets, and paper bags.

Perhaps one year before Alexander, an old bearded craftsman, living several hills beyond the city, in a small, white limestone house, shaped that goddess to please some king ...

In those four young men is not something suggested of the old companionship, of comrades-in-arms assembled for glory? He imagines Myrmidons in the mountains of Afghanistan. But would he truly want that stark, brutal engagement? What he seeks is love, somewhere, and expression. Could he withstand the assault on the self he knows, which violence brings? ... Can he even understand where his marriage went wrong, and why?

Pressed by this latter thought, he reaches out, "Have you spoken to Patrick or Alexander yesterday or today?"

She looks over frowning. "Wren, I would have told you ... Have you forgotten the camp discourages parental calls?"

He turns away. Only with this does he understand that his question was to release pent-up anxiety. He'd thought, if he'd thought at all, that this subject was one of the few unlikely to provoke irritation, but here too he was off the mark.

Soon all oncoming traffic falls away, and twilight replaces the last streaks of sunlight with a purple shell, under which they glide smoothly over the narrow road toward the sea. *Thalatta, thalatta*, that double quote he whispers to himself, looking ahead for the first glimpse.

A young boy, leading two donkeys along the road, halts and stares at the whooshing taxi bearing two pale faces away. His eyes narrow as this meteoric life shoots past, void of awareness or acknowledgement.

Now they can smell the sea, the cool, damp air rising from its depths, from skeletons of the ages. They pass several white-pillared entrance gates to drives snaking off through the descending dark. On one, a life-size statue of Hermes, stepping up into the sky on winged sandals, flashes in and out of the headlights so fast he appears to twitch and glare after them.

A pebbled, half-moon driveway brings them to the front door of the quietly reclining shell, just as another couple arrives on foot. These two Greeks are courteous and excited, insisting the Americans enter first, bowing and gesturing in assistance to their English. The Americans flush that they have no Greek to exchange, but all is erased by the opening door and tall Antaeus, a man of a different scale, stepping out to greet them graciously, wrapping his arms around the women and lifting their supple bodies off the stone, laughing as he alternates his welcome between their tongues.

Inside, the beach house's tunnel ceilings and arcing walls suggest a luminous cavern, futuristic, disorienting, entrancing, as the couples follow their hearty host to the inner circle where he introduces them to other guests. Beyond the half-rings of concentric walls and clumps of partiers, the new arrivals catch sight of the ink black sea. Wren's eager glances discover the structure's outer rim strings together bedrooms and baths, while the successively inner, tightly-curved spaces are for sitting, dining, cooking. Along the beach, a stone patio, sectioned by chairs and chaises, suggests a paddock for ancient beasts sleeping on the expanse of sand.

His excited eyes follow the white stucco walls and sensuous, olive-wood furniture, smooth and limb-like. Abstract sculptures reach from roots or laurel branches anchored in the stucco. Light diffuses from hidden sources atop the walls, aided by a few modern lamps whose bending necks and spindle legs echo the size and shape of Sandhill cranes. Already entranced, he is further excited when told the architect may soon arrive. He hopes ideas may flow as seldom they do at home. Only the arrival of the Caryatids might exceed this prospect.

Around them float guests, brightly clad, or draped in simple whites and grays, moving inside or out along the hard-sand beach. Others gather in small bands or languidly trace the water's edge. Anchored at the edge of light in the rocky cove, the long, white hull of a cruising sloop waits motionlessly for dawn's building breezes and captain's course.

The couple separates without a word when Antaeus invites Wren on a tour. Not wishing to follow, Belle moves toward several women surrounding a single imposing Englishman, tanned and presiding in a deep, British baritone. He interrupts his story to welcome her, introducing the three who have collected at his side, one each from England, Spain, and Greece. He asks her who she is and from where she hails.

A smile spreads across her shapely face revealing life and beauty, and from that confidence she offers, "I am Artemis, daughter of the thundering patriarch, yet I reside in the virgin forests far to the west of towering Olympus."

This they like and laugh. "Heavens!" exclaims the Englishman, "our virgin huntress! ... Welcome. And what is your quarry these days, noble daughter?"

Smiling, each in her own manner, the three women look more closely at this new arrival as they await her reply.

"I have come ... to consult with and to petition my sister Athena, to re-learn the ancient stories and their truths ... to reacquaint myself with the wisdom of those times, through which I hope to better understand the trials of my own."

The Brit's cheeks crinkle in restraint of a wry comment; instead he asks, "And what will you offer your sister and her fellow immortals for this wisdom?"

"Why a sacrifice, of course, as would befit the tradition. But I have come for pleasure too."

"Ah, the Greek balance, am I not right, Marcelina?"

Marcelina, the Greek among them, bows in gracious confirmation.

But the tall Brit is clearly eager to express a related thought. "As it happens, my dear Artemis, I too have adopted a Greek name to supplant the 'Henry,' with which my parents constricted me. In these magical environs, I felt I needed something to match the vivid heroes of the past. So call me Argos, wise Athena's second city and Hera's favorite." And he laughs as Artemis's eyebrows arch. But Marcelina calls out, "You have chosen the name of Odysseus's dog. What shall we infer?"

And Angela cries, "Argos was the home of the House of Atreus where murder and vengeance wrecked havoc through generations, where Clytemnestra slew her husband, the victorious Agamemnon."

"Who sacrificed his daughter for war," mutters Marcelina.

"To angry Artemis, as it turned out," adds Angela. The women send glances to this Artemis, before Angela, smiling, snaps, "Be careful, Henry, whose stories you enter."

Argos seems briefly shaken; his face falls, before he asks, "A poor choice, you think? Is that your opinion? ...Does it attach a curse on me?"

But Marcelina rescinds the sentence, reminding him, "That curse was lifted by brave Orestes, and we hope we have learned from those ancient struggles, to move past that bitter cycle of revenge ... Still I would consider another choice."

He frowns. "And yet I like the name, the sound ... But my apologies to you all, and to my Attic host. As Marcelina knows, both my sceptered isle and eternal Greece need rebirth, and why not seek it in the examples from their glory years when they ruled the waves?"

"Hubris, Henry," warns Angela, "has undone many a hero."

He nods but allows that thought to slip away. The women turn from him to their new arrival, Marcelina taking the lead, "Artemis, I am from the north, Thessaloniki. From where in America do you come?"

Experienced at introductions, Artemis entertains them with her story compounded of the personal and the classical, "Many years ago, when I was but a Naiad, my family brought me here from my New York home, to this cradle of the western world. It was perhaps that trip which pricked my interest in the past, which I subsequently studied and now teach at a university. On that trip, we stopped in Delphi for an interpretation. I remember a striking older woman in long robes and blowing white hair whispered that I would find many connections with the ancient world so that it would be wise to learn its tales. I did not quite trust her – my parents said I had but imagined her – yet I remember she foretold that I would marry a builder of temples, and that if warranted, he would build one to honor me. Alas, on that last prediction, she was wrong by half."

"Is your life history so susceptible to the whims of the gods?" asks Argos.

"They seem to have foreseen, in part, my fate."

He laughs. "I would like to hear your story, then, and feel envious that they deem you worthy."

"It was a gift, like many, that extracts a cost," she laments, with both amusement and regret now twisting in her cheek.

"And yet clearly you have benefited from that divine connection, and it is natural that you would find attachment to the gloried past."

"Attachment and affinity. Something about that ancient life is alluring."

"Certainly if you are a goddess," quips Angela. And Marcelina cautions, "But remember that it is a time softened by the haze of centuries."

And now Argos asks more earnestly, "Do you teach Greek history?"

"European history, but starting with Herodotus and Thucydides, then on to Tacitus, Gibbon, and Braudel. There is nothing that can match the depth and breadth of its creations, culture, and ideas. While Europe has had its up and downs, and now with the rest of the world runs pell mell into an accelerating future whose trends may lead us who-knows-where, it cannot be argued against that, at their best, the nations of Europe have carried the world to new heights, and a few barbaric lows. And so

I come seeking insight and connection to that ancient world and, from a vantage close to high Olympus, hope to see more clearly how to judge the swirling changes that engulf us."

"Good luck, luminous Artemis," calls Argos, interested and amused. "I wish you a successful quest. Happy hunting."

The women murmur their varied reactions to Artemis' pronouncement, before Marcelina adds with deepening intensity, "As you know, our ancient citizens took the lead in many things, and then were cast down by their own mistakes, and changing times, which opened the gates to waves of other empires sweeping over them, starting with Alexander. The two centuries, which saw the first democracy, were an apogee upon which we look back longingly. How did we squander it? ... We were a nation of many parts. Phillip and his son briefly united us under their swords, before others subjected us. Perhaps valuing freedom, at the expense of unity, we have spurned communal sacrifice. Even after throwing off the Turkish yoke, we did not hold together. We glory in the individual and die in our fractious factions. With other empires long ago eager to rush in, we, as a people – the Athenians at least – never had the time and separation that Henry's island and your continent allowed, to mature, improve, and pull together. We did not have the time to correct our mistakes, nor have we had the educational tradition which you embody. And people forget the devastation World War II brought us, with Germans, Italians, and Bulgarians ravaging our land. And then a civil war. We have never quite recovered, and are no longer the proud lords of the Aegean, but mere survivors and vendors, each out for himself. We trip over our undisciplined ways. And so visitors, like you, come to study *not* our contemporary thought or affairs but our ancient ones, as you walk through the tumbled-down blocks of our ruined past."

"Marcelina, you are not alone," consoles Argos. "My much-diminished nation also struggles to adjust to its lesser means and prospects. It is not surprising that *metamorphosis* is a term given to us by ancient Greece. It is the paradigm for surviving on this planet."

"But pray tell us, ancient Argos, what metamorphosis, as a businessman and yachtsman, have you undergone?" asks Angela in sardonic tone.

"I got into business because I had to eat, and pay my way," Argos explains both soberly and with pride, not minding his compatriot's tone. "Our mother died when we were young, and our father rarely was seen at home. But necessity taught us well. I got myself to university, where, on the side, I imbibed a lasting taste for the classical world, which I think can teach us much. Indeed I have on occasion looked there for guidance. And so, with hard work, and good choices, I availed, for myself and others, a fortune which allows me to travel theses ancient seas, in Odysseus' wake."

"Let us pray that is the only wake we shall follow," again quips Angela crisply, while Marcelina murmurs with uncertainty, "I'm not sure that I, as a woman, would prefer to live back then."

And Ileana from Barcelona asks with mischief, "Argos, I wonder if in fact you are seeking a route home to your island kingdom and you're Penelope?"

Argos laughs heartily, if briefly, closing his eyes before confessing, "I've twice been down the connubial path. No more for me. I am not cut out to be faithful or domestic, nor father, sparing myself Agamemnon's agony. Give me instead the freedom of the seas; my boat is my castle, and when not working, I sail her on a never-ending voyage."

"Another quest?" asks Angela amused. "And what is yours? dare I ask. They proliferate with the wind."

Smiles move among the women, but in their silence Argos finds permission to continue, rumbling into deeper motivation:

"To capture life! ... You see I have imagined sailing the Aegean in those open ships, so long ago, not knowing what the horizon might hide. What exhilarating adventure it must have been! To what strange places they might have journeyed, across the uncharted world. With each crimson sunset and star-flecked night, who knew what wild shore or beasts or pirate fleet the next day might reveal. And facing that, how keenly alive must they have been, alert in every cell, in contrast to our deadening office days." Now he turns and stares out upon the black sea. "What fiber had those men to everyday raise sail and set forth!"

"Fiber for early death. And die they did by the bucket-load," Marcelina pronounces pointedly.

But Angela, no longer engaged by this subject, instead asks Marcelina and Artemis what they think of our transforming world, one day positioned for advancement, the next teetering on the brink.

Marcelina defers to the historian, who reaches into familiar, if muddy, waters. "Changing yes, in many ways, and with ever increasing speed. I think we cannot underestimate the impact of the internet and the stirrings of democracy, however imperfect are the various forms. Nor dismiss the problems religions bring, nor the changes in the financial and natural worlds. The question is, like the Greeks, what unity of action will we agree upon, and will it be enough, or too late? But then we must remember it is men, essentially, still, who have it in their hands, and they have long undone us with their miscalculations, hubris, and greed. As I look back into the ancient world, and see the errors even their wise men embraced, I cannot but fear the errors which ours may stumble into."

Angela considers this, as does Marcelina who narrows the focus to her own nation, "My country has her feet in different decades, indeed centuries. Too many cultures have washed through, leaving us cynical and rejecting. Too many of our citizens have lost any sense of a wider good."

Angela, still with a slight edge in her voice, queries her compatriot, "And you, Argos, in your petroleum business, you must wonder what the future holds, and must question what your products do to our world. Is there not something evil in this black gold you sell?"

"There is truth there, Angela, but let's not forget the benefits as well. None of us would be here without it. Yet, it is correct to say that it is time for change. But change, on a world scale, will not come overnight. Right now, in the developed and emerging countries, products and the wealth from oil have lifted many out of poverty. Do we thrust them back, if everything is done at once? But yes, gradually we must shift our focus, change our energy technologies, for our own health and the world's. Indeed it has begun. I am not as fearful as kind Artemis, but then perhaps am not as well schooled in her subject as she."

"But in your industry, Henry, I see no urgency in your efforts," Angela replies with a heavy-lidded look.

"Rome, and even Athens," he allows, "were not, as they say, built in a day."

"All things fall, and are built again, and those that build them again are gay," quotes Angela, then asks, "Are we in our Fall?"

All are silent for a moment, before nodding Argos stretches an ambivalent smile across mouth and cheek, and turning to Artemis, asks, "What does history suggest?"

"History, largely written, and skewed, by the victors, mostly men, is imperfect in its lessons, and yet its patterns all-too-clearly are repeated and repeated: ... rise and fall: discovery, innovation, ascendancy, then hoarding of power and wealth, excess, error, inequity ... collapse, devastation ... rebirth, in altered form. We waver on the path between improvement and relapse. We've avoided nuclear war, so far, but now we undo and overwhelm bounteous Nature. So it goes, from the Trojan War, to Aeneas, to Gibbon's bloody tales, on and on into the present."

Again, for some moments, silence prevails, until Argos clears his throat and changes gear, "Well then ... how will you relax and enjoy your stay, in fair Achaea? Are you here alone?"

The eyes of the four women shift among themselves, then glaze over. Though she does not glance at them, Artemis is aware of their reactions, in choosing her reply. "I'm here with my husband. We're hoping to visit the islands, and Delphi, for a consultation."

Smiling faintly, Angela turns away, saying she needs to refresh her drink, but Marcelina and Ileana eagerly advise Artemis of their favorite islands and other attractions not to be missed. And Argos, watching closely, seconds several of these before announcing, "In fact, I shall be sailing among the islands, with my guests." And he nods toward the sloop anchored in the placid cove.

Peering through the dark to the long white hull, Artemis asks, "That is yours?"

"Poseidon is her name, inappropriately to some, I concede, although in honoring him I have remained in his good graces and avoided wrathful seas, unlike one ancient wanderer. Unfairly these days, I feel, the sea lord gets bad press."

Returning to the kitchen following his tour with Wren, outsized Antaeus is summoned by a six-foot blonde goddess from Stockholm requesting assistance with her hors d'oeuvres. Her almond eyes quickly appraise this new mortal of unexceptional size, discovering no reason to linger, and so she leads the host away, leaving Wren standing next to a short Greek man just introduced by the owner but whose name he did not catch. "I'm sorry," Wren apologizes, "but I'm afraid I missed your name."

The other's lips waver then stretch into a smile. Under opaque gray eyes that do not move, he pronounces carefully, "George ... Nes-tor-os."

"Ohh ... the architect ... of this extraordinary house!" exclaims Wren as if suddenly favored by the arrival of Apollo.

"Why yes ... and thank you." Both reflect on this burst of excitement, before George voices his pleasure, "I am pleased to hear that you like it. In truth, not everyone does. Not to own, not to live in. You are American?"

"Through and through, and one who must confess to never having seen such a unique and delightful design, perfectly placed on a beach."

"At the edge of the sea."

"It reminds me of a Nautilus."

"And me as well, which was my intention, from the day I first held a poor dead specimen in my hand, washed up on the sand," George recalls with deep pleasure. "I wanted to return it to the sea. Its shell is the perfect home for a small creature. And now a man. Which god, I wonder, imagined its unsurpassed design?"

"Hephaestus, I'd wager ... although my wife would argue Athena. Maybe they put their heads together. Did you speak to them? In any case I love it."

"Thank you ... And I did speak to them," he imagines with a laugh.

"Indeed you honor them ... May I ask you something?"

"Of course, but if you are concerned about my eyes ... and sight ... why yes, I cannot see ... and have never actually seen *any* of my designs ... though I run my fingers over the wooden models, and the walls when they are built ... And I am blessed with a good memory, from my earlier life, when I *could* see."

Wren feels awkward, and pictures the pain of this, trying to imagine how it must be. Could he survive this Homeric handicap? He extends his sympathy and again congratulates the other, confessing, "I am honored to meet you and walk through your Dante-esque passageways and curving rooms. I love what you have done, and I speak as a fellow doodler, as one who is also in the business."

"Ahh ... well, you are very kind," bows George, smiling genuinely and awaiting further comment. But before any arrives, he appears eager to correct something Wren has said. "Please allow me, dear sir, to say that I do not consider it a business." Having made this correction, he straightens up from his bow, turning slightly toward Wren.

"Well no. It isn't much of one for me either," concedes Wren. "But it's what I do ... What I can ..."

Digesting this and feeling pleased, George wants to elaborate. "What I mean to say is ... that I take it as an honor, a service, to be able to design a home for others ... to design, to bequeath, something that may last, and reflect the Earth's forms and beauty, and in doing so please others, serve them, and delight them, long after I depart." His expression brightens; his unseeing eyes roll back, perhaps to follow his thoughts, floating up near the ceiling where they deliquesce into strange imaginings.

Wren has listened, and now watches closely. Admiringly, he responds, "I commend you, for your daring and its result. Both are noble, and as with Nature, at once practical and beautiful, adventurous and of the Earth ... How I wish my projects could embody some of that, but I would have precious little work."

Inhaling the sea air, gently breathing through the house, George nods, and assembles an idea he has long been eager to voice, "If you will allow me, may I suggest something for you to consider ... a new approach or ethos ... Namely that you be directed by the organic designs of our Earth, and the love that these call forth in all their individual functions and mechanics." He smiles out across the room; passing guests return his smile, unseen by him. But he laughs quietly to himself, and to Wren, who replies, whispering, "Yes, thank you. I will, I will ... try ...Thank you."

George breathes, "No need for thanks ...For all of this is in Nature, to harvest as we will. It has given us everything and more, of what we require. But if you do so, your passion may be noted by the gods, accepted as an offering, pleasing them, who, even more thoroughly than we, appreciate this paradise."

Moved, Wren touches George's arm. "I hear you and thank you."

George again shakes his head as he resumes, "The gods are sensitive to sacrifice, to great exertion, and they recognize the costs to those of us who attempt it. They know that we may win little appreciation from our neighbors. But to those willing to give their all, to show the gods their love, working to add something new – not the golden ratio of man's proportions that guided the building of the Parthenon and all her children – but something out of Nature's endless treasure-trove, from all her other proportions and structures ... well then, the gods may acknowledge this, and just possibly may grant our wishes, from time to time."

Wren feels his cheeks and forehead burning. He is enchanted, if not persuaded. He notices now that some illumination from no discernible source glows in George's features. Is it his companion's own satisfaction? Wren feels unsettled. It seems that voices from above fill his ears, as if raining down from the walls of Troy, hectoring him to renew his efforts, expand his ideas ... The costs will be borne ...

Leaning close to George, he whispers discreet and repeated thanks, with feeling.

"Homer wrote of this," George replies. "It's in our nature, and we cultivate it through our efforts." And he reaches out to find and clasp Wren's arm, squeezing it encouragingly.

But then it occurs to him that he should explain a bit more. "If I have found the way, you might ask, why am I not better known, famous ... rich?" He smiles at his own questions as his explanation is taking form. "I have done my work, expressed my love, but ... selectively, you might say, to but a few clients. I have no goat or daughter to sacrifice, nor gold to pay for favor and temples. My few houses *are* my temples. ... You see I am willing to work for very little; I have no family and few needs. I offer my services for whatever they want to pay, unless it is to some Croesus like our host, Antaeus."

With this, his attention floats off, and Wren's follows, off through the white tunnels, out over the moonless sea whose ripples suggest unseen presences.

But then George resumes his tale. "When I meet a potential client, I ask that we speak our views, our dreams, our loves and lives. I need to hear what the other wants, broadly. And if our tastes and desires align, and they do not always, then we forge a pact which establishes, in return for my ideas, and drawings, my vision, time, and paper, how much the client will compensate me, sometimes with gold, sometimes with food, or a borrowed home, or beach house and housekeeper. Antaeus has invited me to stay here with Ingrid, when he travels."

"How wonderful ... how flexible ... how freeing," Wren exclaims, even as he adds to himself, how impossible.

"Yes, all ... But, I think you would agree," and here George whispers intimately, "the real payment is in the work itself."

Yes, Wren thinks; he has thought this, sung it to himself, felt the tears of joy when his work was good. But often it gets lost in the practical struggles of running his business and trying to make money. Now, however, he smiles with feeling, indeed with love, over these values spoken so directly. And he tells George, "Indeed I agree that it is the work that provides the deepest satisfaction. ... Not always, but frequently. Yet sometimes, if the work is ordinary, and does not ask for something original, I almost feel wrong in accepting payments ... but of course my family must live and there is no end of bills.

"At the same time, I am concerned that a project is not supposed to be about the architect, although sometimes with the leading lights in our field it becomes so ... but rather a project should be about the realization of some idea, or need, coupled with an aesthetic, or image, as this house was for you. These aesthetics can of course coincide, but one hopes that egoism is not the driving force."

George bows again, tipping forward and nodding, but then straightening, he faces the sea beyond, and inhaling its air, says, "Don't misunderstand me, there are many approaches to our work, and to different projects. Life, as you know, is woven of many strands, but frequently we can select those we would weave. And if we can contribute in some small way – parent, artist, creator – we become part of the inexpressible universe which is ever creating, dying, being born. We are no longer lost and alone but have joined with the particles of this magnificent mystery." The soft glow returns to his cheeks, and Wren feels his own eyes filling with delight.

But then abruptly George laughs, sharply, entertained by his own pronouncement, and he turns toward Wren again and breathes, "Thank you so much ... for allowing me the opportunity to say this. For this too, this expressing to a receptive other, is also a joy. I do indeed believe there must be forces abroad and beyond us, though I am not religious. Perhaps they are those we name Aphrodite or Apollo, forces for love and creation, and somehow we enlist or connect with them, so that they assist us in our searching and efforts. I do not think we could do it alone."

And Wren brings together his palms, upright and before him, nodding, as his mind entertains a rush of ideas. He reaches out and rests a hand on George's shoulder and murmurs once more his thanks for the unexpected chance to speak and hear these things. "You do me an honor in sharing this. And doing so surrounded by this wonderful creation. I thank you for what is a treat of a lifetime."

George reflects for a moment, before replying, "I too am honored." Indeed both stand in silent reflection, heads bowed, for some moments, until a woman sweeps up to George, inquiring with concern, "George ... are you all right? Do you need something?"

Quickly he reaches out to her, and she gives him an arm which he follows up to kiss her cheek before greeting her, "Luisa! How nice. How are you?" And they embrace, followed by a volley of compliments and news. Wren watches, pleased and moved by their affection. Does he have any such friend? And in the low light he gradually discerns that George is attended by a woman of sharp features and dark hair falling in ringlets upon her long and finely muscled arms.

George now turns and introduces them. Luisa spreads her wings for another greeting, and Wren does his best to adjust his embrace to the proper pressure, as they shoot brief glances at one another. George begins filling in the background, "Mr. Wren is also an architect, from America, while Luisa and I are sometimes neighbors in Athens."

She steps back a bit, to take in this American, his face, structure, and shadings, while he seeks rescue from her scrutiny in turning to George. Her dark eyes move over him seriously, evaluating. Wren feels them boring in. But uncomfortable in his avoidance, he returns her evaluation, detecting some flicker of disappointment, which frees him from any need to entertain her. He looks more closely, meeting her gaze, hearing her coolly ask, "So, Mr. Wren, from which coast do you come?"

Wondering what this might mean to her, he explains he lives not far from New York. Immediately her expectant expression wilts, as she announces that it is Los Angeles or San Francisco that she would visit, should the winds carry her.

"Well then, Luisa," cries George amusedly, "I fully expect to soon receive a letter from one city or the other, detailing your discoveries, of their best architecture and restaurants, and of course from Napa Valley. I hope you will invite me to visit." At this she laughs happily, before she sighs that such a voyage is unlikely, and places a hand on George's shoulder. Wren stares through a frozen smile down at the stone floor.

George, now wanting to include his new acquaintance, asks Wren what projects lie ahead. Wren mentions several, small in scope, and one which may be open-ended and exciting. George nods encouragingly, but Luisa shows no interest, and so he curtails his description, instead asking George what projects may be in the offing for him.

George lists several possibilities and expands upon his hopes, one of which is for a public war memorial. As he describes his idea, Wren cannot help noting that Luisa's appearance is dramatic under her long, dark, curling hair. Her face seems almost a sculpture with sharply carved lips, flashing teeth, and graceful, arcing nose, all atop a trim, strong body, recalling Minoan acrobats somersaulting over bulls. Her darting eyes convey a hunger, indeed a voraciousness, and her personality seems primed for pronouncement or passion. Her long sensuous fingers might pluck a lyre or bowstring, and she radiates a kind of coiled energy. Wren wonders what one could calmly discuss with one so fully charged. Though gentle with George, she seems primed to joust with him.

As if sensing this, she turns to him, more interested now. He holds his gaze, matching her detachment. Her expression softens but then, with redoubled intensity, she asks, "Have you come to study this house, this structure that is both Mesozoic and futuristic, or are you here to enlist our Gods?"

Both men are surprised and amused by her question. Wren's eyes blink as they attempt to read her, then slide to George, and back again, before he speaks, "George has expressed a timelessness in the organic shapes he has designed here. As I toured with Antaeus, I felt I'd stepped into the belly of some beast from an early time, and was walking through its organs. What thrill this house gives me ... along with some connection to the deep past, to the strange and giant creatures of prehistoric times. I thank him for this inspiration. And now I meet you, who also seem to join the pure energy of the past with our expanding awareness of the present. Where I come from, few embody these things."

For an instant, her eyes grow bright, and George murmurs repeated appreciation. But Luisa's brief excitement dims, and she suggests, "Perhaps in your home you have not noticed them," and she allows a shiver of annoyance. She follows this, however, with a closer look, before she reveals, "I believe I just met your wife, whom the Brit introduced as ... Artemis?"

His mouth parts with unexpected humor. Artemis now? Can it be? "To me, she is more gray-eyed Athena, wisest of the gods."

"Because she married you?" mocks Luisa. "But Athena had no husband."

"... I am aware ... But she reveres the goddess for her wisdom. And perhaps she shares an Olympian impatience with mortal men."

"Who does not?" snaps Luisa, tilting her displeased face down and moving her jaw in unhappy evaluation. George, seemingly taken aback by her irritation, grows sober. "Nature has seldom been perfect in her creatures. Man is both creator and destroyer, like the gods he long ago fashioned. Even as we progress, we navigate a narrow path along the rim of oblivion. Our little nation, once bestriding the Eastern Mediterranean, wavers in the ever-changing winds." And he runs a hand across his brow and unseeing eyes. Then turning more to Wren, he softens his delivery. "While I have not met your wife, how could she not be thankful for the fortune to call you 'husband'?"

Wren stares down at this kind man and inhales discreetly. "Alas … her expectations have not been met. Where the fault lies seems an ever-shifting narrative. But it's been sad to see her discontent spike into anger."

Unable to restrain his curiosity, he glances at Luisa, who appears, for a moment, to consider this, before her features harden, and she stares back at him through continued contemplation.

He seeks to change the subject. "But tell me, Luisa, what you think of this fine house."

Focusing a beam of energy upon George, she expels her feeling, "This house?! … I love it! I could both live … and die here."

"Goodness," breathes Wren, as Georges laughs faintly at the hyperbole. Wren looks more closely at her, but cannot read the thoughts in her darkly flashing eyes. She shakes her ringlets which seem to clash like scimitars striking in the night. He wonders at the conflicting emotions she exudes, before he looks back at George, and widens his stance as if to balance on a tilting deck. Indeed for some seconds, the surface of the Earth seems as precarious as rolling ocean waves. What are we doing here, he wonders, on this ever-changing planet, pursuing our small purposes, too often solitarily? Are we no more than meteors flaring up as they streak into the atmosphere, or planets confined to orbits, swinging close, then away?

By the water's edge, Argos walks with Artemis, two gods jockeying to position their wills. He asks her how she will travel around the islands, and she reports that their hotel's concierge has described several cruises they might take. Argos is silent for a moment, before quietly and carefully warning: "I'd be a little cautious booking some of those cruises. Some are very commercial ... cattle boats, all about numbers, with cramped accommodations and erratic food and service ... Why don't you come with us? The Poseidon has plenty of room."

She pauses, aware of competing internal voices. "That's very generous, Angus ... uh, Argos. But one problem is that my husband must return in a few days, for work, and we must meet our boys when they come home from camp. So we're limited by time. Perhaps we'll only go to Delphi."

"Oh no, don't miss the islands and the sea, a magical realm. The Cyclades and Dodecanese. You must find a way. Delphi does not compare ... If I understand you, while your husband must return, it does not sound as if that is required of you. Why don't you take the opportunity and stay for a few days? You would be welcome to join Angela and Ileana on board. You needn't place yourself under those same constraints. Everyone should do it once in a life time. The Aegean is the birthplace of the gods, and is their gift to us."

Artemis wonders if he conflates himself with those gods, and yet the opportunity sends exhilaration through her. Her heart misses a beat. She breathes to settle it. "... That's very good of you ... but we need to meet our boys."

"Hmm, yes. Well I understand ... But you would return soon after. We're planning a week or so. I'm sure the boys would understand, and be happy for you. And your husband too would not want to deny you this adventure he himself might wish to experience. He needn't fear he'll be cast as Menelaus." And Argos studies her while she avoids his eyes. "It is an opportunity to discover this ancient sea, on a yacht perhaps the size of Ulysses' ships, and with friends. Do you know how few people will ever make such a voyage? To live upon the sea as the Argonauts or the Phoenicians did. It is a different world, a part of the planet which most people will never know. The islands are individual and fascinating, with much rich history, with which you're acquainted. All the different empire armies landing, swarming ashore ... driven away."

A faint smile steals over Artemis's features, though she is not entirely happy with his cavalier presumption. She needs to clear her throat, and her mind, even as she concedes to herself that the idea is tempting. For indeed when else in her life might she do this? And Argos seems engaging ... intelligent, attractive of a type, and Angela certainly worldly. Of course, she reminds herself, the sophistication engendered in a British accent can mask any number of human deficiencies. But then, what is perfect in this life? Certainly not her marriage. And she is moving on; middle age is no longer distant snow-capped mountains. What memories will she carry with her as the years pile up?

Argos glances down from his six-four height at her as she walks gracefully along. Carrying her sandals now, she allows the wavelets to wash her feet, conveying sensuality ... freedom ... the kingdom of the sea ...

Perhaps he sees the light in her eyes. In any case, he feels encouraged. "Do come, really ... please join us. I'm sure we'd all enjoy your company. You can provide the history most of us lack about this center of the world. I'm impressed with the knowledge you bear us."

She places little value on this last inducement. Indeed its disingenuousness is faintly worrisome, but the opportunity shimmers before her like the afternoon sun sparkling in the waves. She cannot take her eyes from it, this light, the islands, their history. Reaching for these fabled island in her mind, she feels them take her in, imagines climbing their hills, wandering their villages. She recalls that Angela and Ileana made no mention of husbands on board. On the other hand, they did not seem like fools. "I will speak to Wren about it."

"Excellent. I would be delighted, indeed honored, to have you join our crew."

They walk for a short time silently glancing out at the dark sea, holding Poseidon's white hull anchored in the night. She wonders if she sees some god briefly surface, stir the waters, and sink again. At some point, Argos remembers something. "You know, our conversation nearly erased a message from my captain out on the boat. He called a while ago, advising that it would be smart to set sail at rosy-fingered dawn, for reasons of weather. And that will require we gather on board this evening after the party. We could stop at your hotel and collect your things. You will have your own cabin on board, but it is apparently important that we set sail early. The Meltemi is forecast to kick up quite strong and blustery in the afternoon, at least until we get down among the Cyclades, in their lee ... So, what do you think?"

Artemis finds this a little difficult to follow. And what of all the others? Has this been arranged with them as well? Perhaps she should consult with Angela. "I'd like to just clear this with Wren and Angela," she says, meeting his waiting eyes, and swinging around toward the house. But Argos, from just behind, cautions, "It's possible they have left. Angela claimed she was tired and wanted to retire to her hotel for a night's sleep, but now we'll have to rouse her too."

Artemis half turns to him. "Well, let me see what they all say." And she walks quickly back. But approaching the house, she sees someone who looks very much like her husband heading off along the beach in the other direction, with a dark-haired woman. Artemis pauses for a moment, now all but certain that it is Wren, walking with a younger woman. Should she run after him? Rising irritation twists into disinclination. No, she will not chase him. Let him have his flirtation. And so, instead, she continues on inside, seeking Angela and Ileana, while Argos repairs to the bar. But her searching through the rooms fails to find them.

Encountering Antaeus, now at the edge of the patio, talking with his Amazon, Artemis asks if he's seen the two. While he has not, he does recall that both may have joined others in a cab returning to the city. Argos, arriving behind, catches a bit of this. "My shipmates have headed back?" Antaeus confirms this probability, prompting Argos to mutter to himself: "I'd better inform them when we sail. The Poseiden will arrive at the dock before that hour." And he rummages in his pockets for his mobile.

Artemis wanders out again onto the sand, while Argos makes his calls, then follows her. "Shall we take a quick swim?" he calls from behind. She ignores his question as she recasts her own plan, "I need to wait for Wren, following his walk."

"By all means. We can sit and have a drink. Here, let me get you one while we watch the sky." Not waiting for her reply, he reverses and returns to the bar. She pauses, wondering about her decision, then settles onto a chaise and gazes out upon the waters.

At the other end of the beach, two dark figures wind among the rocks bordering the sea. They pause and stare out at the lightless waters. When the second moves closer to the other's side, the first reflects, "We are standing much as contemporaries of Socrates, Sophocles, Pericles ... or other leaders of the age may have stood, staring into the night ... Twenty-four hundred years ago. I try to picture them, talking in our ancient tongue. I try to imagine their lives, and conversation ... I wonder if a man and a woman, such you and I, strangers, could meet and talk."

"Classical Athens was famously open, was it not?" he remembers. "And long before that did not Homer arrange a few such meetings? Paris and Helen, Odysseus's several hostesses and Nausica, on his thwarted voyage home. And how frequently did Athena cloak or counsel one or another to allow some conversation?"

"Still women had little freedom, and those tales were mostly cautionary, or moral. I feel they offer us little for the complexity of our lives today. Socrates and Plato doubted democracy and said little of most women."

While his knowledge is minimal, he notes that, "As the family was central to most lives, women were certainly at its center, running the home, I must assume."

"But with limited scope." She looks at him under a darkening brow. "What chance had they to lead a city or write a play?"

"Some were poets while others were central to many of those stories."

"But seldom were they admirable heroines. And today, in our fractured country, we hear of few, even as we could use their abilities."

"In our country as well. While women have risen and gained much lately, in all areas, still we too could use more widely their abilities."

"Here, we are trapped in the past."

"Why do you think that is?"

She frowns and looks away. "We have allowed the oligarchs and army to run things too often. Many Greek men are not adequately educated, and thus are fragile and want to hold onto the little advantages they think they have. And in your country as well. Look at the power your oil men exert. Your Bush family was financed by them."

"While there is truth there, I believe things are in flux. Hillary was our Secretary of State and may run for the top ... Germany is directed by a woman."

"What wisdom has Merkel been allowed to show? She speaks only of austerity, when the problems are more subtle. But she must appease the men around her."

"... Do you feel harried by men?"

She glances at him now with some irritation. "Many buzz about with little or no understanding. They want physical relations, sex, beauty, but little more. Why must we ever have to fend them off? Why to this day do men remain superficial and insatiable? Drawn to appearance foremost, leaving many capable women unsought? It is a weakness of our culture and maybe the species, possibly a fatal one."

"And yet many societies have grown more equitable and just, and men more sensitized. Even my wife acknowledges as much."

"I'm sure she envisions room for improvement."

"Of course. Even I do."

"The ancient Athenians chose Athena Parthenos to be their advisor, Promachus their protector. Homer made her the most interesting, nuanced god. Why did men place her on those heights, and then turn away?"

"Has that not, is that not, changing?"

"In some places. And yet the world stumbles along from one crisis to another."

"There are many institutions and organizations working for improvement."

"Yes, but where does one find that improvement? It creeps along, one step forward, another back."

Once more he studies her as she stares out upon the sea. She seems to shudder in her anger, and her brow and cheek appear, in the faint glow, moist with ocean spray, or irritation. Tiny beads glisten as if in starlight. To him, she seems as if she's stepped out of the surf. But now, with a single shiver, she shakes the moisture from her brow and hair, which for a second forms a cloud suspended about her head, before her breath dissolves it. With fierce asperity, she spits out a concluding thought. "Across the cultures, alas, and particularly in our own childish one, many still live the old, unenlightened ways. What is the purpose of marrying, or bringing children into a world like that?"

While he believes he understands her frustration, not dissimilar to Belle's, he feels disquieted by her anger. Where can it go? Can she even see someone like him who feels he is not so typical? He hears her continuing,

"Through all the centuries … all the lives, all the women succumbing … what has the purpose been? …"

"A question for mankind generally, is it not? … Yet there has been progress … and do we not each shape our own life and purpose, if we are fortunate? Does that not offer satisfaction and promise?"

"Where? … Where is it, and where does it lead? … But to inequity and exploitation, to where the powerful men lunge for control and advantage, while the rest must struggle and be-damned."

"Not if the laws are well-crafted and upheld. Not if the people take responsibility."

"Maybe they do in your country. Not here."

His country, he tells her, is hardly perfect, and yet things for many are better now, despite the constant crises. But he wonders if her personal life is as bleak. Surely she should have found some worthy man, as he found a worthy woman, before it slipped and slid into ruin ... Imperfection wears upon us all ... It takes great strength to withstand. Relatively few succeed. And they probably find some help, as wise Odysseus did, from fair Athena. But what does that offer we ordinary men?

Now she turns sharply to him. "Both countries are run by men. Until that changes, I see little hope."

"There are more women in leadership now ... I think that our laws and structures and education will keep us on an improving path, which, includes as well, new men."

Yet she seems unconvinced, and while he can understand, he feels now that she has receded from him, into her wrath. Would it help to say that many men recognize these things, and struggle too? But he doubts she would hear what he might offer.

And seeming to expect nothing, she turns away, bringing her arms around herself, and stares out at the silent sea.

His eyes fall to the wavelets just visible in the dark. He wonders if for many, maybe most, life is like these little waves which throw themselves fretfully upon the sands, extinguished without acknowledgement or achievement. Homer's tales suggest ways to live, offering examples such as rounded Odysseus, noble Hector ... But how many, then and now, find a path to fulfillment?

He gazes out at the black expanse, which seems empty and devoid of purpose or connection. To his side, he notices that she takes a step closer to the water, but his gaze falls back to the wavelets. He wants to believe that men have made progress, changed their ancient ways, no longer follow every impulse, balance power with just behavior, strive for a greater good ... Many do ... but many not. Indeed his home is troubled by division. Even in his work, he finds few opportunities for real creation. His dreams outpace the circumstances of his life. Should he reign in his fantasies, or pursue them with greater passion?

Glancing at her, hoping to say something of this to her, he discovers she is bending and pulling her shift off over her head, revealing long white legs and underwear. He looks away, but hears her calling, "I am going for a swim. Come, if you wish."

Looking again, he finds her clothing cast aside and her white form moving through the waves. "To the Mother of us all!" she cries out over the waters of the cove, then dives into the black surface which parts and swallows her ghostly outline.

He watches disbelieving, unsure what to do. He doesn't want to swim, doesn't want to undress and wade in. Now he sees her stroking, kicking vigorously. He glances around. Back toward the house, a few guests stand talking at the water's edge. Beyond, on the patio, a woman sits talking with a man tall and shadowed. Wren cannot make them out, but wonders if it's Belle.

As for Luisa, will she be all right? She seems a strong swimmer, of near Olympic strength. What to do? Wait? Walk back? But Belle will not want to see him, and he feels uneasy about leaving Luisa. He experiences an odd trembling, as if the beach rumbles beneath him.

Glancing out, he tries to find her, but can see only faint, fluttering splashes, whose sounds follow at short intervals, before new splashes flash above the surface. She may be out seventy yards or more. Ahhh! he cries, half-audibly ... Then not so much deciding as giving into a gruff order, he pulls his shirt over his head, slides off his sandals, slacks, and briefs and walks, against all objection, into the cool sea. A cacophony of thoughts drown out his own footsteps through the shallows, thoughts which cannot be disentangled or understood. The only clarity is the cold of the shallows deepening as he pushes on. Distantly he recognizes that what he's doing makes no sense.

Up to his thighs, he pauses, searching, catching glimpses of splashes now farther out. And so he throws himself in, ignoring his protestations, and swims angrily to override their clamor. Kicking and stroking to catch her, and to build up his body heat, he swims blindly on. His brain cries at this absurdity, but his efforts overwhelm those cries as he churns ahead, until he must breathe and search. Does he see her? He kicks again, windmilling for a half-minute, then halts, breathing harder, squinting in every direction. But he can find no sign, no motion anywhere. Fear invades him. Can something have happened? Did he veer off course? He swims left parallel to the beach, but sees nothing. Then back the other way, powering, pausing, scanning the dark cove. Oddly now, he notices the ghostly yacht gliding out to sea, its starboard light gleaming like a covetous eye. She cannot have reached the sloop and clambered on, can she? And yet where has she gone? He's never enjoyed swimming aimlessly, to no destination, paddling for no purpose. She did not seem to need his help, but is nowhere in sight. What now? Where to go? The beach is only a gray rim. He really doesn't like floating with things he cannot see, though the Aegean isn't known to be a problem. Has something happened to her? A cramp? ... Is she crazy? ... Is he? He tries to reason, but hears no clear solution and sees no signs. Treading water, he looks once more around the cove, then slowly, back-stroking, still hoping to spot some glimpse, he swims in, and stumbles out onto the sand, more spent than he knew. When he regains his breath, he zigzags along the water's edge seeking her, her clothes, then his, and finding the latter, begins pulling on each piece over his sandy feet and wet body, an unpleasant, resistant task. Only when finally dressed does he see that her shift and things are gone. He breathes and stares for some time down at the incessant waves, eying him and laughing in brief delight.

Unable to make sense of it all, he turns and walks slowly back and forth along the beach, searching much longer than is sensible. Eventually he heads back to the house, past the chair where Belle may have sat and on in among the few remaining guests. Seeing Antaeus at the bar entwined with his Amazon, he asks if he has seen Luisa. The host detaches minimally, while his lover's lips slide up his neck. He tries to recall, seems uncertain, then remembers, "I did ... not long ago ...but you know, I think she left ... Is that right, Gunnel?" Gravely she interrupts her sampling to nod and murmur, "Yes, she said she had a swim and was going home. Henry gave her a lift. And your wife too, if I remember correctly. You didn't see them?"

Wren feels the salty cold return and reach inside. He twists uncomfortably and notices that Gunnel seems concerned now, or curious. He shakes his head in response to her question, then inhales and leans against the bar.

"You had a swim as well?" Antaeus observes.

"... I did ..."

"It's invigorating, no?" But Gunnel cries out, "Noo, it's too cold, without the sun."

Wren studies both, to see if they are being straight, but both seem quite sincere, and kindly Antaeus asks, "Can I get you a towel? Shall I call a cab? Most of the guests from Athens have headed back."

This seems strange. "So early? Why?"

"It's midnight, my good man. Many have things to do tomorrow. My friend Henry is early setting sail for Crete."

Still, Wren finds it strange that Belle would leave without him, without a word. Did she think he had left, when he went swimming? Had he talked so long to George, Luisa, and others?

He finds it nonsensical. Glancing at them, through consternation, he nods, "Yes ... I guess a cab and a towel. Thank you." Antaeus smiles as he detaches and moves away to the kitchen where he keeps his phone. Gunnel glides away too and soon returns with a towel, again watching him with mingled curiosity.

After retreating to a bathroom to wash and dry and pull himself together, he talks to another guest, while waiting for the cab. The other is a fellow from New York just arrived, tomorrow heading down to the Peloponnesus. But Wren is only half there, repeating to himself how strange it is that Belle has gone without him. Was it anger, or preoccupation? Was she irked that he'd wandered off, with that younger woman, if in fact Luisa is younger? So unusual was she ... he felt that her anger was both strange and familiar. Surely her life could not have been so restricted. He did enjoy, however, his chat with George ... How odd that we connect, or not, he thinks, almost before our minds decide. What is this unconscious perception? ... Some instinctual recognition ... some chemical reaction?

Belle has grown tired of waiting, although chatting with Argos has been diverting enough. Exuding European savoir faire, he can talk about many things, from the islands to theatre, history, politics, and stories from Classical Greece, including the ancient plays. Nonetheless, Belle is anxious to get things decided, tell Wren, make sure that he understands and can live with her desire to go, and will explain things to the boys. She hopes they won't think it odd of her, or unloving. But it won't be long, a week, after which she will return. And the boys are growing ever more self-sufficient.

A dark-haired woman, whose wet hair and partially clinging clothes suggests she's been swimming, walks past them, eying Argos strangely. He asks if she's seen an American on the beach. "Yes ... out there swimming ... back and forth," she says, waving her hand in a dismissive manner, before asking Argos if he's returning to Athens and if he'd give her a lift. "By all means," comes his accommodating reply. Belle feels that this exchange is not one between strangers. Argos explains to Luisa that he is waiting for his friend here to say the word. Luisa gives Belle a disenchanted glance, before asking if she has time to shower. Argos looks at Artemis, who nods through distraction.

And so Artemis and Argos talk some more, until she can no longer quell her impatience. "Well, it seems my husband is taking his sweet time. I'm not going to sit here all night and hold you up."

"Then come. You can leave him a note at your hotel, explaining our pressing haste and your plans. I will give you my mobile number which he can call. But we do need to head back."

And so Artemis prepares to leave, thanking Antaeus, who gives her a drowning farewell kiss, fully on the lips, and Gunnel too, bending down and enwrapping her, as if Artemis were embarking on an uncharted quest.

Walking out to the limo, Belle passes a short Greek man as he emerges from a bathroom. Although she senses he cannot and does not see her, she hears him wish her, "Safe trip." She looks back at him as he makes his way along one wall, navigating like a trolley, one hand tracking its curving path. This strange house, she thinks, collects an equally strange array of guests.

In the car, Argos slides to the center of the backseat and the two women duck in on either side. The driver takes them fast over the same roads and past the leaping Hermes. Unconcerned, Argos tells them of former voyages in the Mediterranean, South Seas, and Indian Ocean, and Luisa adds an account of her own adventures. Artemis doesn't join in but listens amid the wanderings of her mind. Hidden by Argos's bulk, she finds that Luisa does not acknowledge her presence, speaking exclusively to him, while he listens lightly, waiting to insert his bon mots.

In the city, they drop Luisa off at her apartment building. Argos and she exchange a fervent kiss, before she calls a knowing, "Good sail," to Artemis. And then the limo takes them to her hotel, where she runs upstairs to pack, while he waits, talking contentedly with his chauffeur.

Upstairs, in their room, she pulls out her suitcase and throws it on the bed, her mind racing in one direction then another. Doubts cry out, but she dismisses them before they clinch their point. Even if all does not unfold as promised, she cannot now give it up. The prospect is too exciting. A new direction in her life, a chance to stretch herself a little, to make up for the recent unhappiness. Yes, Angus ... Argos, is a little full of himself, but lively and not without interest. She has seen that he is attracted to her. And the two women, while a little odd, are alert and intelligent ... And such an opportunity is not likely to come again. Indeed, would we read of Odysseus had he reached Ithaca so easily? And what has she to lose, but her chains? She shares a house, but no longer a life; they are parents of the boys, but have become strangers to each other. Life is short; for a week or so the three can do without her.

When all is ready, she writes a short note to Wren explaining her plans and hoping that he will enjoy his freedom. She leaves Argos' phone number, asking him to call in the morning, and she instructs him how to explain things to the boys, as he's not always so adept at these things. She guesses she'll be home in ten days or less.

And then she descends in the elevator, tries not to appear too flushed striding through the lobby and out to the car again. Argos repeats that they will head to the Piraeus yacht basin, and wait at the bar for Poseidon to arrive. The women will come on their own, Angela, Ileana, and one other. He sketches the first part of their voyage. "At first light, we'll head south for Crete, past Serifos, Milos, west of Thera and on; we will explore Knossos, seat of Minoans, the Eastern Med's early civilization, then east to Karpathos, and Rhodes, each different, each interesting in its own way; Rhodes is full of history. You'll glory in its offerings."

She closes her eyes, imagining gliding over the blue swells toward the ancient islands, smiling at Helios who winks at her from high in the sky.

"When we push off, you can turn in if you want, sleep for a while, but I would urge you to come back on deck to watch the dawn. It moves the soul. There are few sights more glorious, gliding between Heaven and the islands ... recognizing that we are doing what the ancient Phoenicians and Ionians did, a realization that is beyond anything I can express in words. While I've done it many times, it still transports me, tells me I'm alive. I cannot get enough."

In the bar, he describes the other islands they will visit, Patmos, Mykonos, Delos, and others. His eyes light up. "I love imagining the life that must have flourished centuries, millennia ago. And now we join the procession. A voyage through the ages, following those whose histories we've read ... Extraordinary!"

Turning to their own lives, they exchange descriptions of their work: her teaching European history at the state university, and his executive role in the oil production company, although he seems reluctant to say too much. He does mention, though, that while London used to be his home, Barcelona is now where he lives. But he says nothing more about his personal life, nor does he ask about hers, beyond commending her for studying and teaching history.

Yet ranging over many topics, they speak together easily and fluidly, and she is pleased by it all. In time the women arrive, amid much greeting and laughter. But Artemis cannot miss their evaluating glances. Marguerite, the third, from near Geneva, is more open, offering quips and questions and laughing when Argos mentions Belle's adopted name. "Well, I suppose I should choose one also, if we are all going to be goddesses and gods. Mon Dieu, you'd think we'd hardly need a yacht."

Argos suggests they settle into their cabins, as he attends to plans with his captain. While Angela and Ileana share a cabin, Marguerite and Artemis have their own. Argos asks them if they want to rise at dawn to take in the sun rising from the sea, but only Marguerite and Artemis request a waking, as the other two opt for sleep.

And so Artemis descends to her cabin and unpacks her bag. That done, though hardly tired, she climbs into her bunk and tries to sleep, but not surprisingly she cannot. For hours she runs through reflections on her decision: her leaving Wren, what it will mean, what effect it may have upon the two of them, and the boys. Much will depend on how he takes it, and presents it to Alexander and Patrick. But, in all probability, when she returns, life will resume its established patterns, its hectic, sometimes wearying pace, scrambling in all directions. Indeed the days and years slide by too fast, seeming to lack any clear direction. She wonders how her kind mother would see all of this, traditional and dutiful as she was, of a different era, when women had not so many paths.

She wonders about Argos, his adopted name and persona. Which of the many sources of that name was he thinking? ... Which of the other women are his lovers ... All? A possibility that she finds distasteful, even as she concedes he's interesting, and clearly enjoys his success and means, unlike her husband. While she notes that Argos is not really her type, she confesses to herself that she has never met her type, at least not for many years when she thought it was Wren.

As for the islands, she will take a slew of pictures, for the boys, and colleagues. Write an article? The civilizations of Knossos, the many passing through Rhodes? Her sons have shown little interest in the past. She wishes she had a Greek history book, or books, to refresh herself. Perhaps he does on board. The Emperor

Hadrian spent time in Athens, finding some affinity, and a lover, as Yourcenar re-constructed it. Oh to have travelled in his court!

Wren sits alone in the back of the taxi speeding toward the city. After thanking Antaeus, he had attempted to shake Gunnel's hand, but she had spread her eagle arms and pulled him in. Full lips awakened his for an instant. What was that? ... A stolen taste? Was she high on something? Or did the nautilus transport them all back to the instinctual Paleocene? Slightly taller than he, an Olympian, she drew him up, then let him go, her plush flesh a fleeting, tactile memory. And who was he, so willing to respond? A cast-off plebeian, or some jackal snatching any morsel?

That parting lingered, distracting him from his wife's escape. How strangely mixed are life's moments of connection. How little these fleeting gestures ultimately mean. And yet he hungers for them, with little else.

His thoughts float through the dark with other faces from the party, until, in time, the here-and-now returns, reminding him he feels odd, and empty, that Belle is not with him. At the same time her absence leaves a sense of peace. Her anger had been an omnipresent weight, even as he admits their respective roles in stoking it. He thought he'd reached out a hand, a kiss, but she, he felt, never responded. Her discontent discolored every gesture he made, despite the years of happiness. To her, clearly, he was the culprit in their demise.

At the hotel, he finds her note on the dresser. Sitting slowly on the bed, he reads and re-reads it. Can it be? ... Disbelieving, he searches the room. Most of her things and bag are gone, save for a few guide books. He stands, circles, and sits again. The room feels dark, despite the lamplight. Underworld shadows lurk in the corners; he feels the chill waters of the dark cove.

Turning and turning, he searches once more, noticing a rumpled towel on the bed, a cast-off hotel robe and information packet. On the bath's white tile lie forgotten underwear, and faint wafts of her perfume linger near the bureau. Without energy or purpose, he does not move. Eventually he thinks he should take a shower, wash off the sea foam and the shock. How can that which was so close slip asunder? A god-like trick, or common fate? How did it all change so? He feels a hole deep inside, while overhead an empty cloud pauses as if a sad observer. He stands again on Antaeus's beach searching for a distant swimmer, or another, once very close. The cool waves leap at his feet, their silver tongues reaching up to knees and spine, leaving a deep chill.

III.

Sleep eventually comes, despite the excitement. She sinks away into peace, as if slumbering quietly on the ocean floor. But too quickly a knocking is heard at her door, followed by a squeaking hinge and Argos's deep gong: "The dawn, dear Artemis, is upon us, climbing the virgin sky. Come, awake, and behold the god of light."

Who? She has momentarily forgotten. But then recalls enough to slide out of her bunk, onto the gently rolling cabin floor, where she braces herself and begins to dress. Although she would have welcomed more sleep, she imagines the dawn into which she'll step: the half-dark, faintly-pale canopy strung with points of light, down to where sky and sea briefly extend as one. To be here, as the ancients were, fills her with expectation and a sense of belonging, finally, to the chain of time. Her study of history, which first focused on this contested sea, kept her at a remove from the living world, but now joining the eternal seafarers, as she hopes her boys will someday do, summons a suddenly-swelling yearning for that simple, visceral life which has too steadily fallen fast astern.

Winding through the passageway and main cabin, she steps up into the dark gray world, nodding to the young helmsman whose face, lit by the binnacle light, sends a flashing smile of jagged teeth, as from an ancient mariner, or creature of the deep.

On deck, she sees the sails are set abeam as Poseidon runs with the wind and following sea. Ahead by the mast stand two figures looking at a long low island far ahead. In the east, the first fingers of pale dawn crack the gray expanse. Silently she moves to join them, glancing at reluctant night hanging in the western sky. To Argos and Marguerite she calls, "Good morning." Tall Argos swings around, whispering, "Just in time," and he takes her hand, squeezing it, as Marguerite echoes, "Good Morning," her long brown hair blowing about her eyes and mouth.

Turning ahead, now flanked by his two guests, Argos points to "Milos," the island they are watching, and informs them that with the favorable wind and sea they are making good time, surfing the gray swells south over the wine-dark troughs.

Soon, and almost imperceptibly, a red shawl ascends the lower sky, pulled by blue needles and pale yellow streaks rising from the empires of the East. Artemis watches transfixed by the majestic beauty. She has seen sunrises, but never over such expanse, nor composed of such pastels. Emotion, called by the unworldly light, fills her eyes. It is as if she is witnessing Time paint its hours round the rim of heaven, while below the days of man unfold their wild tableaux. She imagines she is briefly back with ancient sailors and pausing soldiers, gazing up with wonder, pursuing commerce or bloody war. Phoenicians, Persians, Crusaders, Venetians, Ottomans and soldiers of the Werhmacht on the way to Crete – all may have felt the astonishment of existence in this canopied, wavy world, before they were pulled ashore by the lure of coin or conquest, or summoned by dark Persephone.

How sad it has been, she thinks, that our story's dominated by endless struggle and early death, for one ruler's advantage or another. Yet modern theory, and, increasingly practice, has led us to more civilized resolution, where discord that formerly led to wars now may find negotiated accommodation.

Marguerite, as well, is moved to describe sunrises and sunsets in the Alps and French West Indies – magical and magnificent beyond what the bare elements could seem to offer. And Argos recounts the dawns he's awakened into, thrilling in what they prophesy. The three, watching the vault of heaven grow more ornate, stand in awe of its pageant. Indeed their feelings swell to bursting. "How is it this beauty exists for us?!" wonders Argos, his voice breaking with emotion. "It passeth all understanding." Deeply he breathes to replenish his lungs, before his sight falls from heaven to his companions. Belle inhales in accord, thinking it's entirely understandable to imagine gods presiding over this paradise. Her heart races at the prospect of sailing on across this living, ancient sea.

When the entire sky is filled with color, and Milos looms ever larger, they go below deck for breakfast, and then all return, carrying coffees to the foredeck where Argos tells them of Milos's culture and history, and Artemis imagines the fleets of nations gliding, hulls filled with goods and soldiers. She wonders how much this endless acquisition, from Aquitaine to Levant, was born of Nature's ways. She recalls the bees and birds back home ever collecting stores. Yet what a waste of lives, down through the ages, has strife and conquest mostly been, though sometimes bringing new tools and understanding. To Marguerite she breathes, "Why did this divine expanse, and the arc of the day, not suggest the supreme preciousness of life, beyond material acquisition, and that there is room for all?"

Faintly nodding, Marguerite's clear brown eyes take her in, as her own anticipation swells and brightens. But then she expels an old concern, "Yes, heavenly here … but not on every shore, where much misfortune and strife afflict so many. Large swaths of the Middle-East and Africa suffer poverty and war. Not so long ago Bosnian ethnic struggle tore that country apart, as World War II did across the continent and beyond. And struggle still fills the ghettoes of the world, where men steal, slash, and stab for slivers." A sad smile dims the reflections in her eyes; her graceful face grows darker. But then she meets Artemis's gaze as they take in the beauty rising in the sky. After a moment, the American whispers, "At least, here and there, women are gaining power."

Argos, who was not meant to hear, but has, supports the view, "Why yes, as the new media empower the disenfranchised, women grasp the liberation and power as quickly as the mass of men."

"If not more so," calls Angela, to murmured accord among the women.

Argos bows but turns back to the history of his youth. "As wide-spread are the injustices of today, when I was young, we faced the very extermination of our world, from Hitler, Stalin, and then the bomb. The peace the Allies forged gave rise to the possibilities of today. But in 1940, it was in no way certain that England would last out the year, and in 1962, atomic war seemed one miscalculation away."

"Men, again," mutters Angela, to which he responds, "Yes, but fortunately enough good men thwarted the schemes of the misguided, and urged us to put restraining structures into place."

"But still Europe may fly apart," worries Marguerite, her face growing still. "And who can say what precisely the long-term solution is?"

"Where is our protectress when we need her?" wonders smiling Artemis thinking of her mythological sister with amusement and regret. And the other women seem to second her concern.

Yet instinctively, perhaps, all now shift their talk away from this, to the islands and what they may enjoy. Indeed there is shared expectation that for a week or so, they may escape the world, and its troubles, as they sail among these havens.

Later the wind kicks up, which sends the women below for jackets. In late morning, with Helios reaching his apex, the now-baking women peel off their layers and lather on the sun block, before stretching out on towels. Argos takes them in with a smile, before going aft for a turn at the wheel and to discuss plans with his captain.

Soon thereafter, he receives a call on his mobile for Artemis. "From your husband, I believe," he calls ahead to where she lies. A crew member runs the phone to her as she reaches for something with which to cover herself. She takes the phone and settles down on her back, pulling her top and towel over her, then greets her distant husband in an even tone, "Hello, Wren."

"Hi, Belle ... or is it Artemis to whom I'm speaking?"

With this she rolls onto her side away from the others. "Your choice. How are you?"

"How am I? ... Well, as perhaps you just might imagine, a little surprised, a little hurt, to find my wife run off to the islands, without a word."

"I thought it would benefit us both to get away a bit."

"So I gather. It would have been nice to be consulted however, or at least informed. I can imagine the vituperation that would have poured down on me, had I done this."

"I couldn't find you. I was told you were off swimming with some woman."

"Not quite, but you couldn't wait?"

"I did, but it was important, the owner told us, to set off at dawn, which meant returning to Athens in late evening. But how are you? What are you up to?"

"... How am I? ... I hardly know. ... Is this where we are? Where either of us can just run off, without considering the other?"

"I just explained."

"You revealed your priorities ... Do I merit so little consideration?"

At first she doesn't know how to continue. "... I wanted to consult you, but you were nowhere to be found."

"I was not so far away, if you had cared to look."

"I was told it was either go quickly or not at all. It's not as though things have been improving between us."

"No, and this is one reason why. You're pretty much wrapped up in your own life."

"As you have been in yours, your architecture, where you pay your assistant more than your family."

"That's a sad exaggeration."

"I've seen very little coming in."

"Who pays the bills? Unfortunately it does go out as quickly as it comes."

"To her salary, leaving less for the boys and me. Am I supposed to silently and happily accept this?"

"You might try discussing something closer to the truth. But obviously that doesn't suit your purpose. I am hoping, by the way, that this new project may be remunerative, though probably not enough to suit you."

"There are stark financial realities we face ... yet you make no adjustments. I find it frustrating. At this point, my taking a week's odyssey is not going to fundamentally change our relations, but a break just might be beneficial. Might offer perspective, and a fresh start."

"Your perspective is pretty much cast in stone from what I've seen. But it's not that the idea is a poor one; it's the way you broached it. Fait accompli."

"If you hadn't walked off to swim, and who knows what else, with that woman at the party, I could have found you."

He laughs. "While you were wandering with your pirate? ... You hardly know your husband, after all these years."

"Nor you me. But I know men and your so-called dreams."

"I wonder if you do. Your willingness to listen, to talk calmly, honestly, has all but evaporated."

"There is no point in repeating old lines and lies."

"You show little care for the truth or my side of things."

"I have tried to understand."

"Really? ... I missed it."

But now both fall silent for a moment, before he feels he wants to explain, "As for last night, I had no interest in swimming, only chatting. But she disappeared, swimming out in the cove, and I became concerned. Only then did I go in. I hear you shared a ride with her back to the city. I presume she told you where I was."

"She said you were still swimming. At that point, we couldn't wait."

"Couldn't walk to the water's edge?"

"There was no sign of you."

"You didn't care to look."

"There was no time. I'm sorry if this upsets you. It's an opportunity that will not come again. I'm here with three other women, and the boat owner."

"I don't doubt it's appealing. Such opportunities, however, are seldom completely free."

"I've been asked to pay nothing. And I'm sure you would have taken the opportunity, if given the chance."

"I would have discussed it with you."

"When do we discuss? ... We don't. We don't have a normal marriage. I think you should stop pretending that we are in any meaningful way a couple. There is little left. We have been living our individual lives. For me, an opportunity came; I took it."

"This trip was supposed to be *our* opportunity."

"There had been no progress. We were going around in circles."

"... So ... well ... when are you returning? Any suggestions on what to tell the boys? 'Your mother ran off with some oil exec.'"

"Please. I know you get your little thrills with your office assistant."

"That's a self-serving bending of the truth," he expels sharply. "I need help on the projects I have, and hopefully the one coming up. Someone to help draft and bounce ideas off of, and be there while I'm here. Even though the amount of work isn't what I'd like, I still have hope and this coming project."

"You should have asked her to come. You could share your love of architecture."

"Why did you propose this trip we're on?"

"Back then *I* had some hope. But I see you will not change."

"I've tried to talk, but your distortions lead to anger and impasse ... And look now. No hint of apology, or conciliation; no acknowledgement of your role in this."

"Have *you* offered anything?"

"I've tried to discuss, have made gestures here and there, but found nothing coming back. There's no pulling together, and it seems you have lost all integrity, willing, as you are, to say whatever comes to mind. You've become more Hera than Athena."

"To your Zeus pursuing maidens? ... This is getting us nowhere, serving no purpose."

"Certainly none of yours. What shall I tell the boys? Clearly you won't be on the flight back."

"I'll return soon after. Please give them my love, and explain that this came up unexpectedly. I think they'll understand. My relationship with them is not so hand-to-mouth."

"Yes ... I guess they've seen things more clearly than I have."

"I had hoped this trip to Greece might help us heal our differences, but you seemed unwilling to bend."

He laughs harshly. "Bend? This whole trip has been a bend; it was *your* itinerary. I've been suffering from the bends."

"You wanted to go."

"Yes, but made a few suggestions, which went unheeded. Okay, it was to be your trip, fine, but even that didn't please you, as you packed every disgruntlement from the past twenty years."

"I wandered with you for hours on the Acropolis, inspecting every inch of rubble, as we do everywhere ... but there's no point in discussing it now, on the phone, when we'd made no progress together ... I hope you'll be fair in your account to the boys."

"Would a factual account be fair? But what facts do I have? That you disappeared at a party, went off on a cruise without so much as a word? ... I have no idea where you're going or who you're with."

"I mentioned the other passengers."

"Their number, little more, or where you're going ..."

Now she is silent for a moment, then repeats, "So, what will you say?"

"I hardly know what to say."

"Wren, I knew you had to get back for your project, whereas I didn't."

"Yes, that part I understand."

"The boys will want to hear something."

"That too I understand."

"We're supposed to be adults now, and able to put aside our emotions for our children's sake."

"Put aside our anger and wild accusations? Yes, that would be adult."

"I've got to go."

Again, for a moment, silence fills the phone, until he rasps, "Well enjoy yourself. You can give us an account of the islands." Another pause follows, before he confesses, "I don't know what else to add."

"I hope that you have a good time in Athens. I'll call the airlines."

"Yes, well ... bon voyage."

"Yes. You too. Goodbye."

Her last syllables echo in his head. He feels an indistinct contracting. She too is motionless, on the deck, trying to understand and recover, taking in slow, discreet breaths.

In his hotel room he stands turning slowly, trying to think. Their anniversary trip has driven them farther apart ... Inept handling ... misunderstandings, or irreconcilable differences? ... Old lines push into his mind:

Moments follow one another as do, say, sips of sherry,
songs from a singer;
numbers in progression they become.

It is amazing, bewildering, that it has all gone ... that so many couples tumble down this path, stumbling over differences.

He is alone now in Greece, as if on the Moon, in this overwhelmingly Moon-colored city of near-blinding light, in this country of magical history and landscapes soft and harsh ...

So it is not the sip or song
save for a savored, favored first few,
that linger
any more than time's moment does ...
but the tremor in your core,
the warm burn of a flush in your face,
the intertouch of a smile.

These are the animal moving,
the human knowing he is moving.
Move and a mouth moves;
love and set two loves moving;

*green and bring brown coming.
How soon?*

What now? ... Call Antaeus, try to reach George. Five more days.

He circles the room, then calls the concierge, asking him if he can find a number in the city for this architect. The fellow provides several, as the name is not unique. They make an educated guess; he reaches an answering machine with a man's voice speaking rapidly in Greek. It might be George, can't be sure. He leaves a message and his hotel number. He tries Antaeus; same thing, a machine, on which he leaves a second message.

What else? Delphi keeps recycling through his mind. The oracle, the future, Apollo, the musician, archer, healer. He should go. Again he calls the concierge and books a car service, as he doesn't think he should drive. Distracted, he might run off the road, off a mountain. Now he can relax and take in the countryside. He will leave at noon on the 2 to 3 hour drive.

He reviews the guide book, dresses for the day, has a coffee, and then he is ducking into the car and soon chatting with the friendly driver, Kostas, speeding out of the city. They pass the route to Corinth as they fly north then west. Gazing out and talking, he keeps his mind away from the hollowness that otherwise would fill him. Kostas is a fount of information and stories. Wren listens, absorbing some, missing parts, but the constant chatter is diverting, informative. The farther they go, the more rural and rugged the land becomes; mountains edge closer from the north. Passing a turn-off for Thebes, they take a narrower road through hilly countryside. He thinks he should visit those other cities, but another day. He asks Kostas about the islands. "Magnificent!" cries the Greek. "My family is from Paros. If you go to only one island, go to Paros."

"Can you drive me?"

"No, you must fly or take a ferry," Kostas corrects him, missing the humor, but Wren feels better, that he can joke.

As they draw closer, the road dives and swerves, making sharp switch-backs around steep foothills and deep valleys, occasionally providing views of the Gulf of Corinth to the south. Kostas drives faster than Wren would, by far, and so he slides low in his seat, trying to focus on the increasingly dramatic mountains. They blow through small villages and past the occasional herd of goats. "Are the goats for sacrifice?" he calls to Kostas.

"Milk, cheese, meat," Kostas answers, again setting him straight. Wren feels a certain devil-may-care attitude working into him. Kostas is now telling stories of ancient battles and their heroes, ever fighting the Persians or Spartans, the punching bags of Athenians. Why is it we all have *never* gotten along? Different views, different goals. Power, gold, territory, self. Even the animals do it. Why should we compromise with barbarians? The ancient Athenians knew their culture had risen ... but not quite high enough.

He turns his thoughts away. More happily, memories from work, his designs, edge back, superimposed over the views of the mountains. He is stirred by both, the beauty around him and that into which he has thrown himself. Long has Nature inspired him to imagine ... Half of his life, and his love, is of the world and half can be found in his efforts to render portions of it. There, at least, heart and mind marry, bringing joy.

As Kostas speeds them through another small village, Wren sees that it is an outpost in Nature, whose slopes and cliffs rise high above and around it, dwarfing all. In his designs, he tries to remind people of this natural beauty, while the ancient Greeks, surrounded by Nature, and sometimes roughly handled, sought to stand out from it.

He revisits the pleasure he finds devising, drawing, discussing ... most often with his assistant, Margaux, who is so positive and architecturally striking. The optimism and energy of youth. Unfortunately the halting flow of projects is not really enough to occupy her, yet he keeps her on, allowing her to pursue her own ideas and small projects, paying her, though he cannot every month really afford to. There is some truth to Belle's accusation, but inaccuracy as well, a blowing out of proportion. She is no threat to the marriage; for one thing, she has a lover, her fiancé. He simply likes her, and needs her optimism and energy – her friendship, her help, her talk. But Belle feeds her own irritation, pesters him to let her go. Yet it is Margaux's running his office now that allows them to take this trip, something Belle does not acknowledge.

In early afternoon, Argos turns the Poseidon into the wind allowing the crew to lower the sails, and the boat to drift in the swells, so that all might dive into the deep blue sea. Argos leads them, throwing his arms ahead and slicing into the glinting waves, followed by the women, save for Angela.

Artemis has recovered, largely, from her conversation with her husband. What she heard from him on the phone was not new, and proffered little hope. Stuck, he clings to his hobby and little pleasures, unable to change. He will never build the houses of which he dreams. But she must put this out of her mind, for now anyway. Here the water feels fresh and life-restoring, thrilling her as she strokes, kicks, and laughs with Marguerite, Ileana, and Argos. She plays porpoise, diving under, then bursting to the surface to breathe, rising and floating in the clear water, silver in its peaks, blue in its depths. She might be on a different planet, a different world, among the Naiads of her youth.

Back on deck, under the hot sun, she lies on her towel and talks with Marguerite who is also glorying in the warmth. It was work in Marseille that brought her in contact with Argos, and he extended an open invitation to come sailing with him. She laughs. "Of course he did not say who the other guests might be. I imagined other couples – Quelle idiote! –I suppose sometimes there are, but mostly he plays the sultan." A laugh is half-swallowed, before she continues, "But he is all right, not unreasonable, mostly, somewhat predictable; one can manage him."

Artemis whispers, "Are the other two his lovers?" Marguerite smiles, but can only say, "Je ne sais pas. You'll have to ask *them*."

Artemis turns her inquiry to the earlier journey, and Marguerite describes rounding the Peloponnesus from Ithaca and the Adriatic. "The sea there was gray and flat, with no wind to push us. The islands came looming out of the mist, so that I could imagine the gods and nymphs streaking above on errands." Artemis listens with growing pleasure, interrupting only to say, "It is hard for me to believe that Ithaca actually exists. Yet that it does makes Odysseus seem almost real. And if he is, then Athena certainly is. Wisest of men, wisest of the gods. The few from Homer's time who seemed roundly aware."

"And yet Odysseus lingered long with Calypso," Marguerite reminds her.

"Washed up upon her shores, he had no ship or crew to take him home, though he yearned for his Penelope ..."

Marguerite smiles away the other part of this as she resumes, "Yes, Ithaca is real and alive, unlike Troy's scanty ruins. Passing it was ... like a dream ... in the mist ... I wanted to go ashore ... and yet did not want to lose the dream ... To be so close ... But we did not stop, heading south toward other islands and on around to Athens ...The hairs on my arms and neck stood up, having re-read parts of Homer. In some ways, the gods seem more real, and balanced than Homer's men and women, whose concerns are so narrow, unseeing, and sad, save for wise Odysseus."

Smiling, Artemis repeats to herself, "Wise Odysseus," then sends her attention up into the blue sky, with its soft, Rubensesque clouds, which form an arm, a shoulder of that hero, or Apollo, or Hera's hip and thigh, the brow and braids of Aphrodite, all drifting slowly by. We see, she thinks, what we want to see, as sung by our ardent hearts, where past and present flow together in their rendering by our arts.

She wonders if the ancients still live in the ether, for there are unexplained occurrences. And she wonders about her life and marriage. Are they too much like stumbling human history? Promising much, delivering less – a bag of shells, once beautiful, before inevitably splintering into broken colors and jagged edges, which the sea, and time, wear down and scatter on the deepest ledges.

Leaving behind the twisting mountain road, Kostas drives them through the village of Delphi and up one side of a valley to the ancient temples and new museum, where Parnassus towers to the north beyond the rocky cliffs. The temples here, Kostas explains, were Apollo's, where his priestesses, the pythia, served as intermediaries between god and men who came seeking advice and the future. But the predictions issued by the pythia were ambiguous, leaving the advised to ponder their true meaning. With some humor now, Kostas observes that most pilgrims discovered their futures only in retrospect.

Wren gets out and begins walking up the curving pathway between the remains of small temples. The climb is steep, the air still and hot, so that he must soon wipe his dripping brow and pause to catch his breath. Continuing on, with a few other tourists, and surprisingly, two on horseback, he soon reaches the largest temple, Apollo's, sitting on a shelf carved out of the slope. There is little more than its foundation left, but that provides an outline of its dimensions, design, and intricacy. Somewhere on the main floor, a crevice in the original rock was preserved, from which vapors and voices rose, to be interpreted by the pythia.

He looks around. A valley to the south and west plunges down, before rising up the far side. Behind him reclines an impressive amphitheatre carved into the mountain. Close behind that, sharp rocky walls enclose the site, softened only by a line of pines and cypress. Overall it is simple, even plain, except for the view across the dramatic ravine.

Wren imagines the ancient Greeks come to seek the future or the truth. And he wonders if he has come for something of the same. He pictures the architectural beauty of the temples as they were, simple yet elegant in their designs, to honor and please the god of light and music – who he might choose to befriend, if he could. He closes his eyes to listen for some voice or message, should there be one, and maybe to send one back, to an open ear. But no pythia are in evidence, nor any voices whispering.

He turns and climbs on, up along the side of the amphitheatre, where the rhythm of the curving seating bestows a beauty that is both natural and designed. This pleases him, and he imagines the less-hurried life here so long ago. Individuals climbing slowly to gaze down or across to the rising cliffs, wondering what fate may hold. A few of the other tourists pause, as he is, gazing around. Perhaps like him, they are attempting to picture it as it was: more heavily populated and wooded, he's read, home to game and great cats. He wonders how the Oracle's reputation was sustained through centuries, if truth was not forthcoming. Was it the ambiguity of the priestesses or their worldliness?

Climbing farther up the zigzag path, he reaches the stadium where athletic competitions were held. From this mild exertion, in the dry heat, he finds himself puffing and resting in a pine's welcomed shade. Other tourists are also pausing, expelling remarks about the heat, along with the heat itself.

He pushes on, walking next to the stadium's narrowly oval field. Across from him, a dozen curving granite seating rows follow the arc of the field and give the stadium its form. He veers again into shade and turns to study the grass field where the events took place. He imagines runners sprinting, javelins and discus arcing through the sky. What could those young men have been like? ... Simple, focused on the events ... pleased maybe that they could vie for honor in such a beautiful, hallowed place. He was not so different, consumed through much of his teens with sports and dreams, only slowly beginning to truly appreciate the world's wonders beyond.

Turning the other way, he looks once more down into the valley and over at the sharp outcroppings that define the other side. Though dry and rocky too, they somehow support a thin covering of small trees and shrubs, attaching a soft beauty to the sheer slopes. What will happen with still less rain and increasing heat?

When he has taken in the stadium and views, and has again imagined those competing there, he ambles back down to the amphitheater and settles on a rock near the top, there picturing performances of dance and drama. How real to the performers and audiences were those stories? Did they see them as metaphor or historic accounts? He must ask Belle. Some, he's read, saw the gods as symbols, ideals, of love or beauty; others saw them as beings, subject to the laws of the world. How sublime to have watched those performances come alive here so long ago, focused on the crux of life. How well educated were most back then? What did they understand? – something he wonders about many of his countrymen today, and himself at times. Do we make time for deep investigation?

Now carried on the light breeze rising from the valley, he hears a flute, and maybe mandolin. Their chords drift intermittently up to where he sits, as if beauty in one form seeks it in another. The music, and the setting, evoke feelings of spirituality and emotion, doing so with simple grace. And as he listens, it occurs to him that the patterns this music takes are those of Nature. This struck him earlier as he hiked up, following the two horses for a time, whose hooves steadily and rhythmically struck the pathway, smoothly and unhurried – ka-dum, ka-dum ... ka-dum, ka-dum – 4/4. He exults in the recognition that this beat is of Nature, and that man draws it from her, as he himself does in his designs, borrowing or depicting those rhythms and patterns around him.

His attention returns to the amphitheater's stage. The other tourists have disappeared back down, he assumes. The scene is motionless and silent, save for the occasional strains of music. He imagines women dancing on the stage to this music, singing, acting ... And then to the right, behind some trees, he notices the sheer tails of a gown or cape blowing gently in the rising breeze.

As he watches; it seems to move with both the music and air. He wonders who is wearing it and why – a costume? He stands to see, then decides to make his way over. Carefully he edges back to the path, descends, then steps off again, climbing over rocks and in among the trees. The gown has moved farther down, and he follows it to a clump of pines, where, rounding them, he discovers a figure, within the shifting, shapeless gown, facing the valley. The music has stopped. He watches for a moment; almost certainly it is a woman. He takes a step closer, then pauses, not wanting to disturb her. But she turns suddenly and looks up at him. Her face is long and pale. Light blue eyes, which mirror the color of the gown, run over him carefully. He bows a little in greeting. A hint of a smile moves in her cheek. Now he notices that she holds a thin rope which runs to the ground and along to a white goat, feeding on the grasses. Wren is amused; his eyes shine. He is touched that she attends to her goat.

She turns fully toward him, keeping her eyes upon him, and then climbs effortlessly to him. Close, she stops and says something in Greek, at which he can only shake his head.

"English?" she tries. He smiles. "American."

Near now, she is tall, he sees, nearly his height. Her long white hair is tied back, falling over her formless gown. He guesses she must be in her sixties, possibly more, and he can't help but be impressed that she moves so lightly and agilely.

Looking intently into his eyes, she asks, "You come for oracle?"

He feels his eyes smile as he tips his head, yes and no. "To see Apollo's temple and the mountains."

"You want the future ... healing?" she asks.

Again a faint smiles moves across his face. "Is the future possible to know?"

"No," she replies with finality, shaking her head.

He likes this and cannot restrain another smile. He wonders if she's a caretaker of the site, the temples. She seems as timeless.

Studying him now more closely, his hands, shoulders, face, she tells him, "My name, Iscaria."

He bows and extends his hand. "I'm Wren." She takes it carefully with both of hers, glancing at it, whispering the name to herself, finding the single syllable strange. "That is all?" she asks. He bows. "No more." She studies his hand, held by hers, which are large and veined. Her fingers are cold, almost ice ... yet the palms are warm, maybe burning. He wants to withdraw his hand, but he fears offending her. He clenches his jaw to contain his discomfort, then re-directs his mind, asking "You work here?"

Her forbearing smile dismisses his silly question, before she shakes her head.

"You have a handsome goat," he tells her nodding to it with an amused gaze.

Affection and humor play faintly in her cheeks. "His name ... Adonis."

ATHENA

A soft laugh escapes him, and draws one from her. She holds her mouth open as she closes her eyes a little, slyly. "A good name for a goat."

He agrees, smiling with her.

"I must go."

He bows again. "Nice to meet you."

"I am leaving," she repeats, thinking he didn't understand. She then looks at him with frowning scrutiny. Leaning closer, looking into his eyes, she observes, "You are sad. Why? Much beauty here."

"... I am not sad. In fact I'm very pleased to have met you."

"You have a loss ..." she asserts.

He frowns a bit, then tries to change the subject, "I came from Athens, for the afternoon."

"Why?" she asks pointedly.

Surprised, uncertain, he shakes his head "I don't know ... curiosity ..."

"You come alone?" This question, too, perplexes him. Why does she care? What does it matter? And yet maybe it does, but he finds the subject awkward ... not wanting to explain. He tries, "I am not alone. I am speaking with you."

Impatience moves like a ripple across her face; she looks away. "It is not good to be alone like you ... inside." And she touches her chest. "Maybe good for a goat, who needs only grass ... A goat's life. Not for a man like you."

"I am okay," he tells her. "But what about you?"

She looks at him sharply. "I have lived long ... I know how to be alone ... My goat and me ..." A brief brightening softens her face. "But you ... you do not."

Both amused and uncertain, he must restrain the urge to step back. "Why ... why do you say that?"

She looks at him strangely, but then with sympathy. Again she studies his hands and observes, "You work indoors."

Recognizing the evidence on which she has based this, he confirms, "I design buildings." Few visitors here, he thinks, would be physical laborers.

She considers this. "Many temples here, long ago. Many come." He nods.

She finds his eyes again and asks, "Children?" He hesitates, then confirms, "Two boys."

"Not with you?" He shakes his head. "Why?" she asks again. He breathes before he explains, "They are home, busy, in a summer camp."

"Camp?" she repeats, not understanding.

"Sports, swimming, running, archery ... As in the stadium," and he gestures up the hill.

"And wife?" she asks. He cannot restrain yet another amused smile. "You have many questions."

She looks at him seriously. "I like to know ... I see many things."

"You see with your heart," he says, unexpectedly, surprising himself.

She looks again carefully into his eyes. He feels indeed that he is being seen. She asks again, "Where is your wife?"

He laughs to himself, that this continues. "On a boat, in the Aegean."

"Why not here, with you?"

He tips his head right and left. "... We have different ideas."

She thinks about this, watching him, then tells him, "You are dying,"

He starts. "What?" Then quickly he corrects her, "No ... I'm fine."

"No, you are ..." she searches for the word, "... shrinking inside."

He pushes his lips out to convey his doubt, but then offers, "Seeking new life, maybe." He recognizes that he feels increasingly uncomfortable.

"Seeking love ..."

He indicates that this may be so. But how has she concluded this, and what might it mean? In any case, he should end it. But she goes on, "You are not old, like me."

He feels himself frowning as he looks at her, uncertain how to take this. He feels something for her, some sympathy, some caring, and he looks more closely into her blue eyes, trying to see who she is.

A faint smile spreads slowly over her face. She returns his searching gaze, then nods slightly, "You must awaken ..."

This startles him again, though he is held by her gaze, a gaze of patience and concern. With no particular intention, he bows to her.

She looks carefully at him. "I am serious ... you must. You have no woman."

He doesn't know what to say. What does she mean? He has mentioned his wife.

"In your work, too, you are not happy."

Now faintly annoyed, he turns away a little, for this seems wrong ... and yet not entirely.

"Are you?" she presses.

Pushing his lips out, he reflects, then says, "In fact I am ..."

"I think it is not so," she grumbles, disappointed with him. "You make money?"

He finds this intrusive now. "Why do you ask these questions?"

She studies him for a few seconds. "I see you ... you are not stone; you are living; you have come a long way, alone ... I want to know why ..."

"But ..." he begins, yet does not finish. What is she seeking? ... What does she see?

Carefully each studies the other, until she offers, "I see ... that you look ... that you see me ... as I see you. Not all people do ... Are you an artist?"

He exhales a little. "An architect."

Her eyes return to his hands and then his eyes. She appears to study each region of his face, until finally she asks, "You draw your ideas?"

How does she mean this? And yet he nods before he forms a reply. He feels a smile, or light, moving across his face. He feels calmer now. He is amused by her mind; he likes it, and her English. She is direct, curious ... kind.

But now she frowns at him, and he looks more closely to understand why. There is something deeply alert in her, and this warms him. But why is she probing? ... So unlike Luisa, say. Maybe she too is alone, up here, as he is. And unexpectedly, he thinks, as Belle is. He wonders if she has found true friends on the boat; he finds that he is hoping she has. This surprises him, and yet he feels content that he does. If she does not see him anymore, certainly not as he sees himself, she is not a bad person, but sees him through her own discontent. Maybe that is true for most.

"You drift ..." she observes, "in the sea. The world is changing, but you are not."

He frowns at first, wondering at this, and looking into her eyes. After a moment, he allows there may be something to this ... may not be so unusual. He considers her sky blue eyes again – maybe she is from up there. He wants to ask her several questions now, but he hears her continuing, as from a distance. "Your body sleeps ... your heart waits in silence."

He feels himself grow perfectly still, and sees that she does also. But he forms no response to her observation.

"I am serious," she says. "You must change."

He smiles faintly. He's heard this before, from Belle. And now, as then, it feels unwanted, meddlesome. Involuntarily, he steps back, turning.

Seeing his discomfort, she hurries, "You must search. You must see."

His lips part a little, but he wants to turn his mind elsewhere.

"And you must talk, awake, with someone ... if not your wife."

He flexes a cheek. This is enough. For where is it leading? He feels his patience reaching its limit.

"You must try. The ancients understood."

Who? ... To end it, he nods.

"You cannot wait ... you must lead. You have begun, by coming here, to Apollo ... for his healing ... his truth ... his music. You have affinity; it brought you here, and to me."

"You are his priestess?" he tries, softening it with a smile.

"If you want." But her thoughts move on, her eyes growing serious. "You see, together man and woman are one, a whole, an old Greek idea. We balance, two halves, not the same, but making one. It is the way things work ... in Nature. Apollo and his sisters Artemis ... Athena ... Different sides, one family. But all equal ..."

He frowns at this mention of Athena. He's had enough of her. Recent images of goddess, temple, and wife, regal and distant, course through his mind. When he finds Iscaria again, she is looking down at Adonis, and she moves to him as he nibbles. She leans over and strokes him with affection. "We must go home, my pet." Adonis pays no heed. She looks up at Wren, as if to say, 'You see?'

They smile at each other. There is a sudden warmth, and perhaps glints of shared appreciation between them. He feels his heart reach out for her, though he does not move. She straightens and steps close. "You have heard me. You listen. I feel your heart. Do not hold back your love of the world. Speak out, free it, and someone, maybe Apollo, will hear you."

A faint ironic smile moves up into his cheeks, even as his heart beats more noticeably. "I thank you. I like your name, Iscaria. It suggests many things ... that maybe you are a daughter of Apollo."

She looks at him with mixed emotions, until she chooses forgiveness. "It is to your heart, and not only your mind, that you must listen."

He is mildly chastened. Smiling a little, he asks, "Do I not?"

"You are ... guarded ... I can understand ... I have someone I want you to talk with, in Athens ... who could help."

He's not sure he heard right. A referral? The modern world intruding ... He waits, wondering.

"Someone who could free you to speak your feelings and through that, hear another ... maybe your wife."

He feels skepticism rising, and shifts uncomfortably.

She urges him, "Try."

He wonders if she's nutty. Why would he agree? ... He does not have endless time, only a few days, and there are things he wants to do. A waste? A scam? ... And yet ... it might be ... worthwhile, an adventure. "Does this person know Apollo?" he asks gently.

She twists her mouth in disappointment. "I am serious; I don't joke." And now she reaches into her gown and pulls out a small piece of paper with a name and number written on it. She had this all along? A sales pitch, a commission gained? Waiting for the right person and moment? Does she give it out regularly? He looks down at Adonis, who strangely is looking at him as he chews. Man to man? What can we do? Opaque, expressionless eyes, with vertical pupils, like a cross somehow, hold on him. Both trapped in an existence not quite of their choosing.

Finding her again, he asks, "Do you give this out to others?"

She studies him patiently. "... If I see hope ... have a good feeling." She reaches out and gives it to him, and he takes it, thanking her.

"I must go now ... but may I ask you something?"

"Of course."

She moves closer still, her face now inches from his. He waits for her request, but she is motionless, silent, waiting, looking into his eyes. Hers are a piece of the sky ... beyond the mountains, and time. He feels drawn up there ... and as he does, he realizes what she wants. And so he leans slightly and kisses her cheek that, like her hands, is both warm and cool. He holds his lips there on her pale, timeless cheek and his arms bring her close, against him. Closing his eyes, he feels his heart reach out for her. He realizes that he is trembling, while she is calm and still and her body seems to have little weight. For moments they stand like this. Her cheek seems to grow quite hot; it almost burns, yet he holds his lips there ... or does he imagine it all? But he recognizes that his body has quieted, that he accepts, that he does not pull away, that he feels love for her. He feels they have become almost a tree, roots reaching into the earth, enrapt in a single bark. Indeed he hears leaves rustling; her long gray hair blows near his eyes, seems to encircle his head, embracing him, in a temple. He smells a combination of mimosa and wetted ash about her, as they stand as one. A wind rises, coming up from the valley, rapidly increasing in strength so that they must grip each other not to be blown from where they stand. Ever more firmly does he hold her, as the wind continues to rise, now bringing with it a squall which pelts them with fine, stinging rain. Steam encircles them, swirling up from the ground, around their bodies, before it is caught by the wind and swept into the sky. He feels he is soaring ... through time ... feels that they are each a mist passing through the other, dissolving in the wind, that their two hearts ascend together. But then abruptly she pulls away, is no longer there with him. He sees her tugging her gown's hood over her head and turning to yank Adonis's rope before hurriedly she begins to descend the hill, veering behind trees and disappearing. For a moment he is frozen by it all, by the unreality, the strangeness, her abrupt departure, until he awakens and runs after her, nearly stumbling, catching hold of a trunk to save himself. Now he sees that she is far ahead, her gown disappearing behind laurel trees. No longer can he find her, and something tells him it is futile to pursue. And so he halts, breathing hard in the continuing squall, standing there feeling increasingly cold and wet, not certain that any of this happened. A single thunder clap sounds not far behind, up the hill. It shakes him, as if a signal or warning. And, once again, he feels rooted in this place, unable to move, planted. His branch-like arms are lifted to the clouds, appealing ... or protecting? ... His mind whirls; he shivers his length; his arms fall back and around him. He recognizes he needs to find shelter, Kostas's car or the museum somewhere down the hill. And so he hurries back to the path and descends, even as his mind, and heart, are held by the encounter – vivid and piercing ... Was it real, or did he yearn for and imagine it? Pushing his hand into his pocket, he feels the piece of paper he was given, and he presses it between his fingers.

Reaching Kostas's car, he opens the back door and ducks in. Kostas turns and hands him a towel to dry himself, saying, "This is unusual. It seldom rains in this season."

Still shivering, Wren dries himself vigorously, flexing to control and warm his wet body.

"Do you want to visit the museum?" Kostas asks. But Wren recognizes that he is too shaken, stunned, frozen ... He could neither see nor absorb anything more ... "No ... No thank you."

"Well then, maybe we should go. The storm may last." Wren rubs his hair with the towel and wipes his face, then meets Kostas's gaze. The other seems concerned for him. "Yes, let's go," Wren rasps as he tries again to stop the trembling.

Kostas appears about to ask him something – Are you all right? But he studies Wren, smiles, then turns to start the car.

As Wren continues to rub and warm himself, Kostas brings them around and heads back down toward the village. After several moments, he asks, "Did you see any signs? Learn the future?"

Wren feels pulled in directions he can hardly name. "Possibly."

"It is said that sometimes they come, visions, spirits, gods, just before storms."

Wren can't tell whether Kostas is serious. But Kostas doesn't pursue this, and Wren is hesitant to tell of his experience.

As they descend, Wren glances out and sees uphill, through the light rain, a tall, gray form gliding through distant trees. He looks again, wanting to point it out to Kostas, but it, she ... is gone, and the car now dives down past bushes and stone walls. Questions push through his mind: what *was* that? How much was imagined? Did his emotions call it into being? ... Who was she? And why did she speak to him? Because he was alone, and came to her, drawn by the music? Yet her face, her sky blue eyes were not of the here and now ... A single great shiver wracks his body, and he presses into the seat. How to explain it to himself? ... He has never experienced something even close to that.

Now as the car winds back through the mountains, he looks out several times, and thinks he sees other gray forms moving along the mountainsides. But clearing his eyes, he finds them to be small clouds of mist hanging on the slopes of Parnassus.

In late afternoon, the captain walks among the women strewn out on the foredeck, telling them that they will reach Crete in the morning. A short time later, finding that the sea air and sun have made her sleepy, Artemis goes below to her cabin for a nap. When she wakes, it is growing dark, and she returns on deck to watch the sun set, over a distant, dark line of an island. The sky has grown ruddy, almost bloody, compared to the morning's delicate hues. And yet it suggests a symmetry to the day, which pleases her. She reflects, as her husband often notes, that much in Nature is circular. Indeed he never tires of touting the structural strength of a circle, which benefits all living things: eggs, cells, celestial bodies, the day and more ... the arc of life and generations. What are women and men but vessels for perpetuation. And yet why? Or is that the wrong question? Is it simply what is, what has worked, and for a time survived? Random, purposeless life? Or is there some end, some level we are evolving toward? ... The gods?

And what is her career if not a means to understand, know, improve? ... Some societies, or parts of them, have done so ... but has she?

Soon after, dinner is served in the main cabin, and conversation flows among the five, each invigorated by the adventure and sea air, and by a fresh, flakey white fish whose name is known only by the chef and Ileana. Artemis notices that Angela and Ileana accept her now, responding more openly.

Following the meal, they step back up onto the deck where brandies or liquors are served as they watch the purple western sky, while to the east a hint of stars, as Poseidon rolls rhythmically south. The liquors, the night, and the gentle motion of the boat combine to transport Artemis to those long-ago years, far from the hurried, modern life. And, as she talks with Ileana and Marguerite, she wonders if her time spent studying and teaching history has taken her too much away from life itself, confining her to the past. Has she missed spontaneous, vibrant, adventurous living? She had hoped to live in Europe for a time, but it has never worked out. And so, instead of escaping the conforming suburban life, she has been trapped there. Here she might have found, and might in the future find, a milieu more exciting, more aligned with her hopes and values ... But what of the boys? They could come, if she finds something over here, a teaching position, in Paris say. They would resist at first, but then might grow to love it. And Wren? What would he do? A less tractable problem, with his business and career, such as it is. He would want to stay home, which might be hard on the boys. Maybe he could find some European firm to hire him. He's not without his ideas. But all of this would require money, and he isn't really making enough to add significantly to her salary. So perhaps she may come alone, when the boys are in college. Then they would enjoy visiting ... She ought to begin looking.

As the purple sky turns to black and the constellations grow more defined, she feels this dream deepen and grow more palpable, perhaps aided by the liquor. Standing on the deck, thinking back over the day, she realizes how extraordinary it has been for her. She is thoroughly happy and, at the same time, pleasingly relaxed and tired. Conversation is dwindling, and so she announces that she will turn in. Seeing that her balance is unsteady on the rolling Poseidon, Argos helps her down to her cabin, and before she opens her door, he slips an arm around her and pulls her up to him, kissing her powerfully. Floating toward sleep, and assuming the embrace is momentary, she does not resist, even enjoys it for its brief punctuation to the day. She imagines it is Zeus who has swooped down, a scenario garnished by his size and aroma of wine. And then he is running his hand over her shoulders and waist and wishing her a good rest, and she is reaching up to kiss his cheek in thanks, before she backs into her cabin and closes the door.

Bracing herself, against the roll, she manages to get undressed and under the covers, bumping her head once but smiling at it. Pleased by her decision to come on this voyage, she thinks happily of her distant but occupied sons, with whom she will reconnect more vigorously, describing the trip and this storied sea for them. Carried by these images and their faces, she is soon asleep.

At some point, on the drive back to Athens, Kostas and Wren resume talking, about the history of Delphi, before Wren describes his meeting Iscaria, "She almost seemed a priestess from another time."

"I think some visitors hope for such things," says Kostas smiling. "Did she ask you for money, some payment?"

"... No ..." And yet he remembers the kiss in the squall.

Kostas tells him that another fellow he drove up here claimed to have had such an encounter, at which Kostas laughs gently. Hearing this, Wren wonders how he should explain the experience to himself. Was it a performance? She an actress? He considers himself a realist, and yet the experience seems both real and imagined, as it wavers in his mind.

Glancing at him in his rearview mirror, Kostas sees Wren frowning and attempts to smooth over the confusion. "It *is* a magical place, my friend. It must be so, to have kept its reputation all these centuries."

Wren considers this, even as he feels his skepticism growing. But then he remembers the piece of paper and reaches into a pocket to pull it out. Leaning forward, he hands it to Kostas. "The woman, Iscaria, gave me this. It seems to be a name and number."

Glancing at it as he drives, Kostas squints to read the handwriting. After a moment, he nods. "Ah yes ... an Athens number. I know where this is."

"Iscaria said that I should go see this person – I couldn't read the name."

"Yes, I see ..." Kostas nods, glancing at the name. "A woman ... You want to see her?"

"I don't know. What do you think? Is it worth the time?"

Kostas hesitates. "I don't know ... I suspect she is not, you know, a consort, a prostitute."

"No, I didn't think so."

"Still, she may ask for money. Maybe she is an escort, as I think the term is. Some can be very nice ... offering companionship for an evening."

Wren laughs to himself. What to do? Possibly it could be interesting. Iscaria seemed sincere. But who knows?

"It is possible that the Oracle has directed you," offers Kostas, eyes smiling.

Wren is also faintly amused as he continues to consider the idea. "I hope to have dinner with a fellow architect, but otherwise I have no plans."

Kostas tells him, "If you want, I can drive you. You can always call me to take you back, if you are not happy."

Wren absorbs this. "... Maybe I will try."

With this Kostas dials the number as he drives. Reaching someone, he speaks rapidly and unintelligibly to Wren, but after the call, he reports that he has made an appointment for tomorrow evening. "It's not far from your hotel."

Wren thanks him, tentatively pleased that he has this to look forward to. The possibility that these three are in cahoots occurs to him, but his feeling about Iscaria is that she was honest. What did she want from him but a kiss.

At the hotel, Wren pays and thanks Kostas, saying good night until tomorrow. Passing the bar he stops for a whiskey, which he almost never has, but then this has been a strange, wrenching twenty-four hours, reaching back to the previous evening. How to explain it all? Belle's misdirected anger? His own, followed by his drawing away? There is fault enough for both. Yet she will not discuss it, nor accept any responsibility – perplexing, after all this time. Both have changed, have grown "As weary-hearted as that hollow moon." Despite intelligence, they have found no way to reach each other. Their worlds have diverged, rising in different directions as did the ravines at Delphi.

The whiskey soothes, or blurs, his emotions, and bends his thoughts back again to those sharp slopes. He feels her cool cheek, gazes into those pale, unearthly eyes. How much more patient and caring was she than he has lately known. The value of strangers. He pictures the black sea in which he swam, and the white form which preceded him, before disappearing, as if into her anger. Strange echo, strange happenings. Did something of those dark waters penetrate his skin, infusing him with an openness to unexpected connection? Or was it the shock of Belle's desertion that shook him to see anew his life ... and weigh what is important? ... He pictures ancient Athens, hears voices speaking, but cannot grasp their words. Today so much has changed ... We have so much information ... still it is a challenge to find connection. Did the ancients, with fewer words, less knowledge, find it more readily? ... Or were their expectations lower? The sharp crags and walls at Delphi suggest barriers, separation, and yet out of them Iscaria appeared, from the past, she who looked and saw ... who came to him and reached out. Perhaps as his heart did, tentatively at first, but then eagerly, thankfully.

Nearly blind, he walks unsteadily to the elevator, ascends, then follows the corridor wall to his room. Pushing in, he looks around through the dark, trying not to notice the vacuum, nor the smooth, undisturbed bed. On one hand he feels relief, on the other, emptiness.

A noise awakens Artemis from deep sleep. In the darkness she listens then slips back into her dream. But the noise comes again, across her cabin. She turns and looks, but there is no light. She listens. "Artemis?" comes a man's voice. Poseidon? she wonders ... No, Argos. "Yes?" she manages, trying to wake and orient herself.

"Just wanted to see how you're doing?"

"I've been sleeping. Is everyone still up?"

"No, they've all turned in."

She relaxes and closes her eyes again, relieved that she needn't join them. But she feels a weight slowly descend onto the edge of her bunk.

"So did you enjoy the sailing today?" he asks. "It was a perfect day for us. We shall easily make Crete by morning."

"Yes ..." She strains to remember, and slowly things return. "Yes ... a beautiful day, from sunrise to sunset, like nothing I've known," she breathes, recalling the dawn and gazing up into the great dome. And then she pictures the sea, staring into its depth, plunging into its grandly rolling swells.

"I'm having a delightful aperitif," he says softly, "which is like walking through an orange grove in the Peloponnesus. Would you like a sip?"

She tries to think. "... No thank you."

"Inhale its aroma, at least. It's nectar from the Gods." And before she can decline again, he places the small glass under her nose. She draws in the aroma; then feels the glass on her lower lip; a drop rolls in. She holds it in her mouth, finding it first cool, then hot, and yes, redolent of oranges. But not knowing what else to do, she swallows it, and experiences a faint current of heat, and sees a profusion of orange blossoms. Now, it seems, the sea is turning orange. Her bunk rolls slightly with the swells. She presses her head down into her pillow, replaying the pleasure of floating in the sea. In her mind's eye the sun's brightness fills everything, while her body shivers from the night air. Needing to breathe, she opens her mouth, taking in a long breath, and releasing it. She feels happy. But then she becomes aware of more drops on her lip, which slip into her mouth. Now she swims in an orange pool, inhaling soft air and pearl-like drops; the trickling heat returns, relaxing her. She watches as the color of orange deepens and fills her mind. She is gliding through lush groves under the streaming sun, wandering Arcadia, Messenia, Olympia. Familiar voices are heard close by, somewhere in the grove. A small glass returns to her lower lip; a tiny stream runs onto her tongue; she savors it, and swallows. Birds alight into the evening sky. Her body sinks into lush pillows. Now she hardly notices the returning flow or its magic filling her.

Fingers are pushing her hair from her brow, then moving lightly over her scalp. She enjoys this, as she floats. Soft hands, cool fingers, touch her neck, in pleasurable contrast to the expanding heat. She feels her eyes roll back as she ascends into the night. Returning to sleep? A dream? Then remembering Argos, she tries to hold it off.

"Artemis?" comes her name. "Yes," she replies. "Are you sleeping?"

Am I? she wonders.

"I must go," he tells her, "but have a last swallow."

She opens her lips, and this time the stream returns, pleasurable, cool, then hot, with that now familiar fragrance filling the air. She must clear her throat to swallow it all. "Good night," she murmurs.

"Goodnight," he replies, and leans to kiss her, which she accepts, a brief, parting gesture. And yet his lips linger longer than she anticipated. But soon she will return to sleep. It is pleasant enough, and then they are gone, as is his weight from the bunk. She inhales deeply and turns slightly. But now becomes aware that his hands have returned and are moving over her shoulders; the covers are gently pulled down. A hand traces her stomach through her silk top. Sensations stir her, and confusion interrupts her effort to sink back to sleep. Finger tips run up her sides, her ribs, stealing her breath, awaking her and some vague presentiment. It is both pleasurable and somehow disturbing. She tries to roll away from this hand, but another joins to hold her, and press firmly over her breasts. Her breath leaves her; her body rises rigidly; she inhales, trying to awake, but she is in a deep cloud, with nothing to grasp. Other sensations, some pleasurable, run through her, into her stomach ... legs. She gasps, caught in a tension of conflicting inclinations. A hand works up her thighs. Her breath flees once more; her body tries to follow, but her mind is clouded, conflicted.

"Argos," she calls softly, "... what ...?" But now lips return, pressing into hers, accompanied by the color of bright orange and the feel of soft leaves. A hand behind her head holds her to them. She likes this, and yet there is something about it ... Voices whisper within her. Her lips are held to others softly pressing. An arm pulls her up against another ... Him? What is happening?

And yet she likes the warmth against her, in the cool air. Now those lips are moving to her neck, soft and sensual, stirring her. They leave, then return, pressing into her lips, leave and return, leave and return. She lifts her head up to follow them. Wants them, a nearly forgotten feeling. Hazily, she finds she is both desirous and wary, floating in steep, rolling waves.

She feels the covers pulled down off her legs, her pajama bottoms slipped off. The firm, gentle pressure on her lips returns, pleasurable but now more confusing. She remembers the orange grove ... Argos in the Peloponnesus.

The few buttons on her top are undone, sending chills over her bare skin. Nothing is now covering her. And she is being touched everywhere, kissed everywhere, pleasantly ... but it is not what she wants. She tries to turn away ... but hands pull her sharply back and hold her down. She tries to call, "Argos! No!" but lips pressing into hers stifle her words. She twists right and left to escape and manages another "No!" But now his weight descends onto her, and his lips press heavily into hers. She tries to push and hit his head, but his hands clamp onto her wrists painfully and yank her arms above her head. She twists and writhes to free them but has not the strength. His legs have pried and slipped between hers; she is aware of his heavy body along the length of hers. Another heart is pumping over and into hers, and this jolts her as if an electrical shock. It fills her with panic, a spasm of fear. Clarity over what is happening grips her, filling her chest. It is not what she wants. And now with the strength of fear, she pulls her legs up and under his and rolls her hips away. She hears him grunting and appealing to her, trying to coax her, but he cannot release his hands pinning her wrists in order to roll her back. Though it seems some harsh beak grips her, she recognizes that he cannot position her as he wants. His lips return to hers, but she does not want them now. Through her clenched jaw she again tries to speak, slurring it, "Argss!" He tries again to roll her, but cannot, as she maintains her fetal bend. With a release of exasperation and an oath, he pauses, draped heavily on her. "Artemis?" comes his appeal. "No," she answers.

"I thought you would enjoy this, wanted this," he tries. But she spits out another, "No."

For some time, he remains atop, breathing, waiting for something, his excitement draining away. She is acutely alert, on guard. Eventually he pulls up and off, and apparently stands there in the dark. She can smell his sweat, a bitter smell. He breathes and speaks, "Would it have been so bad?"

But she does not answer. With relief slowly seeping through her, she becomes aware of irritation, indignation, a knot of fury. She listens, hears the rustle of clothes. She waits in the dark, then hears him move to the door, where he says, "Goodnight." Then he opens the door and steps out.

She dares not move, lying there listening. But all is quiet save for the slap of the waves against the hull. Now she stretches out her legs, hips, arms and wrists, becoming aware of soreness. After some moments of listening, she sits up and pulls her night clothes back on. She becomes aware of other aches up and down, but otherwise she is not injured. She lies there trying to impose order on the whole thing. How did he think this would be okay? What right did he think he had? ... Yes, they had talked; she came on board, had seen he was attracted, but then had cried "No!" Yet he'd continued, trying to force his will ... Had the others succumbed? Who did he think he was? ... And now what? What to do about this whole thing?

It's too late to consult Marguerite. Tomorrow. But then what to do? Get off, go to the police? They will ask if she was raped. When she replies that she was assaulted, their eyes will glaze over ... Now however, she must try to rest; sleep may be impossible, but she will need to clear her thoughts, decide in the morning. It will be a long dark night, and the day maybe no better.

On his second morning alone, he awakes with a start, seeing through the curtain that the sun has preceded him. Rising and peeking out, he finds the white and beige, sun-splashed city bathed in light. Life and the day move on without him. The ancients rose and retired with the sun. Somehow this spurs him to move, catch up, live.

On the other hand, Belle's decision still knots his chest, feels like the clanking, thumping heating pipes sound at home. He shakes himself and fumbles to get dressed, find his room key, and wander down for breakfast. The waiter asks if his wife will be joining him. "No," he says, feeling his body, and maybe the entire dining room, miss a beat. He closes his eyes, tries to relax, focus on the day, filling it, finding what he should do.

As he was leaving his room, he'd seen that neither George nor Antaeus had returned his calls. So ... what ... ? See the city, a beach ... museums again? He feels he's treading water, floating with temples, columns, and buoyant statues, all bobbing in the swells. What he would like is a living, breathing companion with whom to revisit that ancient world. Belle might have been ideal; it was part of the reason they came, but she has withdrawn. So ... somehow he must find an alternative, someone else to share thoughts ... experience ... life. He thinks of Iscaria – a priestess from the past, yet modern and unstinting. He wonders who she shares her awareness and perception with, her caring. Is that what drew her? Some sense of that? Some like consciousness astonished by, appreciative of, the miracle that so much exists.

Light reaches through her small cabin window and awakens her. When she regains a sense of where she is, she holds her breath, looks around. Dark, unpleasant memories lurk in the corners. Though she tries to turn her mind away, they push in insistently, pressing her ribs. She feels an ache in her wrists, pain in her shoulders and chest. She cannot believe it happened.

Her thoughts escape to yesterday, before ... to its sun-filled moments, the rolling sea, the dark, distant islands, promising then, now sinister ... and to the aroma of oranges, and what followed. Though part of her wants to avoid remembering, she knows she needs to, in order to decide what to do ... How did he think he had the right? ... In today's world? But she knows the reality, and feels her anger rising, churning ... Different paths present themselves. Which to take? Get up and confront? Punch, claw, cryout? Inform the others? Let him have a taste, shoved down his throat. Yet she guesses the others would be ... little surprised ... embarrassed ... pitying ... Outrage from Marguerite, but otherwise from the other two mostly sadness, silence.

There had been signs, looks, suspicions. Why had she not been more alert? Taken precautions, somehow barred the door, left the room when he came in? The liquor ... she should have spit it out ... She swallowed too much of it ... and his act.

But what now? ... Go to the police on Crete? How will they react? 'What happened? ... Is that all?' they will say.' We cannot arrest every man who kisses a woman ... Okay, who gropes her; okay, who tries to force himself ... But he did not succeed ... Do you know how many ...? Did you resist from the outset? Well, what was it that *did* happen? *Why* were you on his boat?'

He will deny all, argue she encouraged him ... But not to do *that, not* to that extent! Kissed him good night, yes, but ... And what evidence is there? Sore wrists? ...

Does she want to submit to such skeptical questioning? ... Would they even care? A woman agrees to come sailing, without her husband? Could she explain it? ... He will have lawyers, arguing that little or nothing happened. Their client stopped when it was made clear; the charges should be dismissed ... She might ask for a female police officer ... Would there be one? ... There must be some women in power on the island. She will call the American embassy in Athens, seek advice, representation.

Her mind rushes on, in one direction, then another. Could she find a local lawyer? Is a fair outcome possible? An indictment, a trial? She's read about Greek policy, all favors and money ... If charged, Argos would be out on bail. Would she, at some later date, have to fly all the way back to Crete? Would he even appear? Oh! ... Fury pours out from several spigots, into a raging stream, which she cannot stop.

He's an important executive, he'll want to keep this quiet. She has leverage ... But it's not fair ... never has been ... Who came up with the idea that men are what women get? Still, in the modern age? Kind and loving women, egotistic, grasping men. Force was a survival benefit in pre-historic times, but quite other now ... Where's Athena? ... Women are leading in education ... ascending. Maybe we should go on strike, maybe men should *have* to pay. After all, we do.

She will go talk with Marguerite, quietly in a cabin, after a shower.

She rises, pulls her robe around her and peers out her door. Going down the passageway silently, quickly, she finds the first shower room free and slips in. It's a relief to wash and warmly rub her sore shoulders, legs, and arms. She forces the images away, his grunting in the dark. She turns her thoughts to the boys, the islands ... Or should she leave? ... She doesn't want to give all of this up ... this dream ... and return to her house and bedroom, a kind of mausoleum ... though she is pleased with the way she has decorated it. Wren, the architect, had only a simple, male idea of what to do.

Back in her cabin, as she dresses, she wonders how to face Argos. Smile as though nothing happened, until she lands on Crete?

Moving into the main cabin, she sees that most of the others are up on deck. Only Angela is present, having coffee. They greet, "Good Morning. Sleep well?" Rote questions, rote responses.

Artemis feigns sleepiness, to keep conversation to a minimum. Fortunately, Marguerite comes in, greeting and heading to the cabins. Artemis turns and follows. In the passageway, she catches her and asks if they may talk. Hearing the urgency, Marguerite motions to follow, explaining she's returned for a sweater, as the morning's proving cool.

In her cabin, shutting the door quietly, Marguerite waits, and Belle, with a rush, releases the story.

Marguerite is stunned ... disgusted, angry, sympathetic. She steps forward to embrace Artemis for some moments, before recounting Argos's attempt with her, near Ithaca, averted only because she had not been asleep and was alert enough to quickly leave her cabin, claiming that she was seasick. "Mal a l'estomach ... je ne peut pas."

In low tones, they discuss going to the authorities, but Marguerite is doubtful that any quick resolution would follow. She reveals that she approached Angela about her hinted-at experience, but Angela grew uncomfortable and made an excuse to leave.

Belle and Marguerite stand silently, thinking. They decide to go to the police on Crete, or maybe a consulate if there is one, and inquire generally what might be done, saying that something happened to another member of their party. But until then, doubting the support they might receive from Angela or Ileana, they decide to say nothing. Belle will stay in her cabin until they dock. Marguerite will remain close by, both avoiding Argos.

Sometime later on her bunk, Belle attempts to read a Greek history, with its endless wars, in a volume from Poseidon's library, but her mind is abducted by memories ... questions. How? Why? ... How best to respond? Glimpses, conclusions, plans whirl through her. But then she is interrupted by a knock on her door. She does not answer, waits, breath held. The door is opened. Leaning in, Argos scans the room, finds her. Quickly she pushes up. He soothes, "Good morning. How are you doing? Get some rest?"

She doesn't know quite what to say. They consider each other, and when Argos is fully aware of her agitation, he steps in. She slides to a corner, unsure of his intentions.

"Are you okay?" he asks.

Finding the question, the concern, preposterous, she glances away. Where to start? What attitude to take, given her intention to seek out the authorities? And yet she cannot restrain herself entirely. "What *was* that? Why did you persist after I said no? How did you think that was okay?"

It takes him a moment to collect a response. "I don't quite understand ... You seemed ... interested, responsive ..."

She wrenches herself around in disgust. "I was asleep ... you poured that liquor ... you held me down ..."

"I thought *that* was what you came for ... We were getting along ... talking. I like you ... You're hardly a novice."

She finds this abhorrent, dishonest, but she must calm herself. Just then there's another knocking on her door. Marguerite calls out, "Belle, we are coming into the harbor, come up and see. I believe we'll dock soon."

"Come in, Marguerite."

Marguerite tries to open the door, but Argos is heading out, greeting her as if nothing were amiss. When he has left, the two women stare at each other, silently sifting through reactions, scenarios.

Today the museums again. He decides to study more closely the architectural ideas, to use or draw inspiration from ... Tomorrow, he may fly or ferry to an island, soar over the azure sea.

He consults the concierge once more, about islands to visit for a day. Mykonos, Rhodes, Kostas' Paros. Afterward, map in hand, he walks back to the Acropolis Museum, where he bends over the models, of cornice and corona, flutes and friezes, then peers down into the ancient rooms preserved under glass. Does he catch sight of a shadow gliding between rooms? A custodian, or ancient Athenian? He imagines living in the ancient city, meeting at the agora, speaking of their daily needs, how to live? Threats from Persia, Sparta? Perhaps life was not so different.

He sketches details in a small pad he's brought: ideas to work from, connecting ancient designs with current ones.

Later, he bends close to study dramatic scenes painted on serving bowls: heroes fighting, subduing each other or beasts. A precarious existence. Death omnipresent. He stretches up eye to eye with the sculpted faces of men and women, whose features are symmetrical, calm, intent ... Not at all like most contemporary Greeks he's seen. But the sculpted faces are mostly gods and heroes, embodying: strength, proportion, beauty ... grace ... Ideals then and now.

By mid-afternoon he is happy to find a café in which to sit, eat, have a beer, rest his legs, and his bruised, silent heart.

Glimpses of Belle come back. He does not dispute her abilities, her caring for the boys, her conviviality ... but her anger toward him erases much. When it rages, it becomes excessive, ugly, destructive. What purpose does it serve, besides venting? Yes, he too can spit things out, but it does not linger corrosively for days, as it seems to in her. He has long recognized that she cannot dismiss anger and criticism as readily as he can. But the result of their outbursts is that they have lost the ability to talk, or reach any accommodation. If they loved one another, they might exchange views and compromise. But that ability seems to have pretty much gone. Their story has become another small, local tragedy. Sad, but evidently all too common. Time witnesses the attrition of caring and happiness, and once shattered, unlike the ancient vases, it seems nearly impossible to fit back together.

His mind wanders to his work. What might come of the residential project waiting at home? He hopes that Margaux is coping, maybe more ably than he. She's good on the phone with clients and prospective clients. Her smile is restorative – no one else smiles at him – hers is bright with youthful excitement, discovery, optimism ... appreciation ... before so much is worn away.

In the harbor of Iraklion, under a clouding sky, all step carefully off the boat. Argos has called for a taxi to take them to the ruins at Knossos, but Marguerite now steps forward between him and the others. Though not as tall as he, she here seems as imposing, announcing unwaveringly that she needs to find a pharmacy for a few essentials, as does Belle. Argos studies the two, his face darkening; he offers to accompany them, but Marguerite insists she doesn't want to hold the others up, and will instead meet them at the site in an hour or so. Clearly doubtful of her story, and perturbed by this wrinkle, he asks how long could their shopping possibly take, but the Marguerite holds to her plan, and unable to think of a reason to divert from his, he accepts it.

Two taxis take them off, Marguerite and Belle into the center of the small city, where they ask to be driven to police headquarters. There they request a meeting with a female supervisor, but are told the sole woman is not on duty today. They ask to speak to whomever is available, and are directed to a small office where a young man, thirtyish, and smiling amiably under his short, dark hair, welcomes them. Marguerite explains that a friend has been sexually assaulted, and they are here to find out what can be done. The supervisor asks if the culprit is Greek. No, they tell him. British. He asks if there were witnesses. They don't believe so, but there may be other women willing to lodge similar complaints. The young man, while sympathetic, explains that it will be difficult to arrest anyone, let alone prosecute. Are the victim and attacker on Crete and will they be here long? The two women cannot be sure.

"You see," he continues, "all of this would take time, to present the accused with a charge, to set or deny bail, to investigate and take statements from all who might have something to contribute. If cause can be established, the accused would be given a hearing, offered the chance to state his case. What nationality is the victim?

The two women hesitate, before Marguerite explains, "We only just met. She could be Canadian, English, American; we don't know." The officer suggests that they contact the appropriate embassy in Athens. But he sees that this seems problematic for them. Now addressing Belle primarily, he asks, "Would the woman want to pursue this? Unfortunately, it can not only take time but can be messy in cross-examination ... The principles' histories would come up, details ... You understand?"

Mouth set, lips pressed, she nods. If the officer suspects she is the victim, he's being discreet. "We don't know what she will want to do," she tells him. "We're trying to figure out what it would entail." He offers, "I would recommend calling her embassy. I can connect you, if you wish." Belle thanks him, but asks, "Is a conviction likely?" Looking down, he breathes deeply. "There are so many variables ... If there are no witnesses, it is difficult to prove that it was not consensual." He sends her a sympathetic look. Marguerite asks if the two of them can talk it over, and he obligingly leaves the room.

"Que pense-toi?" Marguerite asks.

"Je ne sais pas," confesses Belle. In halting French, she lists her priorities: she had hoped to see these islands whose history she has studied, and she had hoped to enjoy the cruise as well. But now she wants to bring Argos to justice; she narrowly avoided getting raped. "At the same time, I don't want to ruin the cruise for you three …"

"Ooh, don't worry about me. This is a crime. We cannot let him off."

Belle thanks her, but can envision no clear way forward. "Should we tell this officer that we'll get back to him when the victim decides?"

"Yes … What else, at this point?" agrees Marguerite. And they do when he returns. He agrees to take down the information, specifying, "I will need the names, nationalities … passport numbers, addresses, e-mail …" Belle nods, but hesitates. He repeats that frequently in such cases a plea or arrangement outside of court is agreed upon. "But I can take the names, and you can let me know."

The two women provide Argos's real name and information about his boat, but only reluctantly does Belle accept that she must identify herself as the plaintiff and provide details. When he has written down what he needs, he gives them his card and thanks them for coming in, adding, "Unfortunately, not so many come forward in these cases, which of course helps to perpetuate the situation."

Their eyes meet as Belle grimly acknowledges this. He then summarizes, "I have the information … If someone wants to proceed, contact her embassy and they may contact me."

The two women thank him and leave. Outside they walk silently until Marguerite asks Belle if she wants to fly back to Athens. She's unsure. They stop in a café for a coffee, and to talk it over. "I couldn't possibly return to the boat, and him ... Do you understand my ... abhorrence ...?"

"Mais oui! Of course ... I am not wanting to either. C'est inexcusable."

"So, we should get off ... But the other two ... how will they react?"

"For them it may be more complicated ..."

Belle stares down at the table, attempting to anticipate how the two will respond. "I suppose there is no particular reason for them to leave ... But rather than return to Athens, I might travel around myself... Or with you, if you wish. We don't need the boat."

"No, I agree. But you must also decide if you want to explore any legal remedies."

"Are there any?!" Belle asks sharply. "Of course I'd like to ... but the officer was not encouraging."

"I'm afraid that that is what I've heard as well."

Belle ponders her choices. "And if I confront him? Tell him that we have reported his assault to the authorities; they have his name and the boat's information? ... What then? Where do you think that would lead?"

"Sais pas," confesses Marguerite. "And again we don't know if Angela and Ileana would join us ..."

Belle breathes and glances around. "I'm certain that I don't want to continue ... What I'd like to do is contact the embassy in Athens, to ask what they recommend ... But I feel badly for you."

Marguerite dismisses this concern. "It's not a problem for me, but I think we should talk to the others." Belle agrees, and so, finishing their coffees, they hire a taxi to take them out to Knossos.

The site is quiet and pleasing, not crowded, as they walk in under an alley of large pines to the entrance. They note, as they read in a brochure, that the lack of ramparts suggests the Minoans had no known threats to their dominating position in the Eastern Mediterranean – a situation that somehow reminds them of Argos on his boat. But they find no sign of him or the women as they wander. The palace's buildings are only partially standing or restored, including a number of clay-red columns and walls. Filling one of these walls, a great red bull stares out from its bulging round eye, also reminding them of Argos with his appropriating gaze. They stare back unhappily for some moments, before moving on to frescos of young servants, males mostly, carrying jars or pitchers, and one fresco of blue-backed dolphins leaping, as they themselves did swimming off the boat. The style is similar to two-dimensional Egyptian art, further evidence of its early period, while the absence of women suggests that they exercised little power or had little presence. As the two survey the murals, they try to imagine women's existence in that long-ago world – evidently even more restricted than in classical Greece.

Their tour completed, as they are ambling out, they run into Ileana and Angela, who report that Argos had to suddenly return to the boat for some unspecified reason. Belle and Marguerite glance at each other, wondering what it suggests, but they say nothing. Instead Marguerite now takes Angela's arm saying she wants to visit the gift shop. Ileana is about to follow, but Belle asks if she may speak with her for a moment. Wary and displaying some discomfort, Ileana slowly turns back. In a low voice Belle describes the assault and the police meeting, before adding that she doesn't want to continue on with the cruise.

At first Ileana is shocked; her head falls with a moan, "No-oo ... Is this true?" But she seeks no confirmation, staring instead through the trees, before murmuring, "Ooh my ... oh dear ... I'm sorry ... You know ... I knew him in Barcelona ... We met and grew close for a short time. I painted his portrait, which he bought ... and hung in his office." She shakes her head at this, then confesses, "I could see who he is ... the egotism ... but I didn't think he would ... I should have ..." Her minds runs back through her time with him, until she appears to shake off the emotion, and finds Belle again. "With this ... I too do not want to return to the boat. How could I?" She leans toward Belle and embraces her companion, whispering, "I'm sorry." Pulling back a bit, they seek each other's eyes, looking heavily and expressing dismay. Belle thanks her for her support, before she concedes, "I guess we're all ... in the same boat." A weak smile pulls one from Ileana, before Belle repeats, "So well then ... we must get off and leave it behind." Both now stare down at the walk as they murmur vague accord.

Belle now proposes, "We should broach this with Angela. Marguerite knows, and is with us. We must decide what we all want to do." And so they swing around and head toward the gift shop, where they find the two just leaving. Halting, and reading each other's moods, the four share a sense of dismay, and that something has changed, confirmed when Belle and Ileana fill in Angela. She too is briefly nonplussed, shaking her head, before she releases a rueful laugh. "Why are we surprised? What did we think he was up to?"

For some moments, each reflects on the situation, until Angela speaks out again, firmly, "But there's no point in lamenting this, which we should have seen coming. We must simply respond and leave. We can travel by ourselves."

And so, with all in agreement, they taxi back to the docks. In the cab, reluctant to speak candidly, they describe the details they enjoyed at the palace. Only on the quay, walking to the boat, do they vent their annoyance and anger, until they notice

Poseidon's captain stepping off the boat and hurrying toward them. He greets them but then quickly informs them that Mr. Henry has been called away by business and will be flying off – where to the captain doesn't say. The four glance among themselves. Belle asks the captain, "Did he say nothing more, about how long he would be gone?"

"I'm afraid not, Madame."

"Well then, we must collect our belonging and bags."

"But, Madame, indeed all of you, Mr. Henry asked me to invite you to stay aboard Poseidon, and we will continue our cruise, if that is acceptable to you."

Surprised once more, the four seek reaction among themselves, before Margerite asks him, "What does that mean? Where would we sail to? Without him?"

The captain bows and seems pleased to offer, "He has directed me to continue as planned, on to Rhodes, Patmos, and the others."

"But you are suggesting he will not return?"

While the captain tries to smile reassuringly, he also faintly shrugs. "I do not know. He did not say when, or where. He only told me that he would be tied up for some time … but of course eventually, he must come back."

Belle glances at the others. What now? Does this change things? Angela voices the need to discuss this among themselves before deciding one way or another. The captain bows. "I am here with Poseidon, so please take your time, and then tell me what it is you wish."

The four see that they must go somewhere to discuss this. They ask him if he can recommend a good restaurant for lunch, and he names one, pointing back along the waterfront. Thanking him, they set off, commenting on the sights, interspersed with sharp comments about Henry.

Walking quickly, emotions churning, they nonetheless notice that the port is not touristy but functional. Winding among fishermen unloading their catches, they pass stands displaying food and wares for sale, until eventually they come to the restaurant. Greeted warmly by the majordomo, they are seated by the water, and soon discover the wine is good and the seafood better. This lifts their spirits, and their conversation brightens, until they remember they need to discuss the alternatives. With returning emotion, Belle speaks first, restating her condemnation of Henry and her desire to disassociate herself from him. The other share this sentiment, until Angela raises a new possibility. "What would we all think, now that Henry has flown off, escaped ... of staying aboard, so long as he doesn't reappear?"

At first the other three express some discomfort in remaining on his boat. But Angela explains her reasoning, "After all, Henry promised us this cruise; we have all to some degree paid to get here, airfare, hotels, putting up with him. Do we not, in a sense, owe it to ourselves? And does he not, in the least, owe it to us?"

Carefully, they glance among each other and more particularly at Belle, who acknowledges the possibility. "I understand; it makes sense ... but I, for one, must consider whether I could stomach staying aboard with all that reminds me of ... Yet I do not want to influence your decisions."

Quickly Marguerite responds, "Do not worry about us. For I believe that we can do something Henry cannot: reason together as to what make sense for all, pour tous ensemble."

Angela elaborates further, "While it is his boat, it seems to me now, that without him, the situation is quite different. Belle, I do not want to minimize the affront to you ... but we had each looked forward to this, with some real anticipation. Now with the problem eliminated, for however long, should we not enjoy what we were promised and have in part paid for?"

Ileana adds her view: "I too do not want to excuse what he did to Belle. It deeply sours my estimation of him, which was already, in my experience, very much mixed ... but as Angela said, he has removed himself, for whatever reasons ..."

Marguerite interjects, "Why this particular timing, other than to flee facing the police?"

"Yes," concedes Ileana, "it is probably so ... but for whatever reason, he is gone, leaving us to ourselves, to enjoy the islands. In a sense his flying off is a concession of guilt. He must understand that we could all go to the authorities. He may think we have."

Belle's eyes fall to the table as she weighs these things, before she concedes, "While my desire for legal redress is firm, at the same time my work and my passion has long been the study of History, and this voyage was going to be a longed-for treat, to visit where so much began and developed. That reason alone, now urges me to continue. But at the same time, there is something distasteful about staying on his boat, with his fingerprints, so to speak, everywhere."

For a short time again, all reflect on this, until Angela suggests, "Perhaps we should all sleep on it, weigh more deeply the pros and cons of staying or leaving, and also, of joining Belle in pursuing some legal recourse. Possibly by morning, we will all have reached some clarity."

While this makes sense to all, their halting discussion persists; for a time they can speak of little else, but by the end of the meal they have pretty much decided to continue the cruise. The disruptive, violent element has removed himself; it might still turn out to be what they had envisioned.

After lunch, for the rest of the afternoon, they wander through the town, enjoying it and discussing what they hope to discover on the other islands.

As they are about to return to the boat, Angela asks if she may relate her own story concerning Argos, and the three encourage her. She glances around to insure that no one can hear, before, with some diffidence and embarrassment, she confesses, in minimal detail, that, as hinted earlier, he had gotten to her as well. While the circumstances seem more ambiguous, the incident now re-summons her anger, spiking into sharp words, then dwindling away into ambivalence. She describes him as both imperious and sympathetic, brusque but occasionally sensitive. She believes that their shared, difficult English childhoods, on the edge of poverty, may have created a bond, or at least a shared history. But that doesn't excuse his behavior. She too explored legal rejoinders, but also found the options limited, and so came to a settlement, which incidentally prohibits her from speaking out against him.

Marguerite, now in more detail, describes the police supervisor's warning of difficulty, expense, and uncertain outcome. Angela emphasizes that she too found conviction on any counts was, and is, unlikely. "Money erects a near impenetrable wall around people with his means."

Back on board Poseidon, they tell the captain that they will give him their decision in the morning. He is courteous and seems content to wait, saying he will be directed by their wishes. But earlier, walking back, the four had agreed to talk openly of the various legal steps they are pursuing, assuming that the captain will pass this on to Henry wherever he is.

Showering and dressing for dinner, they feel a degree of satisfaction in imagining the captain's report to Henry of their legal plans. Belle borrows Marguerite's phone to call the American embassy in Athens. There she is connected to a woman staff member, to whom she summarizes the story. While sympathetic, the woman points out, as the policeman did, that there are a host of frustrating legal hurdles. She offers to help Belle pursue it, but warns that it will be expensive, time-consuming, and very possibly futile. Yet the woman writes down all that Belle provides her, and she gives Belle the names of three reputable local law firms to call if she so chooses.

With that, despite the obstacles, Belle feels encouraged. There is support and several strategies to consider. Returning Marguerite's phone, she tells her new friend that she would never have guessed she would fall victim to such predictable behavior. "I mean, I was not entirely deceived ... But in no way do I turn it back upon myself. He is operating under the illusion that he is captain of his world, which grants him license ... for which I intend to make him pay."

Marguerite reaches out to place a supportive hand on her shoulder. Belle smiles; she'll be okay. Indeed she's recognizes that Henry's venery has brought the four unexpectedly closer, creating an unexpected bond among them.

In the evening, the front desk calls to inform Wren that his car is waiting. Having been sound asleep, he hurries to shower and dress, before heading down to the lobby, where he finds Kostas waiting with an amused smile. "Sorry to take you from your beauty rest, Mr. Wren." And he pats his passenger on the shoulder, as they make their way out the door.

Kostas drives rapidly through the evening traffic to the rendezvous that Iscaria recommended. He reminds Wren that he may have to pay something – she will tell him how much – as the session may include food, wine, and entertainment. Vaguely Wren's still-hazy mind absorbs this, as he sways in the back seat of the swerving car, gazing out at the streaming lights.

Kostas turns off the avenue and navigates at barely less speed through the narrow side streets of Kolonaki. Parking, he leads Wren to the first floor apartment, where he introduces himself and Wren to the woman, Messena. Tall like Iscaria, she wears a burka within whose hood Wren can see only her shadowed eyes. Unsure what to make of this, and still not fully awake, Wren tries to hide his sudden doubt by gazing around her apartment. Is she religious? Why does she wear a burka?

As he's leaving, Kostas looks to see if Wren is content to stay, and discreetly asks as much. Bewildered, glancing about, Wren indicates he'll try it. Kostas hands him a local mobile to call whenever he's ready.

And then, alone with this woman, Wren finds that any idea of what to talk about has deserted him. He searches around once more, wondering what interests they could possibly share.

"Are you all right?" she asks, noticing his discomfort.

"Yes," he manages. "Sorry."

"You did not expect this?" she says running her finger tips lightly down her burka.

"No ... but then I didn't know what to expect."

"I will dispose of it soon, but I want you to react to me not as a woman, but to the person I am."

He nods, not really understanding, feeling disoriented, adrift in high swells. As he waits for her to continue, he becomes aware of other sensations radiating from her: heat, a sense of pulsing intensity, perfume mingling with a floral aroma. Now her voice deepens, echoing through the entrance hall. He peers in at her eyes, wondering if he has made a mistake. Sensing his reaction, she steps back a little and softens her voice, speaking now in a near-whisper, so that he must lean to hear. The effort helps him focus his splaying thoughts; he finds that she reminds him in other ways of Iscaria, then notices the walls of the entrance are papered with great columns, as if leading into a temple.

Now she is motioning for him to follow to a sitting room, simple, spare, with one white and one gray armchair facing each other in the center, and two bronze lamps providing pools of light. She glides to a tray and takes two glasses filled with wine and hands him one. "Retsina. Greek wine," she says and touches his glass with hers. Tiny bells jingle, but again he cannot find the source. He notices now that she is studying him with her large, dark eyes before, her head turning, they recede into shadow. "I hope," she tells him, "that you will forget about me, and tell me about yourself."

He laughs a little. Forget about her? ... But who is she? What does he know of her? Nothing, beyond Iscaria's recommendation. He clears his throat to ask, "Excuse me, but are you a ... marriage counselor, or therapist ... ?"

Light fills her eyes; he can just make out the radiance of a smile. He hears her breath drawn deeply and carefully in. "I suppose that you could say a therapist, although I do not label myself as such, nor do I have a degree. More of a conversational partner. One who helps explore."

He nods, accepting this, if not clearly comprehending. She moves on, saying that she's heard he's an architect. He acknowledges, wondering how she has learned. She asks him how he likes Athens, and its architecture. Closing his eyes, he recalls the sun-streaked Parthenon and other temples, and so begins to describe the delights he discovered. To be in its presence, he tells her, was inspiring; the many buildings together transported him back to that time of flourishing, democratic Athens.

Eyes brightening and seeming to enlarge, she watches, evaluating him with unblinking attention. He rushes on, describing other discoveries in the city: new hotels, corporate offices, and apartments, hidden in the tight crush of Athens' neighborhoods." And ohh!" he exclaims, "I visited a fascinating house on a beach, designed by a George Nestoros."

"Oh George! ... I know George!" she cries with pleasure. "A dear man."

"Yes! His house is a dream, a nautilus crawled out of the sea, graceful, light, and airy. I know no house like it. It is unique, with its curving concentric walls and rooms. It is the kind of thing I would like to design if I got the opportunity."

Her eyes, excited by his, dance within the shadows of the burka. They stare at each other for several seconds savoring their shared excitement. But then she turns back to the subject she feels bound to explore, "And your marriage? Is there difficulty?"

Silence expands around him, cloaking the happiness he had felt. She apologizes for changing subjects, explaining that she does not mean to pry but simply wants to understand. But he's unsure where to go. They watch each other, though she seems to fade within the burka, before from it, comes soft encouragement, "Do not be shy. You have come to talk. Marriages are not easy, I can assure you. But in your case, what are the difficulties?"

Again he laughs to himself. What indeed? And what to tell her, who is not so shy? Already she seems to know much about him. Where to begin, what truths can he extract from the uncomfortable past? From the siege of Troy? ... She must've spoken with Iscaria ... George, even Kostas ... He peers at her, into her eyes, encountering her gaze, earnest, waiting ... He might turn the question back to her, though she seems sincere. He inhales, and begins, "I suppose, not uniquely, things have gone off the rails, fallen apart; we live essentially separate lives, with different views, a loss of respect ... suspicion ... the end of all physical affection."

Her eyes fall. He glimpses pained flashes, yet she nods and murmurs, "And found no way to restore it?" He shakes his head. She breathes and checks, "Neither of you?"

He looks at her with some discontent, for he feels that he has made efforts with Belle, to no avail. Yet to tell Messena that will seem self-serving. "We've tried ... but failed." He twists his mouth regretfully.

"I'm sorry," she tells him. "But it is seldom easy." She looks across the room, noting, "Sometimes one or the other can make a breakthrough, find some tone or key ..." She studies him for a moment in the low, bronze light. Within the burka, her head averted, her pupils are half-lit, half-brown, half-obsidian. He feels disoriented, again, as if suddenly in a different time, speaking with some god. He thinks of poor Paris waiting, looking among the three – having to judge. Yet here, her dark, curving eyes watch him carefully, without judgment. He hears Aegean waves lapping on a dark sandy shore, recalls a ghostly form wading in, disappearing. The first of strange occurrences. Yet now, instead of anger and doubt, an enveloping kindness reaches out and surrounds him, and he hears her ask, "How long has it been?"

His body flinches; a shiver plummets down his back ... He does not know, can hardly think ... Things deteriorated slowly ... Does he even want to go back into it? He'd rather talk about Athens or the Greeks, architecture, culture, books, movies, or even the financial crisis. What he wants is conversation ... with a woman. This woman, for he's beginning to feel that this in itself may be a kind of therapy ... She is, as some are, attentive, responsive ... There is a potential for communication ... at some level, which he could use ... And also, he's on vacation, discovering a part of the world new to him, a part that created so much of what we have. Therapy can be pursued at home ... Maybe he should have invited Margaux. A working vacation. She shares a passion for architecture ... But it's a desperate fantasy ... He had never imagined that things with Belle would collapse so completely.

And so tonight he'd hoped would be more social, cultural, speaking with an interesting person. He feels faint annoyance at this returning dragon's head. Perhaps he can re-direct things. "I ... uh ... a while ... I don't know. Several years. But tonight I was hoping we could talk of other things."

"We will. ... I merely want to understand who I am speaking with. I like architecture. How could one not, in this country? In many ways our ancient culture saw the first intertwining of so much. I love many of the arts, music above all."

"Yes!" he bursts, feeling suddenly released, awakened. He stares into those other eyes. "It is astonishing ... Isn't it? ... How it reaches in ..." As she stares back, he searches his mind for more, "I mean for many ... for me anyway, music expresses so deeply... the emotions, the ideal ... the mere sounds or tones speak particular feeling ... Is it simply the vibrations reaching in ... the deep physicality ... or spirituality? ... I have even read it may originate in the womb, the mother's voice and singing, transmitted through the walls, as through George's curving walls ... Whatever the case, the sounds, the melodies, express what I, and many, feel ..."

Now he hears the music at Delphi, the mandolin and flute carried on the wind, up from the valley, seeming to summon him to Iscaria ... who sent him here. He feels the stinging rain, the cool face he kissed, the weightless body within his arms ... Her eyes shine, here. He can see them reflecting light. Two stars. Light from across the universe.

"Yes," she breathes happily, "we can talk of that, and listen to some if you like, but first ... I hope to learn a little more about where you are. I sense a quiet about you ... something held in."

Still pleased by the mention of music, he takes a moment to consider her observation. Quiet? Sometimes. Other times too outspoken. He glances around the room, at the few decorations: two, small framed drawings of faces, one man, one woman, hang together on a wall; two pottery vases occupy a small table; three wooden sculptures, abstract yet human, sit like a family on the floor. All hold some interest to him, pleasing in subject, design, texture, color. Nature's number, two. Hydrogen and helium, male and female, producing all else. On a shelf sit two beautiful bowls, one blue, the other green, or so it seems in the low light. Next to them, two, narrow bookcases are partially filled. He tries to read the titles, but they are in Greek. "I like the bowls and vases," he tells her, "and the sculpture."

"They're presents, from friends. They have sentimental value. Do you like to read," she asks.

"When I can, which is not as often as I'd like."

She looks at him sympathetically, recalling that this is the case with many men. Not a priority. Now she turns herself a little, glancing around. "If my experience is any indication, I would guess that your wife and you might respond to some initiative, as neither has been able to begin. Am I right?"

She has returned to this. Disappointed, he inhales, then slowly releases it. "Well ... we tried, but not successfully ... Neither of us changed ... Are your bowls local?"

She smiles at his shift. "From Delphi ... Iscaria gave one to me, and I found its mate, far away. She called me about you."

He was right. But "Why?" he asks. Yet he supposes he knows, and tells her, "I enjoyed talking with her ... An interesting woman ... unusual ... kind ... very straightforward ... from a different time. ... Is Delphi her home? What does she do there, through the years?"

"She travels ... sometimes comes to Athens ... stays with me."

He narrows his eyes. There *is* some unacknowledged connection. He recalls the mountainside and valley extending far to the south, and in the foreground, the amphitheatre, and Iscaria, tall, her hair and gown, of similar hue, blowing in the wind. And Adonis planted on the rocky ground. He smiles. "Is she is a spirit?"

Messena frowns, then shares his smile, nodding, "In a way. She believes in such things. Our connections with them influence our lives"

"How?" he asks.

"Listen, and you will know."

His forehead creases. He has listened, but little has come. "Are you talking about our ... core ... our soul?" He feels awkward, foolish, but he forces himself on. "Our deepest self, what our internal voice may say, or dream, or direct?"

She waits, for him to find the answer.

Seeing this, he recalls instead, "She seemed ethereal ... unconcerned with modern life. And yet ... she saw me ... and I her ... she who seemed rooted in another time, and yet she was there ... watching."

Again she waits, and then says softly, "She said you kissed her."

He recoils a little. It was a gesture of appreciation. Love of a kind, he allows. A broad, encompassing love, of the Earth, life ... and yet of her ... He realizes that he cannot define it entirely, nor explain it. "She seemed to want me to. She waited for me to ... Her concern, her listening, seemed warm, deeply gracious. I felt that she saw me as few people do, and I appreciated that. I was moved, and wanted to express my appreciation. Love, maybe. I wanted to embrace her."

She nods, her eyes glowing within the darkened slit. "Is not such an exchange at the core of things?"

The core again ... But how can he know what it is, or if it is? Is it something one merely feels, senses? Such as his feeling for Iscaria. "I guess ... It was a beginning. I would like to see her again, speak with her."

"She sent you to me."

He nods and tries to see her more clearly. What does she suggest?

"Why do you hesitate in naming the love you felt? Should it not be more commonly shared?"

"Yes," he breathes, lowering his eyes. "I have never quite found that before, come so quickly and gracefully. It was not rushing desire but warm acceptance ... interest ... though perhaps I cannot name or explain it."

Her eyes are still for a moment, watching him, before she speaks, "If our soul is what, at our center, we feel or know to be our essential, and maybe best, self ... then to share that ... with another ... is that not something most important ...sublime ... a step toward fulfillment? ... What else should we be doing with one another?"

He nods, feeling this is right. An essential part ... And yet he wants to reason it through. "How is it we manage with so few?"

Her eyes focus more closely. "We are complex ... sensitive and insensitive ... Our histories, our makeup, our minds, hearts ... our situations, needs, and dreams vary ... Often there is no time ... Things get in the way ... We must work ... And yet you did a bit, with her. A beginning."

"A beginning ... but toward what?" But again she waits for him to find the answer. Cries sound in his head. "It was ... so unexpected ... so brief ... She ran away ... I wanted to speak more."

"What might have followed?"

"... I don't know ...This has followed ... Tonight ... I am here ... as if reaching across time. What she allowed to begin ... might continue now."

She waits while he reflects on this. He is thinking that these two women allow a bridging of ... souls ...

Before, he had been uncomfortable with the concept of a soul. But now he feels it is more simple than he thought; it is simply what is ... at the center, our essential nature ... what we might know, if we would listen ... He pictures Sherlock, their dog, running with unfettered joy, as his heart is now.

"What do you feel you are reaching for?" she asks.

"... For breathing life ... for understanding ... connection, where life is drawn to life ... Some we meet share this ... and yet ..." His gaze holds on her even if his thought seems to lose coherence. Yet their eyes do not waver.

After a moment, she says, "There is a current that runs through life, our life ... and it naturally seeks to connect with like elements, with complementary elements, sometimes even opposite elements."

He considers this, wonders if it is so ... and yet somehow they are speaking ... through the differences, distances ... complexities ...

Her eyes hold on his, looking carefully. "When we sense a compatible other, it can happen quickly, nearly instantly, when we see signs that we might share ... And then, if we are truly alive, we respond."

Looking at her, he wonders at this. Is this what is happening? Speaking, exploring, sharing ... This despite the fact that he cannot really see her, only her eyes, which seem to wait for his thoughts ... But her voice reaches into him, as her thoughts reach out to his. He feels a calm, an awakening.

She continues, "Because we are gripped by ourselves, our lives, the discrepancies between our hopes and reality, our disappointments, our pain ... we forget what life can be. I do not dismiss misfortune, poverty ... anger; they are out there ... but if one has a chance, and time ... the opportunity ... to notice life ... one may come to love it ... and wonder at it, deeply, oh so deeply ... and may pass on that love to others."

He tries to absorb this. But it is something, he realizes, that he simply must feel, as he did with Iscaria, as he does with music, Nature ... and maybe long ago, Belle. He can reason a bit, but the elements quickly overwhelm.

"Yes," she concurs, though he has not spoken, "it is both beyond us and in us ... is something that music, art ... and love can convey, for what are these but heightened awareness and appreciation of life's elements ..."

Hearing her words, which feel like strains of music, he imagines the light of day on trees and grasses, on water and living things, and he bows faintly to her, in appreciation.

Watching, she says, "I believe that you knew this, felt it, but somehow had not expressed it to yourself, or another ... yet Iscaria sensed it."

He feels faint tears, that she did, and he looks into Messena's eyes, as they hold on his. He should wipe or blink away the tears, but he does not, instead telling himself that he is lucky, being here, with her. How simple ... Yet how easy to miss, pass by ... ignore ... How many lose, or fail to find, these moments of recognition ... A poor system we have constructed? Poor players ... our failings ... our cultures ...

Blinking within the burka, she asks, "Did you share with your wife?"

He swallows, feeling disappointment ... but then patience. Did they? ... A distant island, and time. There was something then, long ago. Perhaps he was not ready, a slow developer ... "In the beginning."

She sees the distress this brings, and she reaches for something positive. "It is what each sex can give to the other. That unspoken but profound interest, and caring, beyond the solely rational, when sensing the spirit of the other."

"Women more easily and readily share this ... Don't you find?"

"Because you are a man. I find men, some anyway, who share it."

He tries to see her more clearly, as their eyes hold on each other. He tries to understand her distinction, but realizes that he enjoys simply talking with her.

Now she says, "In your life I sense you have pulled back, into a kind of hibernation, because you have no partner."

"I have my work, my two sons ... music ... the astonishing beauty of the natural world."

"Yes ... I, too, am moved by these things ... and am moved to hear that from you." And her eyes now smile into his, which he tries to return.

"What in your work moves you?"

It takes him a moment to release his preceding thoughts. He breathes, then reaches to explain. "When a new idea comes, an idea that works, that connects the world, Nature, with the needs of a building ... An idea, a design, that is both functional and transformative, that adds something, and is beautiful like your ancient temples ... In my case, when something new comes from my perceptions, thoughts, experience, efforts, and adorns the world with a new thing."

"I like that."

"Part is a quote."

"It is how we work, and connect, at the deeper levels, sharing ideas and adding to them, building on them. I would like to see what you have done."

"Come to America," he says quickly, lightly, expressing an idea that though delivered automatically, has awakened him, as if a revelation, and real possibility. Yet he realizes that his emotions have rushed ahead ... But why should he not admit that he is enjoying talking with her, this voice and eyes ... Is it only because she attends to him? ... No, not only ...

He finds her again, watching. He would like to place his hands on her shoulders, hold her. Why? ... To convey fellow feeling ... thankfulness, for her thoughts and feelings, her eyes. To connect, as he did with Iscaria ... and because she is a woman ... and Nature has made us so. Feeling appreciation swell through him, into his eyes, he looks away, rubs them, looks back. But she has seen it, his emotion. "Sorry," he says.

"No need. ... It moves me too."

"Does it? ..." ... Why? ... How?

But she does not elaborate, instead glancing across the room. "We all want ... many things ... but most of all a few simple things: connection, sharing, understanding, contribution, expression ... love ... We are complex creatures, and there is much to living and the world. We Greeks have long espoused balance, a full, rounded life: the physical and intellectual, the sensuous, the athletic, the artistic, the social and political ... but also, wine, dance ... adventure, leisure ... music ... honor ... love ... At the sacrifice, perhaps, of material things." A smile slowly radiates out from behind her eyes, and reaches to him, seeming to call him in. He feels his face flush. Yet now he realizes that he need not hide it or apologize. In his recent life this is new ... extraordinary.

She watches him, as he blinks his eyes clear. Softly she says, "We speak well together."

He agrees, smiling back. Then he hears her, "It is something I too am seeking. I would have thought I would find it more frequently ... than I have."

He attempts to understand, then allows, "I am surprised ..."

She smiles faintly.

For a moment they look at each other, as their thoughts run through moments in their lives. She shakes these away, however, and tells him, "Perhaps your challenge is to both learn to express your feelings and find someone to share them with."

Yes, he thinks. That is all too obvious, now.

"How much does your work fulfill that, would you say?"

He feels himself smile, for this he is clear about. "The work itself is sometimes quite satisfying, depending on the project. But perhaps only with another architect can I really share the joy and detail."

"And your wife?"

His spirits fall a bit. "She has been disappointed, that I have not had more 'success.' She thinks I yearn for my young female assistant and pay her too much. She no longer cares ... No doubt part is my fault, but I find her anger bewildering. We can no longer talk honestly, or at all, really."

"Perhaps talking as we are will help, show you patience and a way," she offers. He tries to smile, and yet he feels that they have stepped back from where they were seconds ago. He searches her eyes.

"Do you touch, at all?"

He shakes his head. She breathes deeply and looks away, then back to him. "No one has held your hand in a long while, I suspect," she tells him.

Not expecting this, he frowns, not sure where she's going. Who has he even hugged recently? His boys saying goodbye at camp, but they were self-conscious. Margaux in the office, also in goodbye, was surprisingly unrestrained. He could feel her youthful body, but he had interpreted it as her excitement to be running the office, being the boss, while he was away. She has her boyfriend after all, who is lively and young. Probably they make love on the office floor after hours, with all the framed drawings watching. Wren tilts his head side to side, pushes out his lips a little. "It's not that bad." But it is.

Her eyes probe his. "Do you have any women friends?"

Surprised again, he wonders, does he? And why does she ask? But before he can puzzle it out, he allows, "One or two, I suppose."

"Female cousins?"

He turns away, laughing slightly. "One or two ... Why?"

"Are you close? Do you embrace?"

Again he tips his head slightly, then shakes it, another faint laugh escaping. "On holidays ... What really ... why ...?"

She nods in understanding, and apologizes, "I'm sorry ... I simply want to know what your world is." She smiles with some sadness. He can just see her nose within the hood. It is smaller than he imagined, a graceful, narrow arc. He tries to imagine her face.

Now she asks him to take a seat in the chair behind. He turns and lowers himself into it, relieved to sit. He sips his wine. Whether it is the emotional strain, or the wine, he feels tired, unsteady; the floor and chair shift. Briefly he closes his eyes and tries to relax a little, leaning back. But when he looks up to find her, she has disappeared. Then he hears her behind him. Her hands, warm fingers, and palms move over his scalp. He jerks forward.

"It's all right. I'm sorry to make you uncomfortable, but if our time together is to have any benefit, I would hope we would become at ease with each other. Only then an understanding of where you are might follow. All of this is to get beyond where you have been, in understanding ... I am not trying to seduce you ... not yet." And she laughs a little.

He slowly leans back again until his back reaches the chair. Breathing he waits. Her palms return and cup and press against his forehead, gently. They rest there delicately, warm, and he has to admit, soothingly. He closes his eyes, trying not to think, trying to relax, wondering if he can be open to this, and what will flow from it.

As she holds her palms on his forehead, she speaks carefully, "We think we make choices ... we do make some ... but may not recognize what may direct our other decisions ... We think we choose a spouse, or lover, but often, initially anyway, we may not deeply know them. We may not know our selves in those situations. Our decisions, then, are based on what? ... Imperfect understanding and perception, attraction, emotion, the practical, the socially acceptable? Our past? How can we weigh all of this? ... We cannot. And inevitably we change, or react to new problems differently. We are influenced and directed by many factors ... How can we manage it all? There is much, maybe too much, to know... It is both simple and complex ... Do we not need ... assistance? A partner?"

She pauses for a moment, allowing him to reflect on this, before continuing, "I was moved that you could be open and giving with Iscaria. It shows me something, as she is not a conventional person. It made me curious; it makes me want to help you."

Once more he laughs a little to himself. "Do I seem so needy?"

"I think you are sad, shaken maybe, by your marriage."

"Perhaps I did not realize what I was doing to my wife, the effects I had. How I came across to her."

"Do you believe that you were at fault?"

"I don't know ... In part, of course. I don't know how much. Slowly things changed; we changed. Over time we each wanted other things, in the other, or things we felt were missing."

"We all change ... our expectations and perceptions. We come to expect, and want, different things. *We* change, but don't always allow the other to do so."

"What I know is that she seemed perfect in the early years, yet somehow that dissolved. She, it seems, grew less happy ... unhappy." He closes his eyes, and wonders, "How do we evaluate these things?"

She slides her hands down over his closed eyes and holds them there gently. After some moments, she says, "You seem a good man, not egotistical ... You have your boys, and your work you enjoy ... Is money a problem?"

"It shouldn't be, but it is."

"... That is too bad ...Without knowing your wife, I, of course, have little to suggest specifically, but I sense that you seem open to an honest discussion."

He nods at this and touches one of her hands with his, pressing it gently against his eyes. "Unfortunately our discussions fall apart too quickly."

"Emotions, anger, disappointment, build up, until it is hard to put them aside."

"Particularly," he notes, "when one says something that the other feels is false, a false judgment, false fact." He shakes his head at such memories. She takes her hands away. He glances around and up at her. Their eyes meet soberly, acknowledging that these situations are not easy. But he must straighten out, swing back around. There, more comfortable, and having expressed his formerly unspoken feeling that Belle's accusations were often false, he is able to breathe more freely, closing his eyes again. She slides her hands down to his neck, resting, then pressing, warm and strong, then slides them to his shoulders, kneading them. He finds it pleasurable beyond what he would have guessed, relaxing, releasing. A massage therapist also? Another weak laugh escapes him.

"One last question: Can you be forgiving of her?"

"... I thought I have been ... not perfectly but ... then abruptly something sets one of us off, and we fall back into anger and accusation."

"What about simply touching each other, as I am you?"

He feels himself tighten. He's not sure he could bring himself to, without some sign from her. Some sign of love, or caring ... In fact, he now remembers, he has made attempts, but her responses have been lukewarm, cold, reluctant. It feels as if there is nothing there. But perhaps she is sensing that in him. When, and in whom, did it begin? He cannot be sure, as it stretches back through the years.

Messena asks, "Would you say she is affectionate, physical?"

"... She is affectionate with the boys. And Sherlock, our dog."

Messena smiles. "I like the name."

"But I would not say she is particularly physical or demonstrative ... is instead maybe somewhat passive, until she explodes."

"Yes ... it is not easy ... Men and women expect certain things from each other, and when they do not appear, it can be painful. If one feels there is no way forward, then one may react in more indirect ways."

"Perhaps we both are waiting for the other to show something ... I thought I had, but maybe not clearly enough."

Taking this in, she allows, "We need signs that we can believe, trust."

As he murmurs acceptance, her palms return to his eyes. "You've been wounded ... both, I suspect."

"... Yes."

In the brief silence that follows, wanting to put away thoughts about his marriage, he concentrates on her touch, which seems to be reconnecting him to the living world ... But there is also the recognition that it is a technique, that he is a client, and it must end. Yet ... enjoy it, he tells himself, while he can. It is part of life. Though not on the deep level of passion, still it is a step ...

Now Messena rests her cheek on his head, and her hands lightly on his shoulders. He is uncertain how to interpret it ... but he tries to accept it, thinking that she is trying to help him open up to his own range of feelings.

"I'm sorry for you, for you both. It is a blow, to lose that. ... It is painful. It is deadening."

He breathes, disappointed with her return to this. But he sifts through his thoughts, before conceding, "Yes ... although, as you know, on almost any scale the two of us are fortunate, lucky. How can we complain?"

"One hopes that all lives may find improvement, and love. Your material fortune is not a reason not to explore ways to find love and re-connect."

He had not considered it in this reasonable way, and so he listens closely as she continues, "And something to consider is that you two have shared much, your children for one thing. Your problems are not that you have fundamentally different values or modes of living. Am I not correct?"

Pushing his lips out, he supposes she is. But all this has finally become too much, and he wants to move away, and so tells her.

"Yes, sorry. " Now she brings her chin to rest lightly on his head. And he appreciates the empathy he thinks it signifies. Indeed he feels a faint spasm of appreciation run through his shoulders. He becomes aware of his own breathing ... then asks what else they might do.

"Talk about other things, certainly, but I want to give you the suggestion that love is more sturdy than you may believe. It lives in us, sometimes getting buried, and needing only to be released ... uncovered."

While he concedes this may be true, he tells her that he has seen no signs of love in Belle, for years. She was kind and loving for a considerable time, but look what happened. "What is lasting? What is sturdy through time? Is not life more about change than longevity?"

"I understand; change is natural, but I want you to find the strength, the love, in you, to approach your wife, who may be as lost as you. I want you to understand, to feel, that love and caring are still possible. Many people are struggling as you two are. Many women would care for and even love you ... and men love your wife, I suspect. I want to provide that understanding, that there is love in the world, from which to begin to work your way back."

He nods, and while he feels that her words are kind, he does not quite believe them. "That is generous of you ... I thank you. But I am more doubtful; I have lived through the acrimony, the accusations, the anger."

"While I believe you are faithful in your marriage, what does your wife believe?"

He emits a faint laugh. "As I said, she thinks I lust for my assistant."

"Do you?"

"Sometimes. For what do I get at home but anger, coolness, disinterest. As for my assistant, she will stay only until she finds a better-paying job."

Messena ponders this for a moment, before responding, "Of course it is not unusual that in walking through our lives we meet many, or at least some, we could love and maybe many we could sleep with, but we opt for something else, something more profound and lasting."

"And if that changes, or disappears?"

"That is where you feel you are?"

"Yes …"

"There are no quick and simple answers. And that, in part, is what we are exploring."

"But I don't know … what might be found."

She brings her cheek onto his head now, which stirs buried feelings. He wants to put his marriage out of his mind, but she continues, "We are the masters of our fate. As music deeply moves you, so can your belief in a relationship move you and give you strength."

"I wonder if I have that belief, in her, any more. I think she has changed, as perhaps I have."

"Changed, yes, probably. But I think you may underestimate what you had, which is not unusual, in our disappointments."

"But this change is real … She calls herself Artemis here."

Messena frowns and reflects, before reminding, "But you must remember the profound value of what you had."

"Yes … but is it recoverable? Is there anything left? … Change is part of life."

"Think of the many good things that brought you together."

Although he had wanted to move on, he tries to recall. He can name a number of good things, but they feel distant, intellectual. With a shudder of frustration, he shakes his head.

For a short time she says nothing, until stepping back a bit, she releases a breath and says, "Come, we will try something else." And she asks him to sit on the floor, as she will do, back to back. And though hesitant, he does, and she follows so that they sit supporting each other, leaning against the other. He finds her back warm and firm and not uncomfortable, and reaching for his glass, he throws down the rest of his wine.

"We all want to be known, understood," she resumes, "accepted, find support. For some it may start out as physical, simple desire, but this may raise hope for more complete knowing."

Listening, he finds himself compelled to ask with faint humor, "Should I be taking notes?"

She is silent for a moment, before responding, "I'm sorry. Am I lecturing?"

"No. Sorry."

"I'm afraid I can fall into that. In attempting to understand, I start listing things, generalizing."

"No no. Maybe you're going a bit too fast for me, or I couldn't follow the leap."

"Thank you for alerting me."

"... I guess that I can't help wanting to know about our conversation, and now sitting back to back. What does it tell you? Are we complementary, or to some degree like-minded, or are you merely a sympathetic therapist?"

"What do you think?"

He smiles at her again turning his question back to him, but he is willing to answer. "I hope that we are complementary ... It would be nice, after a long ... hiatus."

"I think we are doing well, but it is too soon to define things. Trust yourself."

"But I find that slowly I am being drawn by your voice, and kindness ... and I suppose by the fact that you are a woman ... with whom some sort of sharing ... or something ... seems possible."

"That is good, no? ... Perhaps we will find the answer."

Again he smiles. "In leaning against your back ... a nice backrest ... are we not connecting? Can I love a backrest?"

She laughs faintly and says, "Yes, I like that. We are talking well together, which is good'"

"Yes ... but that cannot be unusual for you."

"Each conversation is different."

He thinks for a moment. "But the specter of sex must arise, regularly, no?"

"Of course. That is natural."

"... Perhaps it is a good thing that you keep your burka on and we sit back to back ... I've never met anyone quite like you, so open and direct. No holding back. Like Iscaria."

"That is good. That is what you came for."

"I didn't know what I came for."

He feels her nod before she speaks. "I am enjoying our talk, our conversation. We are finding openness ... sympathy."

"You're not just being professional and kind?"

"Do you not trust your instincts?"

"How can I know? There is an increasing jumble."

"Of ...?"

"Oh ... appreciation ... communication ... recognition, history ... We share humor, a bit ... My mind and hopes run ahead ..."

"Yes, that is normal, to be attracted ... to want closeness."

"But this is one evening ... What do we do with it?"

"We take what we have discovered with us."

"But this is your work."

"Of course ... I learn ... We are both learning about each other ... how we are together."

He weighs this. "In gaining a sense of you, I feel that I am being drawn out from my loneliness ... but ... to where I don't know ... There are limits for us ..."

"Yes, limits, but recognize also what we are discovering."

"... Yes, but taking us where?"

"To self knowledge ... and understanding others."

"... That is something ..."

"It is a lot."

"Yes ..." He shifts slightly so that he can feel her back. "What about sex? Where do you place that in importance?"

"However nice it is, and might be, it would be ... fleeting ... distracting, taking us down a different path, robbing us of the communication we have been discovering."

"Really? ... And yet I cannot help but wonder."

"To want it is normal, natural."

"More so for men, don't you find?"

"Don't forget that women have been designed for love, including sex. Our destiny generally involves others: lovers, mates, children, mothers who have shared and can share our fates, and families who surround us, who need and support us. Sex can be even more important than it can be for men. Just because men think about it frequently, and rush after it, doesn't mean that it fills their souls in the same way. Women think more about the other, the lover, who reaffirms them, when they feel loved. Connection is more important, as we see it in our mothers and experience it ourselves. Women know that they can give forth another life, maybe many, and with their mothers and children, are part of a continuum. That all of this flows from sex, makes it important, and adds to the desire, a desire to feel but also to join. It is complex, an encompassing desire. And there is also the responding to the greater physical, male presence, and sometimes the greater energy, and desire. That can be exciting."

For some moments he digests this. She has described contrasting elements in women. How, then, to balance this knowledge with emotion, with passion? He asks as much.

"With experience, caring ... understanding."

It sounds simple enough, he thinks, until he wonders, "Do you believe that people can learn, change? Have you seen it in others you've spoken with?"

She leafs back through memory. "Yes, some. There is variation, as with everything."

"And have you yourself found friendship, companionship ... love?"

"To different degrees ... We individuals are of many parts."

While he understands, he asks "But you and I, to take one case, we come from such different places and lives. How deeply can we share and speak together?"

"We have taken a few first steps. We have already learned much."

He wonders how true this is, and yet he wants to tell her, "I am pleased to be talking like this. It is something I have longed for ..."

"We are relaxing, trusting each other, and talking well, even about sex."

"It moves me ..."

"I am enjoying it too."

Surprised, he laughs a little. "Ahh! ... Isn't it wondrous: all the people, souls ... stars, galaxies ... all spiraling through space and time ... Occasionally colliding, interweaving, connecting. Macrocosm and microcosm, planets and bodies ... patterns repeating and recapitulating at the different levels."

They are quiet for a time, attempting to find a way through this. Though strangers, in this brief time, they have communicated, and he has reached some new frame of mind. But he remembers that she draws other men to her, as clients ... lovers, no doubt. What then can develop between them? "Since we are being direct and open, I confess that I cannot help wanting to know what you feel about us. Will this 'we' survive as friendship, and possibly grow?"

"I am making an effort to keep our idea foremost, to help you understand and explore your situation ... But I am also moved, as you say. And we are making progress; we can go back and forth on ideas and feelings, which is not all so ordinary. Something is taking form."

"But which you must find elsewhere."

"... With some ..."

"And also, I am paying you. I am a customer. How profound can that be between us?"

"That is just the arrangement that brought us together. If we speak and connect truly, then that initial arrangement will not matter."

"But in one evening, what can develop?"

"Maybe nothing, maybe something. But do not decide yet. Already we are speaking openly. ... I want to move again. I am going to lie down on the floor on my back; I have a pillow. I want you to lie also on your back and place your head on my stomach."

Once more he finds this strange. Holding his breath, trying to see what this might offer, he doesn't move. Something resists, in his chest. But there is also now the faint hope that it will lead somewhere ... He has faith in her now - a bit. And so after a moment he complies. Her stomach is firm yet soft, and he can feel it rising and falling with her breathing. After a moment, she asks, "You feel me breathing?"

"Yes ... Does this mean we are one?" he asks lightly.

She laughs quietly. His head bounces on her stomach. But then both fall silent, lying still. As he feels the rise and fall of her breathing, it reminds him of the sea, and from that sensuality, the murmur of desire returns, but also the desire to reach in and speak of things, expressing and exchanging. There is already conversation, and perhaps some friendship between them, or is this her professional talent? And yet even if this is the case, it is an opportunity to reason things through – his life ... and yes, maybe his marriage, what's left.

But can they, from two different cultures, deeply connect? And who is she? ... Who are they together? ... two living creatures among the billions. A random coincidence, or something set in motion by Iscaria ... by Belle, by all the decisions? Should he not embrace it whole-heartedly? See where it goes? What else might life bring him?

Yet it is hard for him to identify what he might have to offer her ... Companionship, communication? ... She must have many ... But for him it is odd that he had to come this far to find this – perhaps as Odysseus had to sail so far, for years ... until Athena saw him.

And so he reasons that what she offers is companionship, responsiveness, which Belle no longer does. It has awakened him, he who felt half-understood, half-dead. For years he made love to his wife and had thought that was profound, but somehow canyons opened, the result of shifting tectonic plates. Now this seems to offer a new connection, possibly ... But what does it offer her? ... He cannot say ... beyond fellow-feeling, and conversation.

And so, for the moment, he is alive ... Even if he cannot see her, there is harmony. Probably it is better that he doesn't see her. We want beauty in our lives, as we see in Nature, hear in music; encounter in many ways. We want to see and hold that embodiment ... Yes physical beauty might distract him ... or its absence disappoint. A weakness? Could he get past it, either way?

She must have foreseen this, encountered it before. How could she not? Men are, in part, simple creatures.

"We have so little time!" he expels suddenly.

"We have a beginning."

"Is it a tease? Will it vanish when I leave?"

"If it moves you, you will carry it in you, our time tonight. And it need not end ... If we are truly drawn, we will find a way."

In this she is different from all he has known. Willing to speak openly and simply of her feelings. He feels suddenly stretched between futures, so that he must breathe deeply. He draws in a deep breath, reaching for clarity. Having come this far, he must go with it, wherever it leads. What she has given him is a revival of awareness ... life, hope, intensity. He must thank her. And he does, "I thank you ... for your ... patience and kindness and insight."

"I have received something too, much as you said."

Again he is struck. The floor shifts, once more. What does she suggest? "Explain ... to me."

"I think you know."

Does he? He floats with vague explanations ... Dare he name them? Does he fear the possibility, or the disappointment?

"I believe you do."

He thinks, trying to name what he has felt. "My feelings ... are clear ... firm, alive ... but ..."

"We are moving slowly toward understanding, and sharing. We don't need conclusions now. They will come. We must simply reach out."

He focuses on her stomach rising and falling, like the waves. "I cannot help but want you ... in all ways."

"We must both be patient as we continue to explore."

For seconds he reflects upon this, pondering where and how it might go. She is there; they are talking, touching; she seems caring ... sincere ... How can he not treasure this? ... But where will it go, if anywhere? "Messena, this is such a gift to me, something I have long not had ... How can I not want to hold on to it?"

"As you know, we are all complex creatures. There is more for each of us to learn and understand about the other. We are both experienced and must use what we have learned to weigh what we might have."

"Tell me then what I must learn about you, that I have not sensed or heard?"

He hears her laugh a little, and breathe deeply. "I will start with the simplest of things. I like you, feel love for you. There is something in the way we are together, the way we talk and hear each other. I have not found that recently. It reaches into me ... but I cannot tell yet how much, how deep. It need not be everything immediately ... but if you are patient, we may discover what has awakened in both of us."

He considers this. A moan escapes him. And she responds by bringing her warm hand to his forehead and holding it gently there. His heart beats strongly, loudly. Can she hear it? He inhales to calm himself.

"Are you okay?" she asks.

"Yes …"

She relaxes and says, "Unexpectedly, I feel drawn to you as someone to share with. Part of me wants you, now, and into the future, does not want to lose you … but we come with different lives, which will not be easy to sort out. We must both be patient and put away impetuosity, not because it is bad, but because we are mature and have others, our children, and your wife, to whom we are tied."

"My work has trained me for patience," he allows, smiling.

She too smiles at this. "I like you as a man."

His feelings leap; a voice cries out. But with some humor, he pronounces, "That is a start."

She laughs, joining his. He wants to turn and hold her, but feels her about to speak. "Yes, but you must learn who I am."

"I am here, eager, listening."

"… I have known other men, as you have realized. I have been married twice … And yet, what is between you and me is gentle and moving … and in that, unique".

He reflects on this slowly, trying to imagine what this means to her. Now she adds, "I feel love … for you and the world you carry in you, as I carry a world in me. I don't know how deep this will go. We must recognize that we are at a beginning. But also, if I can help you find some way out of your emptiness and into connection, between us, and maybe others, I am willing to try."

"You are a saint."

"I am a woman. And you are a man. If we can reach each other truly, it is something that will become part of us, and that we will never forget."

He reflects upon all of this, until a question pesters him. "Do you mind if I ask how often you do this?"

She is silent, restraining her breathing.

"I'm sorry. But I ... must understand ... and understand why."

"I do it periodically ... In your case because Iscaria and Kostas recommended you ... Because you will pay me, and I need money to live. And because we might speak our souls."

He tries to fit this together. "Are the people who come to you ... adrift?"

"Yes ... trying to get home ... Life is a challenge, a puzzle, ever shifting. We are all shifting, trying to meet needs, others' and our own. We need help, companionship. If we can find a true friend, with whom to go deep, how wonderful."

"... Yes, I agree ... how wonderful ... I am shaking ... that we are speaking in this way ... I want to rush ahead, even as I realize that it will take time ... to see what we have. Yet how, in the short time I have here, will we discover the depth of what we share?"

"Much is possible, now, tonight. But we can also stay in touch, and meet again somewhere, if we wish, if it seems important enough."

"I am beginning to feel that it is. There is no one else."

She nods at his confession. "We are making a start. We are both open to what may unfold ... Come, I will stand."

And so he raises himself into a sitting position, while she stands. She asks him softly. "Can you kneel before me?"

"... To offer my devotion?" But with a smile he does.

She touches his head softly and with affection. "Come, let me hold you." She brings her hands once more behind his head and presses him gently against her stomach. The source, the sea, he thinks once more, turning his cheek to her, pressing in so that he can feel her. His hands slide behind her and bring her firmly against him, while hers trace his head, ruffling his hair, touching his neck.

Is this just sex-light? he wonders, and yet her touch allows him to believe in her and what may be between them – beyond anything he has experienced, that he can remember. She is alive and alert, and kind and patient ... Is this because she knows the pain of a failed marriage, twice over ...is aware of what re-evaluation has taken her through? Through profound emotional upheaval? He feels his own emotion ascending up from the depths. His eyes leak ... that this is possible, happening ... He must wipe them on the rough burka.

"Okay?" she asks.

Afraid to speak, he nods, not wanting to show his tears or lose contact with her. He wonders if this is some maternal experience, or is it, really, two adults finding a receptive other, trying to reach out? Still he is doubtful of her need, if no longer of his. He wants to touch and be touched by her and to go on doing so. If he cannot articulate why exactly, his wanting is certain ... Is it finding another half? Is it mostly instinctive ... physical? He pictures dear Sherlock who loves to be petted, and petted. Nature's needs, across her array of creatures, the subtle and infinite mechanisms of evolution ... Wren has needed this; it was in him, but he had lost his opportunity to share it ... Is this a reprieve, a second chance? A chance to be stirred, heard ... to stretch himself, to embrace the fullness of life?

He presses more firmly, deeply, into her stomach, then lap. Does he want to see her naked and to lie with her, and in her? ... That is always there. But he has begun to feel that there is something else, something that might be drawn out between them, and he wants to see what that might be, where they might go together. That is less predictable.

Gently she lifts his head, then indicates, touching his shoulder, that he should not move. Dimly he becomes aware that she is stepping back, undoing something, and allowing the burka to fall from her. Staring, he sees that she stands in a beautiful blue and purple silk dress. Her head and dark eyes are lowered, in humility, until they, with sharpening feeling and attention, rise to find his. Her softly abundant dark hair is woven in an invisible design around her head, a few strands falling down behind to her shoulders, all gently crowning her pale, sculpted, exquisite face. She stands tall and perfectly still, a statue of beauty beyond what he could imagine. He cannot take his eyes away, nor fully breathe, while her eyes, attentive and kind, do not leave his. Is this reality, or a dream? A god come to earth? Somehow he feels her perfect grace has entered him, chest and heart, so that there remains no space to breathe. He tries to move, to free himself and draw in needed air, but she fills him entirely. She is not of this world, but is some gift … the real Athena or some sibling. He tries to restrain, then re-compose, his emotions, but they cascade, carrying him beyond all thought, washing out from his eyes.

As he blinks clear his sight, he thinks that maybe she should put the burka back on before he can breathe no more. But now she is kneeling in front of him, on a pillow, and bringing his head next to hers, on her shoulder, and lowering hers onto his.

"You are beautiful," he says. "In many ways."

"I hope I please you …"

"Me … and any man. More than I can express, or understand, or deserve."

"You come well-recommended … … Many of us are alone, for one reason or another … What we can do is console each other. You bring me conversation and caring … Our souls need partners too. Perhaps ours see another who in some way mirrors our self ... shares sensibilities, modes of talk and touch ... Will you tell me what you dream?"

"Dream? ..." He swallows a broken laugh. "I dream of you." But in the instant he has said this, he regrets it. And yet, with his mind and feelings racing, blurring, he is also thankful that he has spoken this truth that floods through him. Struggling to articulate anything, he breathes, "But tell me yours, first."

"After..."

He fills his lungs at last, in this unreality. "Well ... it is true; I dream of you, as I'm sure countless men do. Perhaps as all of Athens did, of Parthenos, so long ago." He cringes at this too-saccharine thought, yet it is what he feels. "Sorry ... I didn't know it was possible, on this earth. I have never met someone like you ... But please, won't you tell me yours ...."

She smiles and softly kisses his cheek. He tries to return it, but she moves her head onto his shoulder, and begins: "In many ways my life has been fortunate and rich; I have been lucky ... but not always wise. I was married, twice ... each time mistakenly. ... The first was an actor, lively, passionate, attractive, romantic. My heart was captured; I was overthrown ... I went to every rehearsal and performance ... but soon saw that he was not meant for marriage ... pursuing, falling for, bedding, every woman whom he met or acted with. He was never home, travelling across Europe. And I had been a fool. He was not dishonest; simply incapable of belonging to one woman ... It ended ... I see him occasionally when he passes through ... We have, I have, a six-year-old daughter, Arethusa – Aarrie, I call her – a follower of Artemis." She smiles. "Not really. I am teaching her to love men, but recognize that they are different."

Wren has pulled his head back and is studying her, his heart reaching. She touches his cheek lightly and goes on, "Several years later, I met and married, too quickly again, a local politician, an idealist, energetic, charismatic. I guess I had not learned ... He was essentially a Communist, although he did not admit it, but he was adamantly for the left. All capitalists are corrupted by greed, selfishness, materialism, exploitation, to the point of being evil. He worked tirelessly to oppose them and their representatives. But this was not possible in Greece of recent times. He was jailed, which only made him more intent on working for his cause. When he found that my views were inadequate, less strident, believing that those on the left could be as egocentric, as authoritarian, as the right, he abandoned me, and soon hooked up with another, a zealot ... We are not in touch; he has no forgiveness, no room for the personal life; all is to be devoted to the cause. In a way it is admirable, and maybe necessary, but we Greeks are too often like that, intolerant of other views. It has kept us in political turmoil."

They study each other carefully, closely. Both are refugees, he thinks, maybe as we all are. He cannot imagine what he, a mortal, offers her ... Peace maybe ... communication, attention ... passion newly born. But how can he match the dynamism, and excitement of her husbands? Much of his world, his work, is interior, silent, produced on paper. He will seem dull compared to them. How will he engage and captivate her, as his own marriage sunsets below the horizon?

"So, you see?" she whispers. "We each have a past to digest. You may want to reconnect with your wife, or maybe there is no hope. You must find an answer ... for yourself, first, then for us. Possibly I can help."

He looks at her, a stifled cry inside. Having been sent to her, how could he ever part? ... Iscaria must have seen ... He leans against her, and she against him. Is it possible that they could grow close? Are they already? Some shared sensibilities? The music that she is. What was it that Iscaria discerned?

Now she urges him again, softly, "But please ... more completely, tell me what you dream." And she inhales, preparing to listen. As her body moves, he can for the first time feel her fully against him, and once more a spasm shakes him. Yet he must pull his story together somehow. He twists, flexes, seeks to loosen, to breathe. He girds himself, fearing his story cannot deeply be understood or interest her.

She presses her head against him, and turning, he buries his face in her soft hair, sinking into it. She rolls her head in a pleasurable way as she repeats, "Please, tell me."

He tries to collect a few details, whatever he can. "Before you appeared, I dreamed of ... of someone ... A joy I had experienced, for a time, with my wife, before we lost it ... In the beginning there had been harmony, happiness, a sharing of much. But things chipped away at it all. Increasingly I found I was alone; she sees me through the darkness of her disappointment and anger ... Looking around alone, I found Nature, an exquisite companion – its perfect, endless beauty, its essential goodness, though there is catastrophe and carnage too ... Perhaps it is the inexpressible harmony of many things that you embody for me. How could I not come to love so much of what is around us, cherish it, the trees and landscapes and water, the creatures ... all changing with the light of the day. All the many living things. All of man's extraordinary creations ... which he draws from Nature and the miracle of existence. I watch and listen, and appreciate her systems and structures, her architecture, and our own ... which mirror, but also go beyond, adding and honoring ... And I think: Is this not the true value in life? This joining, this appreciation, this experiencing, this contribution ... this love ... such as even our dog, Sherlock, feels: his joy, his love of us, and ours for him; and mine for all the local birds and animals. Sometimes I come eye to eye with a squirrel, a bird – a silent exchange, and maybe recognition, with another. And so, in a sense, much of what I want in my work is to express that grace and harmony, its beauty, its music ... and our own, the expression of our feeling, our spirit ... An ideal design, and structure, to me, conveys something of all that, as you do ... I know it is an unfair to burden you with this, and perhaps unfair to others ... but Nature presents it to us, her ineffable beauty, and we add to it as we can. And how can we not want to hold it, possess it, embrace it, love it? We who are part of it ... and yet ... who seem, who have, gone beyond ...

"The designs I imagine, when not working on a purely practical project, embody something of Nature's ideal, her harmonies. My ideas come from both what I see and what I imagine, representing and maybe embellishing Nature. It is possible, too, that what we may sometimes be reaching to recreate are those moments and feelings we experience: flight, freedom, rhythm, tone, melody ... Or maybe the sudden coming into light, each day, as we did at birth, into a perfect, simple peace, encountering others who see us with caring ... And with luck we find those who share that, over time, a few, occasionally ... And to create is to express those experiences, the relationships, patterns, structures, and maybe recapture them, to, in a sense, re-experience or express them, so that we might walk again together through the fields of beauty and praise.

"And in life's progression, and in mine, I find myself dreaming of my sons, of moments together, of occasional, innocent joy, of what they find and will find. And I pray, in my dreams, and in some waking moments, that the world they will inherit will continue to be as I have found it, as inspiring and deeply beautiful, with moments of grace, as you and I have found here ... And sometimes I dream of being able to sing or dance ... or play some music ... write a poem that captures, or expresses, something of this feeling ... of this beauty, as much inner as outer ... And some of these dreams come as daydreams, and some at night. And among them, the desire for goodness and justice, in contrast to their opposites, which insert themselves too often ... And I find not infrequently that the goodness can be symbolized, and realized, by a woman, or a considerate man ... And also, I must admit, occasionally I dream of making love, not so much the full throes of desire but of the first recognition of love, approaching one another, touching and anticipating what may be revealed. And finally, repeating myself in part, hovering over all of this, the strains of music, expressing so much, such profound feeling, and perfection, our highest experiences and imaginings, and the beauty of the world, beyond what I can define."

He feels her move and feels her bring her lips to his neck, then cheek, full and warm, and she holds them there, until he moves to find her cheek, and lips.

After a time, she pulls back and studies him carefully, and then confides, "I share so much of what you have said ... and am deeply happy that we do ... I tremble with feeling at this and what we might come to share ... At the same time, I cannot forget that you have a most difficult decision to make, unlike me, who has found them made for me. It cannot be easy. I am ready to help, even as I hope we may find a way ... while recognizing it may be wrong or mistaken, and we may not know for a time."

He finds her eyes and looks earnestly into them. "I am moved by you deeply. My wife and I have had our time. While we should know how to work it out, it seems we don't. She has not responded to my overtures, nor cares about my work, or who I am really. She is not a bad person, can be quite good, but she has withdrawn, and is not inclined to return. I feel that she has already decided. She offers no signs that she wants to talk openly. Her dark views of me insert themselves at every pretext. There is no honest talk, or forgiveness, or signs of love. She may want some interesting, successful man, but not me. I don't make much money. She resents my young assistant, and while I know the history of men, I feel that she does not see *me* as I am, nor does she care to make the effort. Maybe she carries prior disappointments, maybe she has made her choice ... I don't know. As you may guess, I am something of a romantic, ever picturing the imagined, or ideal. Maybe she has grown tired of that."

She takes this in soberly, then allows, "Yes, a romantic, as am I too, I fear. But the ideals of my husbands led me down impossible paths. The actor would say he is also a romantic. But alas these simple terms cannot sum up all that we are. There are many different ideals ... Yet you and I, it seems, share a number."

He studies her anew, seeking to understand. "So, what ... do we do?"

She thinks for a moment. "Explore these feelings, see if they last, reach into each other. Use patience and experience to understand and decide."

It sounds simple, he thinks. Yet how to accomplish? And in reality, an ocean divides them, and a culture as well ... and circumstances ... children ... Is the recognition, and acceptance, of these, the 'understanding' she speaks of?

For some moments they reflect. He presses his eyes closed as he leans carefully into her soft hair. He imagines that Belle, who seems so distant, and he might limp along, for the boys. But there will be no joy. No communication. Without their sons, they would surely split.

"I could speak to her," she says quietly, somehow sensing his thoughts. "I don't know her, of course, don't know what she wants ... I am just beginning to know you ... But I don't think you have closed out that option entirely, have you?"

"I don't feel there is a real option. I suppose that if she made any effort to reach out, there might be some hope, but she hasn't. She puts all the blame on me, which means I alone must change."

They look at each other before he asks, "And you? Are you connected to someone now? You must have a hundred men ..."

"... No ..." she whispers. "There is no profound connection. And so my dreams are not so different from yours, dreaming of someone. Perhaps that is why we talk well together ... I too dream of harmony, of finding the right person, a common hope. And this, the third time, I must be lucky, no?" And she smiles a mixed smile. "But no one has appeared recently ... No one like you with whom I enjoy talking. I dream of sharing, complementing ... I would like to find a man for my daughter to love, and appreciate, so that she can see what is possible ... I have a sense of the life I want: to see more of the world; I may want to write, about my culture, and my experiences ... about women. I would like to live in George's nautilus for a time ... I will ask Antaeus ... but right now, I am mostly thinking of our conversation, wondering what it tells us about each other ... even as I understand that you must resolve the issues of your marriage. And that we live far apart ... But relating, sharing deeply, is too important to be obstructed by solvable problems. We must not ignore the profound gifts life brings. My marriages have taught me that. Which does not mean there will be no challenges or hurdles. There are always hurdles."

Acknowledging this, he tries to weigh it all. What do these first rays of hope and harmony between them mean? How, and where, might they develop? Would all the practical differences wear away the closeness? ... Is it love, truly, that he feels? ... He presses his head against her.

"So you, Wren, must decide, for your part, as I too want to see what we might share. Choosing each other, you and me, *would* be in some ways difficult. Our lives are separated by much. Your wife and you already share many things ... except for the essentials."

His chin brushes her shoulder, as he hears her adding, "I say this with some difficulty, because we have barely met ... though we have talked well. Part of me wants you for myself, to see where we might go, yet part recognizes the unknowns, and difficulties ..."

He pulls his head back and finds her eyes. They are wet; she closes them.

He kisses her cheek, holding his kiss. She trembles. A stifled cry escapes him, "Ohhh …" as he's thinking, we have found this, all of this, and still it will not be easy … and there is no time …

For some moments they are silent, wrestling with these things.

Finally, he asks, "From your experience, can people sense enough about another to take a chance, build on intuitions?"

She smiles a sad smile. "Sometimes. There are no generalizations, there are so many variables … I've seen it work; I've seen it fail."

"Even good beginnings do not necessarily last."

"No, and yet, if we remember what is important, and you and I have had experience, we understand that if people talk and listen and understand, then much can be worked out, though none of us is perfect … But if we can explore together, how wonderful." She looks at him thoughtfully, before adding, "I have had, and still have lovers, although they are not … you know … serious, or even well-suited, but this teaches me to appreciate, deeply, what you and I may have found."

He reflects on this, then tells her, "I suppose the loss of love between my wife and me has taught me much the same, to appreciate connection."

She looks down with sad smile. "You were sent to me by she whom I have long known … After my second marriage, she suggested that I take up this … therapy, knowing my experience with pain and disappointment, yet somehow seeing hope as well. I was already a good listener, which allows me to offer … ideas, reflections, much as you said."

Yet the sadness in her voice pulls at him, and he brings his arms around her, saying, "I'm sorry that this came from disappointment."

"You needn't be. It is part of life. In my first marriage, I saw my mistake early, even before Arethusa was born, and I withdrew, emotionally. The second time was perhaps more painful, because I thought our ideals coincided, but I did not understand his extreme view of society, so unbending and intolerant. While I did not disagree with all of his positions, I did with his methods and fury. And he had a blindness toward communist government; he couldn't see the ruthlessness, perhaps because he saw the right as equally bloody, if not more. But he has no time for me, nor people like me."

He nods and tries to smile at her. Gravely she tries to return it, saying, "It is hard … One must recognize that there will be differences."

He studies her profile. "And where is Arethusa tonight?"

"Upstairs. A woman who lives here takes her, almost like a grandmother. Arethusa loves her; they read books to each other, tell stories."

"What does she say, if I may ask, of your lovers?"

"She likes them; they're fun; we take her to the beach, to the mountains, the islands. For her, this is the way life is. She understands that they are just friends. Even with her father, she seems to understand he arrives only rarely. She would like to see him more; he writes her … In fact she has several fathers, whom she likes … But this may cause confusion later."

His thoughts rise and swoop. He wonders if part of her attraction to him is that he is a father of children he loves. At the same time he wants to respond to her story, "I find your life, that you have not been happy in love, surprising."

"Why?" she wonders, her eyes moving over his face. But she turns her thought in another direction. "I am not unhappy," she says, with a half smile.

"To me you are extraordinary."

"Remember that even our Greek gods and goddesses were all too-human, were conflicted characters, with powerful emotions, anger and desire, keen for revenge ... Of the men I have dated, if that is the word, George Nestoros is the one I would choose now, but he doesn't want another entanglement after several marriages of his own ... He enjoyed talking with you, by the way, at Antaeus's house."

"And I enjoyed it too, very much ... But you know Antaeus too?"

She acknowledges, but with no sign that it is significant. Instead she explains, "Tonight however, we focus on you; another time perhaps on me. It is not so unusual that we want to make each other whole, at least one who seems kind and open, as you do. It is natural to want that completion for another. Sometimes, it simply takes one person to start it. This can begin when eyes meet and recognize some shared feeling or sense of things ... Other parts may come slowly, hesitantly, yet successfully with patience and love."

He wonders at her calm, her certainty, despite her history. She simply accepts that there are parts of her life that were disappointing, painful, yet manages to look ahead.

Now she asks, "How long will you be here?"

"Three more days ..."

She leans forward, so that her head touches his, as she laments, "That is not long ..."

Nodding, he pulls back to see her.

Kindly she smiles. "... Let's not allow these concerns to come between us now. Neither of us is what might be called typical. To an extent we are both autonomous, and we must design our own pathway and structure. I believe, from what I sense about us, that this is possible. We share that awareness, openness, and hope."

Taking her hand and squeezing it, he beseeches the Fates to make this so.

Now she leans back to stand, indicating that he should too, and when they are facing each other, she embraces him gently ... He cannot resist imagining making love to her. It constricts his breathing; he presses against her, but then controls himself. He no longer feels it is urgent, paramount, however extraordinary it might be.

As if reading his thoughts once more, she confesses, "Yes, it would be nice ... but it would overwhelm everything we have achieved so far. In relation to our growing closeness, it would mean little. ... Believe me."

And now that he knows something of her story, he understands and agrees, even as he cannot entirely dismiss the hope.

A smile slowly emerges in her features and summons his. They lean and touch cheeks. But he realizes that his body is shaking, from the intensity. He tries to calm himself, tries to assert mind over matter, over his feelings crying out. Watching his face, and interpreting the ripples that run over it, she feels sympathy for him and presses against his shoulder, bringing forth a smile in both. "We are together in this moment," she says, "quite unconcerned with the world or others. Join me in this."

For some moments they stand in this manner, not concerned with time. When finally they draw apart, she speaks, with brightening feeling, "You know, what we might do is ... dance."

Surprised, he laughs, eyes widening as he imagines this. Once again he sees the spiral arms of a galaxy, slowly waltzing, drawing in tiny stars. He loves dancing, moving to music. Is it muscles producing emotion, or emotion moving muscles? Either way, it expresses the physicality of expression, more so than any singing or whistling he can manage, his entire body moving, attempting to express music, its grace, rhythm, harmony ...

"What do you say?"

"Yes, let's."

And so she leads him down a short hallway to a long room, a dining room originally, empty save for two dining chairs at opposite ends. Asking him to wait, she goes on, to turn on a player and select some music. When she returns she carries two sparkling dance heels, which she drops and slips on, then lowers the light, and comes to him as a waltz begins, a familiar Viennese melody that lifts them around the floor. While he has only the vaguest recollection of how to do the one-two, one-two, she is so light that she adjusts to whatever he can manage. As he feels her moving with him, as the room circles around them, as his emotions and hopes rise up together, as every dream collapses into this one, as the moment extends forward into what might be, then back into what is, all cries out that life and dream have joined as petals do, opening in the sunrise, crying out that they are alive. His eyes leak, then stream with joy; his heart sings out thanks to someone and to her in prayer ...

Other waltzes and ballroom dance tunes carry them around and around, improving as they go, gliding along the walls, their shadows turning and merging, as they twirl and laugh and pause to kiss, before remembering the music and moving on gracefully, sometimes lurching, misstepping as their bodies join, then turn and part, allowing the cool air to flow in between them, before clasping once more.

European pop songs alter the tempo; they fox trot through smiles, eyes moist, gleaming. He presses into her and she him; all existence feels centered there. She, he tells himself, in her beauty of soul and body, in her kindness, is music squared, existence at its apogee.

Next come reggae, rock, and soul, thumping with them. Joyously she sings a few lines, as they move parted and mirroring each other, drinking in the rhythms with growing intensity. Smiles and eyes reach out, and in. He has not danced in years nor felt this in his lifetime. With swelling life, they laugh and press cheeks. Love songs bring them together, so that where one ends and the other begins is not noticed. Different voices, in different languages celebrate and soar, as their lyrics and melodies express all that comes with caring. No, he has never danced like this, never joined music and two selves so completely.

Without pause, they move around the room, achieving grace, smiling at imperfection, open to variation, to everything they can think of, twirling, spinning, shaking and twisting to syncopated beats. He is thrilled off the floor, where he finds her as well. Gaining feel, trust, confidence, they try almost anything, delighted at their successes, dismissing the missteps, transported beyond where either has lately been.

At length, tired, sated, they stop, leaning against each other. Kissing her hair and neck, he exclaims, "You are magical, in being able to follow me … You don't know how deeply this has moved me. Beyond all experience, imagination, what I deserve."

"For me as well." And she adds, "When you mentioned music earlier, I thought we might try. We have each simply needed a partner." Reaching for and taking his hand, she urges, "Come," and she goes to one of the long walls and sinks down against it, sitting upright, her legs spreading so that he may sit between them and lean back against her, which he does carefully, tilting as her arms encircle him. A hand moves up over his neck and hair. He feels caught between pleasure and the desire to see her, to gaze at and hold. He searches for the words. "It is as though some image, some statue, slipped into reality, arriving from a mountain, and I must do all I can not to lose it or let it disappear."

"We are lucky," she agrees. He coughs, to clear his emotion. She feels his body jump, and rubs his chest, reflecting, "I so much enjoy dancing. In fact it is what I should have done professionally. Modern dance, ballet. Tonight I would have liked to dance all night, if I could," and she squeezes him firmly, urging him to, "Relax your body, relax …" And slowly he does, allowing himself to sink against her.

For some minutes they sit trying to understand what they have discovered. At length, she observes, "Nature insures variety by the impulses she implants in us, our different make-ups, across her ever-changing environments. What in you drew you to Delphi? How was it that you met Iscaria on that hill? How unusual that she saw something. Without those impulses, those decisions, we would never have met. Is this luck, random Nature, the gods, or some physical, electrical force that draws us?" She pulls him tight against her. "Tonight, we should thank … someone … something … the gods."

"I thank *you*, you who are god-enough for me. But I too am trying to identify what led me to Delphi. Was it several things lining up? The series of decisions, my vague decision to go, guided by something, or nothing."

"We cannot know, but after speaking with Iscaria, I was eager to meet you." Yet he wonders what she imagined, but she goes on, "Part, I think, is that I have learned from my failures. And have slowly learned to deeply appreciate what seems to be the good."

"As it was for me. Our deep sadness, in each, has opened both."

For moments, they reflect on these things, before she looks ahead. "So it appears that our lives have led us, primed us, for this moment."

He nods, his head lightly touching hers, and he murmurs, "Thank Iscaria for me ... deeply."

"I will ... Do you feel? I too am trembling ..."

He feels something, but cannot delineate which is which. Or maybe it is Parnassus shaking the city where they sit, its root reaching east, under all the buildings and temples.

At some point, she ponders, "The urge to find love is embedded in us, but also our yearning for independence and fulfillment." Yet she laughs unexpectedly before continuing, "Yes, are we not filled with contradictions ... as we march along, hoping for some resolution, and that our virtues will outweigh our vices."

He smiles at his own recognition of this.

"One thing I do not worry about is my daughter, who is mostly quite happy. We spend much time together, simply, and enjoying each other."

"Would she notice if you changed lovers?"

She laughs. "Of course ... I would have to explain my decision."

"I somehow believe my two boys would understand. How could they not delight in meeting you?" He closes his eyes, but then twists around to look at and read her. Each takes in the other, then smiles as they kiss. But he cannot hold his contorted position, and so swings back, relaxing against her shoulder. He tries to imagine a future between them. What would be possible, what would be different? Could they survive the wearing of everyday life? What would hold off disappointment? But if not this other, who? ... Where would they live? Half here, half there?

But what of Arethusa's schooling? His boys will soon be off to college. She brings her head to his shoulder, resting it there.

After some time, he reflects, "What we need to do is figure out when and where to meet again." Thinking of possibilities, she nods. "I believe that we will be in touch ... on Skype maybe." And she smiles at those shadowy images. "We will meet, and see what to do. We cannot know all at once."

He reaches for her right hand and takes it to kiss. And she presses her lips and face into his hair and ear, before pulling back to ask if he wants more wine and food. He would, and so she pulls herself up as he slides forward to stand with her. She hurries away, soon returning with goat cheese, bread, and wine.

This time, on the floor, they sit shoulder to shoulder, talking about where they might meet, before he remembers, "I have two more days; I leave on the third. Surely you must have some time."

"For lunch, not tomorrow but the next day. Your last day. I know some excellent restaurants."

"Want to fly to an island?"

She laughs, "I'd love to, but I can't ... this time. Another time."

"I cannot let this fall away. I will hold you to it; it will keep me going, looking forward to our meeting." Yet he wonders what will keep her occupied tomorrow. Another client to counsel? But he realizes that he trusts her to tell him if she wants to.

She leans and runs her fingers over his cheek. "We will have lunch," she says, smiling and studying him, before thoughtfully she says, "We are trying to find what is best for all. I don't know. Surely your wife must encounter men she would like to love ... Could she not speak her heart, talk this through with you, see where we all are?"

He understands, but cannot imagine Belle responding in that way. "She would doubt it all, think the worst, that it is all sex. Her personal history and perhaps our cultural history have left her with a dark view of men. She is not a trusting person. I believe she must have been burned by misplaced trust before we met."

"Perhaps if we find a sensitive way to explain it."

He nods. "I don't know. I have little optimism."

She waits to see if he will add anything. But his thoughts return to her. "You have shown me something not experienced before. A new way of talking and being with another, direct, attentive, responsive, interested ... I'd never quite found that before."

She leans over and kisses his cheek, not quickly parting.

He reminds himself that, as she said, they will need to spend more time together, and learn about the other. And yet with all the signs so promising, his heart rushes after them. She too is moved by this affection, and is also calmed by it, that such a thing is still possible, even if she cannot predict where it will go. For it will unfold in its own way, which they in time will discover.

When they part, her mind turns to their future. "I am touched by you and by who we are together ... And yet our lives, your life, will take you off. We must talk, and write.. We will have lunch and will communicate and perhaps meet again, in Paris, New York – who knows, and we will see what grows between us, for we will be open to all things, and will welcome all things, as our hearts lead us ... through the difficult realities. ... " And she wipes her eyes. He reaches to embrace and gently hold her. As they stand together he cannot help but wonder if they are playing out a Homeric tale, pawns in a god's game. And if so, what is the likely outcome? Should he be wary? At the same time, dare he hesitate and maybe lose her? He would never find another. Homer reminds us that life interweaves the exalted and the all-too-human. But for now, all he can do is picture her wine-dark eyes and ardent soul, her honesty and openness. Out of a kind of death, has come life – an old story reaching back forever, the eternal cycle of existence.

Heeling on a close reach Poseidon knifes through two-foot waves blown by a cool north wind, passing Karpathos to the south, heading toward Rhodes. The women sit on the aft deck, or in the cockpit to avoid the stiff breeze and sheets of silver spray. Gazing out at the distant island, they reflect on their decision to continue on. Without him, it will be quite different, and each is eager to visit the islands. But all remain adamant that if he does return before the end of the cruise, all will disembark. For now, however, they can begin to relax and enjoy being out here on this other great rolling natural world.

Eventually the chilling wind and penetrating spray send them below to the main cabin, where they exchange information about the islands. Belle has found other volumes on ancient Greece in the library which abduct her back into that world. But its combination of enlightenment and brutality summons Argos and the incident. The outline of his long face, smiling in the dark, lined and determined, unsettles her. How did it happen, in our civilized times? How was it thrust upon her by one educated and supposedly enlightened? Of course she reads the papers, hears the broadcasts, but still she finds it hard to accept or explain. How is it that this urbane Englishman would do this? Yes, the veneer of civilization has long been thin. Perhaps, unwittingly his choice of 'Argos' encourages part of him that otherwise remains restrained, releasing him from the modern world. But what in some men still permits this? Is their focus still so narrow, their perceptions channeled by their desires? Is it possible to reconcile their contradictory sides? Animals kill for what they need. Do those impulses reside in the primitive regions of men's brains? They, with their superior size, have long dominated women, but less frequently now ... Yet why, in modern societies, are there not adequate mechanisms to control these assaults? And why are the possibilities for redress so limited in this 21st. century? ... Who are the legislators? ... Men, mostly ... Maybe she should pursue prosecution for the sake of all women ... But the difficulties she would have to surmount seem prohibitive. Instead she forces her mind away, so that she might enjoy the books and sail. Yet images from the attack repeatedly intrude, tightening her stomach, which, with the pitching boat, nauseates her, obliging her to return to her cabin and lie down.

A light knocking pulls her out of near-sleep. At first anxiety, even panic, snap through her as she struggles to stand, but then a woman's voice calls, "Belle? Are you all right?'

Surprisingly it's Angela. Belle sinks back onto her bunk, through a cloud of dizziness, until she remembers to reply, "Come in, Angela ..."

Angela leans through the doorway. "I just wanted to see if you're feeling all right. I have some medicine for seasickness if that's the problem."

Belle thanks her and says she may request some if she doesn't improve.

Angela studies her, before asking, "May I speak with you?"

Looking up more closely, Belle guesses the subject, and waits uncertainly. After glancing back along the passageway, Angela steps in and closes the door. Reaching out to the wall to steady herself, she inhales and begins, "I'm sorry about what happened to you ... It's inexcusable ... criminal ... And I should have warned you."

Belle looks down, feeling both relief and annoyance. Angela goes on heedfully, "I have ... nothing but condemnation for what Henry did ... I hope that you can find some ... appropriate penalty ... But, as you know, you're not the first."

With eyes flashing, Belle looks up. "Why did you not say something?"

Angela looks away. "I should have ..."

Their eyes stare half-seeing at each other through a rush of memories. Only as these ebb is Angela able to resume. "This undoubtedly will seem odd. I can't entirely explain it myself, but Henry called me a while ago, to ask about you, and to apologize."

Belle emits a caustic snort. "Apologize? ..."

"He asked me to convey that to you, as you don't have a phone." Angela peers more closely to see if Belle has understood, and then, with her hands fidgeting, she adds, "He claims he misread you."

Angrily Belle glances away. "Misread? ... Forcibly misread ... You can tell him I've contacted the police, and I've spoken to Marguerite and Ileana, *and* the American embassy."

Angela takes this in. "Good ..." She inhales deeply, then steels herself to complete the message. "Henry is ... He says it's incumbent upon him to make amends, beyond apology, to do something. One idea he mentioned was to offer the Poseidon to you and friends or family for a time."

Belle cannot restrain a sardonic laugh, before her eyes return to Angela. "Is he serious? Is that supposed to ... erase ...?"

"It is what he asked me to tell you."

Thoughts jam Belle's mind. He thinks he can buy me off? Indeed it may be worth the aggravation to go to court. "Tell him, I'll see him in court," she snaps looking fiercely at Angela.

Breathing and wiping her moist brow, Angela understands but also wants to warn Belle. "May I add something?" Belle glares at her, then turns away, saying nothing. Angela can sympathize, yet feels the need to complete her advice. "As I said, you unfortunately are not the first ... And I found out through much difficulty, as you may do, that there are limits to what can be done."

"I can take legal steps; I can go to the media and internet; I can make sure that many, many people know about this. And that he pays."

Angela nods, "Yes, you can do all of that, much as I did. It will take a huge amount of time, and it will take money, and will keep the assault front and center in your life for months. Please don't forget that as he's been through this; he has a series of defenses he can mobilize, top lawyers, investigators, resources, to refute everything you say. And attack you in return."

"Did he pay you to say all this?"

Angela is quiet for a moment. "... No, I understand your anger; I experienced it too. But I tell you to try to help you decide, so that you do so with your eyes wide open ... Unfortunately there are many cases like this. It's no fun and infuriatingly frustrating. You may not even get a hearing, let alone a trial, for a year ... And where would it be? ... And how will you pay for everything? ... Spending time in Crete ... time away from your family ... I don't want to minimize the crime against you ... but you will be dragged through all sorts of inconvenience, expense, and mud ..."

"What did you do?"

"I explored all of this ... spoke to people ... Finally I had a lawyer deal with Henry's lawyer ... There was a settlement ... Afterward Henry came to me, outside the agreement and apologized, and offered to make it up in additional ways ... I have no family, really. The friends I have are in Brighton ... He offered me, in addition to a payment, this cruise, with no strings ... As much as it bothers me to say so, he is, in some ways, not a bad person.

Men with power try this sort of thing, in all sorts of ways ... Maybe I'm weak ... but pathetically I had little else. Returning to Brighton and my dreary job seemed even more pathetic ... So here I am ... I figured he would try with you. I thought you might hold your own ... or maybe were open to it. I could see he likes you, your spunk ... you're attractive ... I don't know ..." She blinks back frustration and memories, then manages, "I'm sorry ... I should have said something straight off ..." She expels a breath, recovering.

Belle reflects on all of this. "I'm sorry that you went through this too. Still I can't believe there's nothing we can do."

"There *are* things. It's just you have to weigh the costs, or at least I would. For me it's past. I don't want to dwell on it. That's one reason I think I didn't say anything to you. I wanted it to be in the past."

Belle wonders why Ileana said nothing either. She asks Angela what she knows about Ileana's experience. Angela's expression falls. "They were lovers briefly ... She's said little about that, preferring to speak about her paintings he bought. She and I have become friends, and I will visit her in Barcelona. She's a good person ... can be surprisingly funny." Angela shakes her head and falls silent.

Belle tries to understand this, imagining how Henry might have appeared to Ileana, before the shock that contorted her face at Belle's news. She wonders how it is that Ileana came on the cruise at all.

Watching Belle ponder these things, Angela reminds her, "Henry now lives in Barcelona, I think for tax reasons as much as anything, and he keeps the Poseidon there ... but being with Henry for a while means putting up with things. ... Oddly, I think he's aware of that. There is business-Henry and personal-Henry, and while the latter is improving, sometimes they step on each other. Or that's my theory, anyway."

Belle digests this and thanks Angela. "When we return to Athens, I will talk to various people at the embassy, lawyers ... and see ..."

Angela nods and repeats her willingness to help in any way she can.

"I appreciate it, Angela. Thank you."

With this their conversation ends, and Angela steps back out of the cabin. Belle lies down again in her bunk reflecting on it all. That she is not alone provides some relief, but also stirs her anger. That Angela is warmer, more personal and concerned than she had thought moves her. She concedes that she herself should have been less quick to judge. And yet, despite this support, her own options for justice and redress appear frustratingly limited.

A living Parthenos, she hovers in his mind, so clear and direct, so exquisite that she must be, if not a god, a dream. Qualities of music are what she brings: melodies and tones of profound feeling and hope ... If life is a weaving of harmony and discord, these are the bright moments he will carry with him for life.

Does he load her with too much, an impossible ideal? And yet the ancient Greeks embraced and sustained those ideals, the gods, based on living men and women. And Nature too, in many of its shapes and stripes, produces beauty of form and behavior beyond words. If we are fortunate, it is all around us, he has noticed, filling him with deep appreciation. For years he found no love in his marriage, so that now this new voice, expressing caring and honesty, circles through him. While their evening did not culminate in love-making, it so deeply stirred him as such a departure from what he had known that he fears he can attend to nothing else. He laments, softly in his chest, as he lies in his hotel bed, that he must live on without her.

Although she made no mention of it, he left a wad of Euros in one of her beautiful bowls. And before Kostas arrived to take him home to the hotel, they held each other with him keenly aware of every utterance, every response, every emotion, all rushing together like that wind coming up from that valley.

Late into the morning he sleeps, before rising and staggering into the shower. Toweling dry, turning in circles by the foot of his bed, he sees the red eye of the phone blinking. Is it her? He hurries over. But it is a message from George, inviting him to have dinner this evening. Wren calls back, again reaching only a machine, but replying that he is available, eager, but needs to know where to meet and when.

Dressed, but still drunk with emotion, he wanders unsteadily down to breakfast, where he sits feeling both weightless and heavily hungover. Her sharply defined, beautiful eyes float before him, leaving him smiling like a madman, searching the ceiling for her. He whispers greetings, hums a tune they danced to, until the patient waiter asks if he'd like coffee or a wine. Wine? So late? It would send him back to bed.

Concluding that he is good for little but dreaming and recuperating, he takes a bus to a beach she recommended. Arriving, he steps unsteadily out into the bright, burning sun of early afternoon, and *wynds* between sunbathers, hoping not to trod on any fine fingers or trusting toes. Eventually he finds a quiet spot, spreads out his towel and sinks onto it, closing his eyes under hers. A light breeze, her breath, blows in off the water, carrying, it seems, her words and phrases, indeed herself, so that he hardly dares move, lest he lose connection.

But then he remembers to work out of his clothes, as his bathing suit is on underneath. Freed, he falls back into bliss, thanking Helios for his heat.

In time, he senses something burning, feels some discomfort. Sitting up, wiping his face, he realizes that it is his skin sizzling, and so he fumbles for and applies his forgotten sun block, wincing, and staring out through chastened eyes at the pale blue sea. But his discomfort and agitation do not disappear, and so he pushes up, tests his balance and bearings, then reels away toward the water, finally running and diving into the pearling wavelets. The comparative cool jolts him as he swims out, but soon the physical exertion calms him as the salty density gently holds him. Floating on his back, gazing up into the infinite blue of Iscaria's eyes, he is thankful for them and the new world they introduced.

Regaining his energy, he strokes slowly along the beach, just beyond other bathers, mostly kids, who stare at him strangely. What is this smiling back-stroker doing?

He swims on to where he is alone, and there floats squinting up ... this time into Messena's darker eyes, which stare back into him, as has not happened for so long ... Still his doubt resides: what does he offer her? A renewal of hope and connection? ... Communication? She too has been seeking someone, after her marriages ... And yet she has not been the despondent soul he's felt he has been. Very possibly her work has given her perspective. Yet how randomly do the world's elements swirl and collide, sometimes merging into something new, as best as science can explain ... Will this be their story? Transformed into new awareness? Odysseus returned?

Held by this, he floats heedless of time, until eventually he sees that the sun has moved. He paddles back and wades out, lying again on his towel, thankful for the reflections that came to him, and for the heat penetrating his chilled body. Warmth and cold, light and darkness, man and woman, life and loss ... What can he do but adapt as he can, remain open to the new, and give expression to his heart, filled with the beauty of the world and her. No longer a wandering, solitary soul, he now feels the energy that shines through the heavens, reinvigorating life on Earth.

Sitting up, refilling his contracted lungs, he looks around. He is surrounded by others, playing, shouting, quietly reading. He watches kids splash and dive, wishing his sons were here. Some of the women, in their minimal bikinis, summon a second look. But last night he met a goddess, and there is nothing more he need ask of life. Someone, something has favored him. He will not ask what or why, but will go on now, filled with that light.

Shortly after eight, George arrives at the hotel and takes him in a cab to a favorite bar that is dark and airy where they sit just inside to watch and listen to the passersby. They talk easily and about many things. He wonders how to mention Messena. But they begin with architecture. Although Wren recalls George's views expressed at Antaeus's, he asks again what design means to him.

Ever happy to expound on this, George begins by listing his many approaches, Nature being his primary source. Yet, he tells Wren, he must prod himself, practically beat himself, to open his mind to new ideas and paths. "Although there is little that is entirely new under the sun, I find that if I stretch myself, squeeze my poor brain, I can devise something that is new to me, at least, and to much of the world."

Turning the question back to Wren, he asks how he will approach the new project at home. Wren confesses that he hasn't seen the site yet, but he hopes that its woods and field will suggest a mixing of elements. He likes the natural complexity of a habitat and wants to reflect it in some way, interweaving what the land and his mind can offer.

They go back and forth on these general ideas for a time, until Wren, unable to hold it in any longer, announces that he met someone compelling last night, whom George knows ... Messena.

"Ah yes. Did you? Is she not a delight?" Smiles illuminate their faces.

"She mentioned you, that you are someone very special to her."

"She is a star," George pronounces happily.

"She is," agrees Wren. "The evening star ... For one evening, I was given a sense that I was seen, heard, and perhaps understood, that real sharing was possible, as we spoke of many things."

"Yes, she is a woman of great heart ... though she has been disappointed in love. But so many things come together in her, I can only think her mother must be a god."

"Or Iscaria. Do you know her?"

"I do." And he sighs tilting back his head back as if to search the heavens. "She taught me much, when we were young. She was wise, with crystalline sight. As it turned out, she was the last young woman of beauty I saw, before darkness came to my eyes. Her face is lodged forever in my mind."

Wren is quieted by this revelation, as he imagines and mourns George's darkness. He tries to picture the universe without stars, the day without sun; he tries to imagine young George and young Iscaria, still hopeful of love.

But George, not at all subdued by this, speaks with rapture, "Those two women are to me what make life a shining joy, in addition to my work. They have a great generosity of spirit ... Iscaria embodied beauty internal and external, those many years ago. That memory lifts me still, as do my memories of the land and sea."

"Are the two women related?"

George frowns and shakes his head. "Not to my knowledge ... but I know what you suggest." After a moment's further reflection, he adds, "Messena's two husbands were intriguing men, in very different ways. Strangely she did not see them clearly, but I think she has grown and is not at all embittered."

Wren feels happy to hear this, even as he continues to wonder how he can be important to her. But now George asks him, "You are married, are you not? I think I heard your wife speaking at Antaeus's."

"I am … "confirms Wren, wondering whether to get into it. Instead he recalls Messena's confession. "But George, Messena told me she would choose you, were you open to it."

"She is very kind, but she deserves a whole and younger man."

"You might bring her true companionship."

"We are occasional friends. But Nature did not intend more than that for those at my age. That is the role for someone like you, were you not married."

Startled by this, Wren experiences a stab of pain and sharp cries. He twists to escape them, but then he looks more closely at his companion, for some moments unable to speak. George, however, sits quite happily and calmly, content with his assertion.

After some moments, George chooses to add, "She possesses a kind of creative goodness, which she bequeaths us, a germ of kindness, which too many men see as an invitation to other things."

Wren finds this not hard to imagine . Indeed his mind had cried out for that as well, before he came to understand what she truly offered. Now he observes, "She combines most unusual qualities, sensitivities, not often found in someone so attractive."

"Nor anywhere." George leans closer and reminds Wren, "You understand that I have never seen her. I have traced her face, her cheeks, her head, her breasts and stomach; her legs, her hips and shapely seat. I have a sense of her physically; I know her voice, her thoughts; they move me ... and yet, in some ways, she is but a sum of parts, a page of notes, for me. Oh how I would like to see her, her smile, her eyes, the whole."

Wren is moved and places his hand on George's shoulder. "She places you above all men she knows."

George does not move or speak for a time, and only after he carefully inhales does he whisper, "Her husbands brought her such joy at first. But she has recovered. She sees them as they are, not through her needs."

Wren imagines the losses she experienced and feels the sadness that his friend must feel, that he cannot see her. He wonders if he himself sees her through his needs ... And then partly in response, he asks, in spite of himself, "Do you not know of any men for her?"

A smile slowly spreads over George's face. "She is capable and free. She will find what she seeks." And an ironic smile chases away the first. "Ask not for whom the bell tolls." He laughs silently. "I have long wanted to use that phrase. Thank you ... You know, I have lately turned to poetry, which I must commit to memory, since I cannot read. Like another old Greek."

"I wrote some long ago. Will you recite one of yours?"

George smiles again. "It is in my language." But he nonetheless delivers what seem to be a few lines. Wren can barely make out the words or syllables, but at the end he thanks George.

"It is half-nonsense."

"I thought I heard music."

"If you did, it was in your head."

Yes, much lately has been in his head.

But George puts away his ironic mood and returns to Messena. "You know, thinking back to women like her, the few, I was never wise about them. I held myself off, fearing to be disappointed. While now it is too late, in the past I fear I was mistaken ... But maybe she is Artemis, not destined for men."

Wren feels a faint constriction as he remembers hearing that name spoken at Antaeus's party by his wife, and then attached to her. At the same time he recalls that Messena has loved men, husbands, lovers, and maybe him. Should he remind George of this? But captured by their respective thoughts, they distractedly sip their drinks. After a while, he asks George what else he should visit, with the little time he has, or if he returns.

George describes a few of the various regions, the north, Mt. Athos, several less popular islands, the western islands, Ithaca, Corfu. "It really depends on your interests, or preferences."

"I'd like to see many of them ... Ithaca, perhaps."

"They are full of history ... and tourists. I need to travel very little – I like to smell and feel the air, to hear the sounds, feel the spray ... elements which then reside in my mind." Wren pictures this. Although George's limitation is sad, a tragedy given his work – indeed Wren feels it slowly suffocating him so that he must thrust it away – he hopes that George has found compensation in the wonders of his mind. But Wren recognizes how little of the wonders ... of Greece he will have seen. Belle will have visited much more. And yet now, who knows what the future now may bring?

Shifting in his chair with some agitation, George now returns to their earlier subject, "Allow me to say a bit more about Messena ... She is unusual ... not consumed by women's cares but dispensing a woman's full heart. She recognizes the gift that is her beauty, at all levels. Like Iscaria, when she was young, she wants to give back in some way ... to we mortals, with whom she has generous sympathy ... And, for that reason, Wren, if you are serious in your appreciation of her, in the love I hear in your voice, you must be sure she knows. I suspect too many men, including myself, have shied away, intimidated by her fullness of feeling and being ... It is daunting in a way, to become aware of her profound awareness and concern ... How could we match it, or return it? What could we give her? ... So you must be very clear, first to yourself about what you can give ... but then to her. Do not fail ..."

Wren feels once again launched into the night sky, called by the aurora that dance in its dark dome ... Yet he too is daunted. How could he not be? – even as he is drawn irresistibly. He grips the side of his chair to hold himself in the here-and-now, shaken by what George has counseled. Moments from that evening come into focus, filling him. The intensity heightens, throbbing into ache. He rubs his temple, shakes his head, to awaken, relieved that George can't see him. Why has she offered herself? What is she seeking? Is she, like Odysseus, or himself, seeking a way to the heart's home?

"George ... do you think I could find work here?"

The other smiles. "With some help ..."

Wren closes his eyes, imagines returning, living here, working, perhaps with George ... and seeing her. His heart quickens; he struggles to breathe as he envisions conversations with her. But in the mean time, in reality, how will he live? How *can* he, after that evening? Her natural perfume, her aroma fill his lungs, her astonishing fullness .... He feels awakened ... rising through glimpses of her. Is this how men's minds worked in those long-ago centuries? Dreams became gods? Why are not many more like her? Why is he not, himself? Maybe he will become. She has opened a door.

ATHENA

The long, dark hump of Rhodes inches closer. Above, the blue sky is softened by a few white clouds, at which Belle gazes lying on the deck. Under calmer winds and over a rolling sea, the Poseidon surfs the swells, accelerating down, then yawing at the bottom of the troughs. Belle finds this world pleasingly simple: sea, sky, and sail – with nothing urgent to consider, for now. Perhaps for the first time in the trip, she feels she's on vacation, though shadows hover like myths at the edge of history. But she turns her mind away, to the approaching island, imagining the faces and styles of dignitaries and soldiers through the centuries. She pictures the different swarms of them come to rule, for a time, before forced to retreat … Yet never did women govern, their lives mostly held in subordination. Only now in the Western world are many finding a full range of possibilities. Life, she quotes to herself, has been a nightmare from they have struggled to awake. Light spray moistens her legs, as if the distant past reaches up to remind her. Together the gently rolling sea and its sparkling drops, like tiny emissaries, call her back through time to the extraordinary 5th and 6th centuries B.C., when, as with women's rise today, whole new paradigms were conceived, delivering more rational approaches to problems – a heady time now, as then, in which she wants to participate and contribute … She wonders if letting go of her marriage, with its limitations, would facilitate this.

Nearing the port of Rhodes, they pass, for the first time, other vessels: several yachts draped with bare sunbathers; a large ferry plowing a white furrow through the royal blue sea, returning clumps of gazing passengers to the continent, passengers who wave, futilely at first until Belle raises a hand. Two fishing boats slowly circle, drawing in their nets, snaring sea nymphs from the curling waves. The brilliant sunlight seems to alter and magnify detail, as if Apollo transforms the scene. Belle's gaze moves from the bare-armed fishermen to the ferry passengers in colorful, new outfits, pleased yet sobered by vacation's end, and again to the white limbs and pale torsos of the yachting sunbathers, stretched out, as the four women are. Why do we choose to brown our bodies? she wonders. To improve appearance, regain youth, certify our travels, the desirability of our lives? She smiles. While it's not important to her, still she does it.

The captain brings them in to the public dock along the extensive waterfront, and leaves them to walk through the town and up to the Grand Castle, built in the time of the Crusaders. Belle wonders if in some way the four are not unlike those crusaders, landed to assert control and take what they can. Though each of the four comes from a different homeland, they share sensibilities around what life might be; indeed for several reasons, they are developing a closeness. Angela and Marguerite are sharp and realistic; Ileana is kind, funny, artistic, aware of the ironies.

Pleased with this harmony, Belle wonders how different the ancient lives and cultures must have been: the Dorians, Ionians, Persians, the Alexandrian and Roman empires, the Crusaders from all over Europe, the Ottomans, and later the Italians all came, conquered, left – leaving what? Today the Rhodesians remain, combing which strands? ... The island is a vacation destination, crowded and commercial. Are the locals happy with this? It might be interesting to find out, might be of interest to her field, even instructive, to the closely knit, modern world. She sees that researching such a book would require returning to the island and the region – both an allure and a challenge. Would the boys accompany her next summer? Would Wren?

The four wind their way uphill to the Grand Castle, where inside they join a tour. Afterward, Belle speaks to one of the custodians about access to museum archives and other sources of island history. She is told permission can be obtained, and that there are additional archives in Athens and Venice, all of which makes her book idea seem more substantive and feasible, if she can interest a publisher. And so, slowly, like a distant island across the sea, this idea begins to rise, take form, and spawn excitement.

Returning to the town, they hire a taxi to drive them to the nearest beach where they swim for an hour, before returning to the boat and then waterfront, selecting a restaurant overlooking the harbor. There they settle in for an early dinner and earnest talk. Used to leading discussions, Belle steers the conversation, first mentioning her book idea, which surprises and intrigues the others, and then turning again to Argos. Is he, she asks, any different than an ancient pirate, pasha, or crusader? All sought control, treasure, the fruits of power, submission, or the extension of belief. "He loves to hold forth and tell wild tales of his life," laughs Ileana, "which I notice vary with each re-telling."

"He is a mountebank!" cries Angela. "Amusing from a safe distance." Mixed smiles and squinting eyes move among them. Marguerite recalls, "He's like those swashbuckling buccaneers from the old movies I would see on television." "Yes!" agrees Belle, "A George Sanders-type."

"But from the 19, 18, or 14-fifties?" queries Angela. "All!" cry all, laughing, amid which Belle adds, "From the age of men." Smiles and reflection ripple through and behind their expressions, until Ileana sighs, "And yet we love them ... for their energy and amusement, and the attention, and sometimes adoration, they give us." The other three consider this, with reservations, before Belle, growing more serious, observes, "Henry's behavior is not unlike that of adolescent males I've recently read about. With their partially-developed brains in transition, they focus on excitement and reward, not risk or pain, or others certainly. They simply don't calculate repercussions. When they see something they want, they go for it ... It's clear that they must be re-educated, taught to understand and control their urges, informed of the consequences. Exactly how to do that, however, is a challenge; it may require a little shock therapy, metaphorically speaking."

The others laugh uncertainly, as they consider this. "Maybe we need to bring back the rack or stocks?" suggests Angela under an arching eyebrow, and the others call out, "Here, here ..." and laugh again, whereupon she adds, "Henry, however, is a complex fellow, not averse to learning, quite capable of absorbing something new, even if he usually applies it to his own ends. He is both adolescent and prince. Maybe they are of the same mind-set. But we should not underestimate him; he can surprise you, negatively and in positive ways. If we understand that, we are less likely to be thrown by his behaviors."

"Has no one informed him that he's several centuries out of date?" asks Marguerite.

"I don't think he is entirely blind to that," Ileana cautions. "As Angela said, he is a complex character, not without his sensitivities and endearing qualities. Not only did he commission my portrait of him, but he bought several of my paintings. How can I not be appreciative, in part?" And she laughs a mixed laugh before glancing at Belle and adding, "I'm afraid I must confess that his worldly success was both intriguing and exotic, at first. He was unique in my life. He made me laugh and cry."

In purring accord Angela expands on this, "As a self-made mogul, he tends to think things, and people, can be brought in line if he simply exerts enough pressure or will. He thinks everything is manageable in that way."

"Has he learned so little from all of us?" asks Belle.

"I don't think it's occurred to him to learn, in that particular vein," responds Marguerite, eyebrows narrowing into a frown.

"If it hasn't," smiles Angela, "Belle has the opportunity to make it a very expensive oversight for him. For money is something he *does* understand and appreciate. It's possible that his childhood years, difficult and without much parental attention, warped him. He trusts money to bring him the things he wants, not people."

"A distortion that affects us all," deplores Marguerite, before Ileana responds, "You may be right, Angela. I don't believe Henry ever experienced what a mother can bring. On top of that, he works in a very male world, where all is focused on maximizing profit, cutting deals, expenses ... corners. They are unacquainted with modern psychology; women are still for diversion ... pleasure ... to bestow admiration."

"Where was he during the consciousness-raising of recent decades? How did he manage to miss it all?" wonders Marguerite with amusement.

"He was in the oil fields," answers Angela dryly. "Where none of that permeated their Permian world, where all is focused on drilling ... wherever they can ... pumping up prehistoric residue." Their eyes meet, acknowledging the seriousness of this and the humor. After a moment or so, Angela adds, "And his success confirms it all for him, that his way of life is rewarding." Another pause sends their eyes around again, before she offers one additional observation, "He was married ... but it had little impact, it seems. He sees it as a misstep or two, not to be repeated."

Again the four ponder, until Marguerite asks, "I still wonder if, by staying on the boat, are we sending the wrong message? ... Are we suggesting that his behavior toward all of us wasn't so unacceptable? In fact, are we conceding that, like him, we are out there, ready to take what we can get?"

"That's a good question," Belle concedes, "but we might well argue that we should be no more emotionally invested than he is. Therefore why not enjoy this odyssey while it's possible? We owe him nothing; it is he who owes us. On the other hand, to deny our emotions might be to fool ourselves and live a false life. I think we should resolve this, for ourselves." And she looks around at the other three, who nod at the complexity, before she adds, "Of course I am going to pursue legal redress. His leaving the boat to us does not erase his assault, nor does it pay for it. That should become clear to him when I take him to court. I assume our captain has communicated my intention to do so. But having made that point, I see no reason to deny ourselves this opportunity promised to us. We all have committed time and money ... Nor can I dismiss the fact that to sail among these islands is an extraordinary experience, which may lead to other things, such as a book and subsequent visits ... And so, I for one feel comfortable with our decision."

Although Marguerite seems to agree, she points out, "Angela won a settlement, but Ileana and I have not expressed to him our disapproval of his behavior. I guess for both of us there has been some ambivalence in our attitudes, before this latest transgression."

"You can join my complaint, and possibly win part of the settlement," suggests Belle. But glancing among each other, none can be certain of the feasibility of this or where it would take them. Angela warns, "While we are free of him now, I would predict that he will be back, possibly within the week, and we should be ready to respond if he does." But frowning Marguerite now asks Angela if she feels adequately compensated by her settlement. Smiling somberly, Angela allows, "Not to be equivocal, but yes and no. It was an affront, an attack, which can never be fully expunged or paid for, but in the practical, everyday, compromised world that I mostly live in, where my work was for years a compromise, it is somewhat balanced out. At first I felt some affection for him, but then he went too far. Yet this cruise is not something I will have another chance to experience, seeing the Aegean, and maybe I will meet a man, some adventurous Greek, or male Calypso ..." And she laughs uncomfortably, and the others smile through mixed feelings. "And so, I guess I have concluded that for me Henry is the price I pay ... as he paid me ... but that is only me."

As the others weigh this, Belle concedes, "My feelings are, I'm finding, surprisingly close to what Angela expressed. My life back home has not been without unhappiness and compromise, while this opportunity, as she noted, probably will not come again. History has been my passion, and to be here is astonishing to me ... thrilling! ... So while yes, I will be pursuing legal redress, even if, as you know, a settlement is probably the best I can hope for, still I am happy to continue our cruise."

The others nod and murmur their assent, until Marguerite, with a laugh and flashing eyes, offers another approach: "Possibly, mes chères amies, we could hire a Mafia hit-man or unemployed jihadist to stalk Henry, turning the tables on him. That might keep him in seclusion for a long time. Why not be pro-active?"

The others laugh and cheer for a brief moment, but then they accept that in reality, as they cannot eliminate uncertainty, they must live with it. Tomorrow they will speak to the captain and see where the cruise will take them, but all agree that they would like to stay another day on Rhodes as there is much to see and explore.

Alone in her cabin, Belle runs it all through her mind. One drawback, she had earlier recognized, was that in returning immediately to Athens she would encounter Wren, and have to explain, during the long, unhappy flight home. And what would she tell him? ... If she mentioned the assault, how would he react? With sympathy, or silent gloating? ... And she had also realized that while the four of them could tour the islands on their own, arranging travel from one island to another and finding lodging might be complicated and expensive. And so she now reaffirms that sailing on to other islands is the best alternative. While there is some chance that Angela was right about Henry returning, it seems unlikely that he would want to face them all. More likely, he will stay away until they disembark in Piraeus. And in the mean time, with just the four of them, it could be quite enjoyable, as it was today, sailing up to the island, walking through the castle – her new ideas beginning to take shape.

Once again the sun-bright day has risen long before him, on this his final one. Its arrival confirms the oft-noted, inexorable beat with which time proceeds. It may seem to slow here and there, but it catches up when one is not looking. All that he, or anyone, can do is to passionately fill his allotted span. Soon he will see the boys, his home, and return to work, prospects which shoot excitement through him, followed by an even stronger surge in picturing her who shimmers like the sun in the sea. While he may well exaggerate her and the possibilities, his hunger for love rushes ahead of all reality or restraint; imagination overwhelms all warnings of experience. His mind whispers that he should reign in these dreams, in this modern, mechanical world, so far from Homer's. And yet his romantic inner voice pleads that this is his chance. He must do all that he can. Tears cloud his sight. To have this unexpected reprieve seems a gift beyond measuring or deserving.

He takes George's recommended walk to Lycabettos and rides the cable car up to the small church at the top. From there the city spreads out around him sunny and largely uniform, a rolling, white and beige carpet. The Acropolis and Parthenon, so massive up close, seem nearly lost in the pale sea of buildings, a mere lattice of lace. He tries to imagine living here in those distant centuries, and wonders what to make of the countless lives, each so precious to its host, each aware of so much, yet lost in the stream of time.

His ruminations curl back upon his own consciousness which seems at times autonomous, an entity outside his physical self, and yet with whom he is in constant consultation. Both seem sturdy, but both, he knows, can also be as evanescent as a breeze, as vulnerable as a spider's web ... What point, then, for most, our temporary residency? What are we? ... With our built-in drives we hurry, or meander, as best we can. But going where? ... Some speculate that we, like atoms, combine and evolve randomly, seemingly in a slow ascension – The system of the universe? But if most men and women are mere drones or worker bees, what significance, what point? Cogs or bricks for a cathedral beyond our comprehension? Or the basic foundation on which the few break-through creators rise? But of course it's more complicated, and we must find or make our own meaning. While some are pondering the grand-unified theory, most are consumed by seeking their next meal, or love ... Artists bring pleasure, insight, and maybe heightened awareness. Astronomers explain the heavens. In either case, their contributions permeate slowly. Yet now, as our numbers push up into the billions, and we're all interconnected, it seems everything accelerates. Toward some plateau ahead? How far? ... Wren acknowledges he's an optimist. Our momentum is taking us to a higher life – at least so he hopes. Or should we, as Tolstoy professed, seek meaning and satisfaction in ourselves, developing in every way we can? Society will benefit as well ... Or are these empty intellectual constructs unrelated to the world?

What he *can* be sure about is that having been without love for so long, its unexpected arrival has transformed everything in him, penetrating like the Sun ... While there were many good, early years with Belle, they come no more, and their residue has all but vanished – perhaps the mode of life. He cannot help but wonder if this new caring, this love, is stronger for having experienced emptiness. For him, indeed, it feels so intense that all other activity seems inconsequential. And while the physical world is exquisite, is the source of all that is, as far as we can understand, without the animation of love, existence seems of little purpose or import, unless and until evolution reaches or reveals some higher plain.

Trembling with these thoughts, Wren tries, nonetheless, to reason how physical substance, atoms, come to know and love? Yes, he's read of our MRI-captured neurological system fashioning activity, forging pathways of memory and connection, of how mind moves muscles and muscles create emotion, but still the leap from signals to concepts and the interior galaxy that is personality, seems, if theoretically explainable, no less a chasm to cross. And what is it that we can really know about how we make our choices? And understand how those other eyes do see, and what those ears do hear. How close do our ideas of conversation, kindness, and beauty converge? Before, Wren would have placed his work, his boys, the early years with Belle, above all, though lately it's placed him alone – until Messena.

Indeed he now wonders if without the possibility of mutual love, all the great architecture he sees is just cold stone; all the great music mere chromatic patterns and variations ... But in fact, they are symbols and expression of great feeling and perception, and as such awaken our minds and our hearts, and connect us, and in this give us purpose, be it focused on mankind, virtue, or creation. If life is fragile, fleeting, wrenching, as it often appears, does it not, in its aggregate and variation, prove to be resilient ... much as love feels at first. And thus is not *love* Nature's gift to the living, in its echoing and affirming one another?

George had touched on these things at the café, noting that while existence may be simply what is, or what has evolved, yet mankind through the ages has searched beyond, for understanding and meaning ... and in the process has conceived god-like abilities, taking us toward increased knowledge, capability, and caring, despite the many, terrible setbacks. George also noted that science has found that our brains are growing and our bodies changing as we change their tasks. And our hearts may be growing as well, metaphorically. Finally, the two men agreed, it was people like Messena and Iscaria who helped spread the recognition of connection between us all.

With a smile, George had then added one final speculation, "The processes which have created us, and which we use in turn, link us with the universe and reveal that we are an integral part." And he'd laughed, noting that despite this slow ascent, we nonetheless continue to tightrope between progress and annihilation. "And maybe for that very reason," he concluded, "you and I, above all, must remember that what those two women have given us is the insight and oxygen of great generosity ... which they breathe upon us, and which we inhale, and must ourselves pass on."

In the streets, with no protestors marching, the morning is quiet and still, as if subdued by the sun. He tries, mostly successfully, to hold his mind away from her, fearing that it will not happen, that she will be called away, or be different, or that all was a chimera.

Down from Lycabettos, he walks half-seeing, in and out of sunlight and imaginings, as if passing through centuries. It is both stirring and calming; doubly so as he comes upon, and pauses to study, unique buildings from all eras: embassies, businesses, dwellings. Later he sits for a coffee, picturing sailing the glinting, age-layered sea, then being home with the boys and Sherlock. Together this richness and range, his witnessing and joining in, bring tears to his eyes, once more.

Suddenly the hour is upon him. He has followed her directions and is at the address. He stops and looks around, reaching out to a white wall to steady himself and reassert reality in touching the cool stucco. And then a figure is approaching, walking quickly from the other direction ... It is her, smiling with excitement. He spreads his arms, soars to her, barely able to contain his pounding heart. They clasp each other, straining, alive. He closes his eyes. Parthenos returned, out of the sun. Any doubts vanish as he feels her lips on his cheek and neck, as he turns to find hers with his.

When they pull back a little, he sees that her appearance is somewhat altered. Her hair is different, pulled back and down behind. She seems less formal than in that stunning dress ... more casual, younger, sensual ... as she too studies him happily. "You've been to the beach, taken some sun and are looking healthy!"

He smiles and asks, "Are we the two who met and spoke and danced the other night?"

Her smile broadens as she leans to bestow another kiss on his cheek, its faint moisture lingering in the sun, a benefaction from the centuries. He closes his eyes as he leans into her, sensing her attentive, smiling, ardent soul. He hears her add, "You seem stronger, happier."

"How could I not be, anticipating you ... wandering the city, imagining the past and future." And he smiles. "Revived, redeemed, reborn."

She presses into him, and he holds her, feeling her energy. He leans back to check the reality of this; she is there, her dark eyes watching his, with no signs of concern or hesitation. He breathes, happy beyond all imagining.

She laughs and takes his hand, holds it for a moment, squeezes it, in a strong, warm grip, then motions toward the door.

As they enter, he feels light, floating over the stone walk without effort. They are led by a waiter to a small outdoor courtyard, partly shaded by trees and walls and then up a curving stair to a small roof garden and tables. An older couple dines silently in one corner; a mild breeze carries the aromas of blossoms and cooking.

They are seated near a railing, from which the downhill terracing of the white neighborhood drops away. Water, bread, and oil are brought. He laughs at this perfection, as if upon Olympus. He thinks, then voices, "I cannot conceive of a more exquisite moment."

She covers his hand with hers. "If you did not conceive it, we would not be here. You asked to meet. You understood that I would be in your mind, as you have been in mine, and my heart, since our evening."

This steals his breath; his head pounds in the stillness; he must breathe, he reminds himself. Time stutters – a series of still lifes fill his mind: her face, the sky, sun, each too bright to fully see. He hears her speak, "Somehow, so unexpectedly, yet foreseen by Iscaria, there is something between us, something we sense but cannot entirely know. A perceiving of the other, a deep appreciation. I would have never guessed it possible, with someone so far from my home and life." Her eyebrows rise. He studies her, moved by her confession. He whispers to himself, as she seems to be suggesting, that what they have found may be stronger than the sea which separates them. Although their understanding of the other is not fully formed, even gossamer, yet it reaches deeply, drawing each. But why should he be chosen from among the multitudes? Did he please a priestess?

In winking glimpses, he imagines talking, walking, wrapped in embrace, dancing again, as music envelops them, as the tide flows in around. The intensity of the images nearly overwhelms him. He presses his soles against the deck, clenches his eyes, shakes his head.

Softly she says, "I know what you are thinking." Her words are barely audible and yet he hears, as she adds, "And I am too ..." Her face grows serious, even as it shines. "We are lucky ... truly ... and yet ..."

Yes, he agrees covering her hand with his. He understands and promises himself that he will do all he can.

The waiter returns. Messena asks Wren if she may order for them, as she knows the menu. He is happy with this; he has not thought of food. Speaking quickly she tells the waiter what they will have, along with a bottle of wine. When the waiter leaves, she tells him that she has some news that she wants to share. "In addition to you, I have found something else ... taking me in another direction, perhaps encouraged by our meeting, riding the energy you have given me. It is what kept me busy over the two days since we met. And I want to explain."

Refocusing on her announcement, he waits as she begins, "I have found a publisher who will commission a book I want to write, a history book."

Not sure he's heard correctly, he checks, "A history book?"

Her shining face brightens as she again covers his hand. Yet even while he smiles happily for her, he cannot help but feel a tremor at this odd coincidence. She goes on, "I have just begun the research, making a second trip to the national library, which took most of the last two days. I was asked to write up my proposal in more detail than I first submitted." She watches him closely as he digests her idea, before she elaborates, "It will be a book on women in Greek history, starting of course with mythology, Homer, Athena, in all her guises."

Again he feels the floor shift, maybe the entire building. He makes an effort to smile, though his mind spins. "Athena?"

"Yes, what do you think?"

Sounds, syllables, music, and images collide. Emotion closes his throat; he swallows and swallows again. What does he think? "I am happy for you ... Very ... A subject for us all to investigate here in the birthplace of so much ... I have little idea of their history, their roles ... but my wife teaches history and writes books.

She does not move, again reading his thoughts, until she observes with some humor, "Perhaps I should consult her ..." She cannot restrain a smile. Nor can he. "Yes ..." Both consider this, but his sight clouds, his mind stumbles through blurring images, which do not quickly clear. And yet, after some moments, a brightness replaces them. Her project may be simply what is most natural, seeking understanding ...

He congratulates her, "I applaud you and embrace you. The publisher cannot fathom yet who they have enlisted. Lucky them. I am envious, that they can work with you."

Her dark shining eyes move over this face, searching, before her excitement spills out, "I will begin by talking with Iscaria.

And of course analyzing Athena, her origins and identities and qualities, as she is by far the most interesting, nuanced god. I will interview many Greek women, a range, for I have only an approximate idea of all the different ways they may see our turmoil and contemporary life here."

Squinting, he tries to see her clearly, but she fades as if within a penumbra. Instead he gropes again for her hand, squeezing it, a little too hard. She withdraws it, asking, "So what do you think? Tell me your reaction."

"I want to read it. Discover what you discover."

"It will take time."

He bows. "As all of these things do ... While I know so little about your subject, I think as a starting point it would be fascinating to explore what Athena might have meant to the various ancient Greeks."

Pleased, she begins to explain, "It is possible she originated in the Minoan world, centered in Crete, for that civilization worshipped goddesses, nature goddesses. But the end of the Bronze age, with the Dorian invasion, brought other gods, and possibly she was adopted by the new mix of Athenians and integrated into that world, first as protector of the city and later as the source of wisdom and justice." Eyes excited, she studies him, whose eyes shine back at her as he murmurs, "Like you."

Her smile deepens, before she concludes, "She is, in her later incarnations, a model for all of us." He agrees, "From the little I know ... Perhaps her even-handedness helped foster their democracy."

"That is a part of what I will investigate. If women had been included, it might have lasted longer, with their social abilities. Still that world was mostly one of struggles for power and war.

Only Cleopatra and Xenobia are recorded as queens. Perhaps we are seeing significant change in our time."

This echoes sentiments his wife has expressed. He breathes, "I hope so, and I look forward to reading your book."

"It will be in Greek," she says laughing a little. "Possibly some publisher may want to translate it."

"American women would read it. And elsewhere."

"Would the Chinese?" she wonders with amusement. "But yes, into English. I hope so. But I must ask Iscaria for some direction," she says smiling. "And Athena, too."

Happily he requests, "Ask her to help us also, in finding a way." She bows that she will, before another practical thought fills her mind. "It will take much time, the book, and I will need to work, in order to live."

He grasps her point, that these things will hold her here, prevent her from travelling ... But he too has a project and children. How will the two of them meet? ... Will these other commitments intervene? Their attraction is so new, who can say what tensile strength it may have. It is not that he is uncertain about his feelings, only about the interference and weight of the practical. Sacrifice will be required. Abruptly he understands that if he wants to see her again, it is he who will have to fly, through a cloud of complications.

Watching, she sees these concerns move through him, and she waits. Their eyes hold on the other, serious, aware of the implications, until quietly, he tells her, "While I'm uncertain about the path, I'm certain about the goal."

She looks down in still-eyed reflection. "We need not solve everything at once. We must be patient. Things will become clear. Maybe in time short visits, meeting halfway ... in Rome ... Paris?"

He smiles, then nods once, adamantly. They study each other carefully, gently, looking into the other's eyes, similar in their dark watchfulness. Abruptly he recognizes, "We see each other with interest, patience, understanding ... What is more important?" She nods murmuring, "We are lucky to have found this." For some moments, they continue to read the other, before he extends his palm to her, waiting for hers, and when it comes, he whispers, "Palm to palm is holy palmers' kiss." She shares his smile, as his fingers now trace her palm. He has changed, he feels, from someone alone to someone connected to this other. He sees her and senses her thoughts and feelings, as he feels that he is seen – something he has long missed. It is a new life. And even if things do not work out, he will have these memories for his lifetime.

Briefly their minds wander through these reflections, until she observes, "How strange that these new directions for me have come together, nearly as one. I cannot help wondering how it is so. Pure chance? Or can it be some energy or synergy ... or spirit? Though usually I avoid such explanations."

"I, too, have believed, 'til now, that we make our own fate, to a great extent, once we have grown. And yet what but chance, openness, and Iscaria's insight could have brought us together?"

"It is for both a strange twist of fortune."

"A coming together of choice and chance," he muses. "Of harmonious elements, as seen by her ... While we cannot yet explain precisely why it is so, it could lead us both to a new depth of living ... through the things we might share, such as your book. How strange it is, to me, that both you and my wife look to Athena for understanding and direction, each finding what has been long sought."

"It is natural that women would look to her." As he considers this, she continues, "How she evolved, through the different eras, mostly in the minds of the storytellers, is something to investigate. I found out that 'Athens' and 'Athena' are not originally Greek names, but may be pre-Greek. It seems she had many influences on her development."

Their eyes hold on each other as they ponder implications, until she observes, "That we share interest in these ideas may not only draw us together, but take us in new directions. We talk well together; you listen, and we share dreams of what life might be – something that moves me deeply. After two mistaken marriages, I welcome the harmony in shared searching and conversation. Perhaps that is what Iscaria saw."

Their smiles brighten. He feels a burning in his brow, his chest, which seems to contrast, he imagines, the deepest cold of the universe, or infinite solitude, where all shatters into nothing. What she allows is the hope for warmth, heat, life ... communication. With the brief flaring of our match-like lives, such a partnership may start a fire.

Sensing his thoughts, she repeats: "Yes, I will ask Iscaria what she saw, and her views of all of this." He peers more closely at her as she holds still for him to see. His palm finds hers again, and then he slides off his chair and kneels on the floor next to their table, and he asks her to join him, and she does. And they embrace, pressing each other close, feeling the other, eyes closed, in hope that they may somehow find a way. As he pulls her closer, he sees a flash in her eyes and feels a spasm which sends her hard, and sensuously against him, and he presses back. Only after some moments must they release and embrace more gently, until they hear the waiter returning, prompting them to rise and sit. Glancing at the older couple in the corner, he finds that they have turned and have been watching, a soft light in their faces. He smiles, bowing a little, and Messena seeing this, does as well, smiling warmly, so that all four share a moment of appreciation.

On through lunch their conversing draws them in and holds them as ideas leap back and forth. They discuss additional aspects of her project and his potential one, and the travel which will be necessary. And they talk of books and music which have moved them and have lodged in their hearts. And each reflects on his and her culture and countrymen who too often seem misguided – even as both acknowledge the good fortune that has befallen them. And they share concern for the changing natural world, about which there is much new knowledge but less consensus about what to do. Will mankind, he asks, come together to address these challenges, or will it destroy this heaven, decline, and fall into chaos? Will it be the story of Cassandra rather than Athena? And she sees that this issue is something she should also address in her book.

At the end, they stand and descend back to the garden, where they stop alone for a final embrace, lasting uncounted minutes.

And then on the street, they exchange addresses, and she affirms, "We will write. We have much to exchange. Perhaps it will be you who flies first, but I know the difficulties. Yet I have faith that we will find a way, that we shall listen to our hearts."

Firmly resetting his jaw, he bows to her, then reaches for her once more, for a final kiss ... committing it to memory, then looking and committing all to his internal vault, before a backing away, blowing kisses, both, turning, swinging back again, each waving, smiling, then pulling around and walking off.

Morning finds the four returned to their harbor-side café for breakfast and a sharing of thoughts. All remain committed to continuing the cruise, even as they support Belle's intention to pursue legal recourse. And to this end, she again borrows Marguerite's phone to call one of the recommended law firms in Athens. Connected to a friendly, English-speaking female attorney, she summarizes the situation and explains that she would like to make an appointment to explore legal steps, when she arrives in Piraeus.

When they have finished their coffees, they hire a taxi to take them across the island to a ruined castle at Lindos, where they explore its broad terraces above the sea and the small, art-filled village at its foot. Afterward they swim at the local beach, and lunch in a simple restaurant. In many ways, this is their most pleasing day. It's not crowded, and exploring the narrow streets they find culture and beauty in the galleries and shops, and in a studio where pottery is being shaped into bowls and cups by a craftsman spinning his wheel with a pumping leg. The vivid architecture and art from different eras delight their eyes and stir their emotions as they imagine those long-ago times. They wonder how they themselves would have withstood the constriction and boredom. Would they, as products of that time, have accepted the limitations, aware of little more, appreciating the available joys? While they acknowledge that perspective changes with each era, they agree that modern living has brought women to a vastly different, and improved, place. And yet they concede that possibly those more constricted, long-ago lives may have been deeply felt and more viscerally experienced.

Over lunch, they speak of their own lives and what gives each a sense of worth and satisfaction. As each lists her own criteria, they conclude that it's the depth of experience, rather than the number, that pleases, and all agree that finding work or a partner, which or who, facilitates that depth would be ideal. Yet their recognition of where each stands in this is sobering. Margaret alone has, at the moment, such a partner. And they conclude that, as stimulating and engaging as their odyssey is turning out to be, it probably will not deliver the most profound of experiences.

Ileana is surprised to find that of the four she can voice the broadest satisfaction. "Perhaps I am a more simple soul," she sighs. "Mais non," reassures Marguerite, pointing out: "You have your painting and your lovers – even Henry. You seem to know how to take them, even him, more wisely than the rest of us ... As for me, I vacillate about marriage, and wonder at the true value of my work."

In contrast, Belle acknowledges the pleasure and satisfaction in her work, and her boys, but concedes that her marriage has dwindled into emptiness. And yet, she has found new friends and re-acquaintance with the ancient world, together, possibly, presenting a new beginning.

For her part, Angela confesses lagging in most areas, save for travel. Her eyes falling in silent review, she concedes she needs change. "I must move beyond these Henrys ... It may require luck, or a god's intervention."

"We are here!" cries Marguerite throwing her hands up, and the others join with laughter and support.

Slowly, then, each comes to recognize that this cruise, initially with its high-handed captain, but now together, exploring remnants of antiquity, has roused them to question and re-evaluate, so that, just possibly, for each, it may be a turning point.

Belle speculates that the experience may be transformative, with the book and spending time in Europe. If she returns to Rhodes for research, she may well stay in Lindos, which seems to reach back through the centuries. Indeed this prospect fills her with excitement.

After dinner in a different, elegant restaurant, with several solicitous, even flirtatious waiters, they consult with the captain. He suggests they continue their voyage as planned, proceeding to Patmos in the morning. To their inquiry about Henry, he reports only that they have not spoken – an assertion all find dubious.

Sitting on her bunk later, she pictures the boys joining her next summer, pleased by the beaches and opportunities to sail and explore the castles and ruins. It would be a sunny, deeply engaging time – the one uncertainty being Wren.

The next morning, under a pale sky and light wind, they sail slowly across to the small port of Skala on Patmos. Alone in the main cabin, Belle reflects on her likely acceptance of a settlement, and she ponders her marriage, where rapprochement seems less and less likely. What then? In contrast, she's aware of how happy she's been with her new friends. And with the one obvious exception, the tour has been all that she hoped. The possibility of the book deeply excites her, while in Marguerite she has found the potential for a truly close friend. Their attitudes and styles are similar, and she likes her French directness, her willingness to discuss in detail almost anything, and her sharp humor.

Reaching these conclusions brings peace, and she enjoys visualizing next summer, particularly if her book materializes. What she does conclude about Wren is that the distance between them has widened; she feels she has left him behind, held as he is by his dreams, symbolized, perhaps, by the ruins at the Acropolis. He will not change. What would he do over here? She doubts he would come, or find work here. There seems to be no way back, or forward, as a couple ... The more she considers it, the more it seems to her to have run its natural course ... Why press things? Many Europeans no longer bother with marriage. What alone connects the two of them is their sons, who will soon be off to college. What many women come to learn is that men, in many cases, are self-involved, frequently insensitive to, or unconcerned with, others. He lives in his unrealized hopes, holding onto and paying his assistant with little justification. If he insists, why stay tethered? Nature draws the sexes together for the mating years, but then the differences assert themselves. Even her father had his escapades, and her boyfriends as well ... So why suffer extended unhappiness, as her mother did? With the divorce rate around fifty percent, nearly half have made this decision. The reasons, long evident, are unlikely to change.

Nor is there anything holding her in the town. Maybe when the boys go, she can move to Europe, find a receptive department, and join her three new friends who she finds increasingly interesting and open. And she may meet others, as the European lifestyle and values seem more in line with hers. Her current home has provided no deep female friendships, such as is growing with Marguerite, and maybe the other two. It's too bad Argos turned out as he did. But there are other men, for diversion … or, from time to time … affection.

Following the established pattern, the captain docks to allow the four to get off and stretch their legs. They walk through the village, then take a little bus up to the monastery in Chora, noticing that the island is greener than the others and less touristy, less crowded. Arriving, they wander the grounds, peeking through doors at dark interiors, Marguerite tells her that while she enjoyed Rhodes, it would be to Patmos that she might return, perhaps with her fiancé, or Belle.

Inside, they explore the rooms, chapel, and cave, trying to imagine St. John exiled here by the Roman Emperor in AD 95. Belle closes her eyes to see the man – she would like to meet a saint – and to imagine the small armies or delegations coming ashore with each succeeding empire. These waves will constitute the segments of the history she is contemplating, a subject growing more interesting as she explores and thinks about it. At the same time, she recognizes that she herself is now part of this pattern, the latest invasion, of swarming, affluent tourists, a signal, possibly, of the end of war, in this part of the world.

Gazing down from the walls to the small harbor, and imaging the different eras, she again feels that she has joined the continuum of history, however small her role. It locates her in civilization, as both participant and contributor, and at a point when things are accelerating. She wonders what a sensibility like Athena's would think of the present. She has never met anyone with her qualities. Yes she was an ideal … still there must be women today who approximate her intelligence, abilities, empathy … Hillary?

Elizabeth Warren, Christine Lagarde? Michelle? ... Certainly there are others ... Marguerite, to an extent. But Belle does not envy Hillary's marriage. So who then? Who embodies the full range? ... Is it even possible? And what male might match someone like that?

She pictures St. John, writing his accounts, bent over his work table day after day. What did he look like? Was his goodness visible? She feels a strong sympathy for the man, doing that work, confined to the island. Excitement throbs in her imagining him weighing belief and events – another chapter for her book. That he was actually here, writing, just as she may be next summer, seems an inspiring parallel. What to take from it? She tries to imagine his thought process, considering history and the new equality ... the beginning of change from the dominating hereditary elites to equal souls ... a road which women still must negotiate ... She needs to re-read his epistles and Revelations. She sees him in his cell, alone, scratching it all down with a stylus. How extraordinary to feel that he had been given that task, even as his world was circumscribed. How she would like to walk the island with him today, comparing eras, imbibing that very other life. And she attempts to picture life two thousand years in the future – impossible. Everything may be transformed ... utterly ruined or greatly improved.

All of this fills her with eagerness to begin. At the same time, she concedes that much of what passes as written history is but scaffolding, not the real, impossibly complex, interweaving of power, ideas, belief, culture, societies, states, conquests, trade, money, agriculture and flesh. Multilayered are the foundations, let alone the interpretations by each generation, each historian. Can she gain and convey an accurate sense of those times by studying the archives? Will there be enough to interpret? Or will it be reaching in the dark for something that vanished long ago, like her marriage?

She imagines craftsmen building the monastery brick by brick. Through much of history, the island was a kind of haven.

Even Poseidon and Artemis visited, according to myth ... The huntress ... What was it that drew her? Its green hills and peace? ... Was the idea of the good life back then not so different? ... Zeus of course was ever pursuing women ... What does that say? The way things were, for kings? Does Argos think he's a royal descendant, inheriting the right? Le droit du seigneur? For all of civilization's advances, in some areas how little has changed.

Through the mists of Olympus, and the brush of soft lips, under the cliffs of Parnassus and the stare of dark eyes, after shower and shave, shirts packed up or put on, through coffee and toast, check out and walk out, faint smiles and the nods of goodbye, he manages to step up into the airport shuttle, side-step to a seat and drop onto its cushion, to be driven away. Winding through streets and gears, the bus carries him out of this white city of antiquity and deity. While no Odysseus he, master of skills, yet fortune has delivered something as rare ... a maid of the myths, filling his heart, as he sways in the bus, leaving her town. He knows why he must fly off, for his boys and his work, but he feels inside a wound of incalculable cost. For two brief intervals, he was called out of his solitude, through interchange of thought and concern so generous that he wonders if it were real. Yes, he's doing his duty, heading back to his home, but inside he is numb.

In time, the familiar procedures of airports and planes distract him from his loss. Automatic steps follow automatically. With senses closed down, he wanders the corridors, shows his ticket, finds his seat by a window, stares out at the wing, down at the tarmac, watches the plane gather speed, the ground fall away. He turns to a book, a novel he found in the airport, splaying Ozark mountain life of clans and drugs, brutal and bare, yet richly told. It holds him for a while, so bleak and so narrow... all hopelessly trapped ... In contrast he is thankful for the world and his work ... and now for her ... He runs over pages and pages of lives constricted, then torn apart – after a time he can stand no more and puts it away, closing his eyes. Her face returns, attentive, clear-sighted, and warm, like no one before. Why to him? ... He cannot justify. Yet she has re-opened life, changed perspective, revealed what he'd lost ... Too good to be true? He cannot entirely dismiss this fear, as all slides through his mind. The architecture of nautilus and white columns, the rhythms of rows, in amphitheaters and stadium, Acropolis and Delphi ... her face and brown eyes, floating above the blue sea. Outside white clouds cover the earth far below, as his ship races west with time and the sun.

And then, through the last sequence of steps, he is home, pushing into the house, musty and still. Sherlock is next door; he will go collect him – happy both. He opens windows, turns on the radio, not to be alone. Tomorrow the boys, office, and project – his world, yet he feels altered by her.

It's warm and windy out between the islands, sailing toward Mykonos. Surging through the swells the Poseidon seems as eager as its passengers, for the captain has told them the island is lively, with many things to see and do: good shopping, good clubs, good beaches. The women see that he thinks they yearn for these things, but he is only half-correct. Yet they smile and thank him, pleasing him in conveying that he is pleasing them.

By midafternoon they are ashore, stepping onto a wide promenade bordering the harbor. White shops and eateries line the walk, and a sociable Pelican waddles toward any with food. Unlike quiet Patmos, they are not alone; all descriptions of tourists mill and wander, but the numbers are not oppressive as most disperse through winding alleys to shop and eat, or take buses or taxis to the beaches. The women see signs proclaiming music, night life, dancing. Maybe they will try, if it is not all for the young. Tempered expectations whisper with the warm breeze.

Despite a cuteness calculated for commerce, they enjoy investigating those shops they find inviting, and buying a few things for family and friends – t-shirts for the boys. Angela and Ileana note that the island has some of the same energy that Barcelona does, with people from everywhere, smiling, laughing, sweeping here and there.

After a while they split up, Belle and Marguerite circling the village, out to the old windmills, then back through the alleys, as Marguerite needs to photograph views and detail for her article. They stop in a café by the water for a wine and some cheese, watching the strollers. People from most continents amble by, pausing to record, with their cameras or phones, the harbor and white village, built for them. In place of triremes, huge white cruise ships drift into the wide harbor and disgorge beetle-like shuttles crammed with more shoppers. "Has Greece, here at least, become a mall?" laughs Marguerite gazing at the groups passing by. "Is there anything left of the simple, island life?"

"Patmos," Belle reminds her. And yet both enjoy watching the scene and their fellow tourists, even as they wonder if this is what American culture has given the world, or is it the inevitable form of modern middle class existence?

They attempt to pick out local Greeks among the strands of strollers. Are the waiters the sole representatives? In time, they spot a few older men standing together with glazed smiles as the throngs push past.

The two women speak of their lives and plans. Though Marguerite has not been married, she has been discussing it with her beau, or fiancé – she's a little unclear to Belle about their relationship. He works for the foreign service, currently in Africa. She's not sure she wants that life. It may not work for them. And yet ... there is something that holds her.

She asks Belle about her marriage, but Belle demurs, not wanting to return to that troubling subject. Marguerite cannot miss the discomfort it brings and does not press. But Belle is willing to express a few general thoughts. "I have observed that as women reach equality in society, they want men who are capable of true and profound exploration and feeling, neither dreamers nor holdovers from prior periods when men presided as the breadwinners, soldiers, and predators they often were. As I have said before, it seems a paradox that ancient Athens, lord of the Aegean for a time, adopted Athena as its protector in that male-dominated world. What does it reveal about their thinking, their traditions? What values did she embody?"

But Marguerite remembers that Athena was an evolving goddess, in the Iliad fierce and punishing, in the Odyssey supportive, rescuing. In later Athens, long after Homer, she symbolized wisdom, justice, purity. Belle smiles, remembering that once some years ago Wren said she reminded him of Athena. She wonders which qualities he was thinking of. To Marguerite she allows that at home occasionally she does encounter some admirable men, capable, aware, flexible, not consumed by themselves.

Marguerite vouches for her friend, that he is sensitive and open. "But you see ... I'm not sure what to call him, or how to define us." She explains that she wants a man who appeals to her as a man, although that can be a little hard to specify. "But I want something different, not the same as me. I need that balance. I am not thinking of a Neanderthal or Achilles ... but Odysseus's fair example ... however difficult to find. Maybe I already have." And she smiles.

Faintly Belle nods. "Yes ... but I'm afraid to me that seems as difficult to define as to discover. In Odysseus, Homer created the highest of Greek men ... but is it reality? Is it at all possible? He was alone back then ..."

"Hector too was admirable, if trapped by his fate ..."

"I suppose ... and some of the older men, Priam, Nestor, were wise and kind, as some are now. But not in adequate numbers."

Marguerite laughs gently. "It does take some looking ... and luck. But I would think you would attract them."

Belle now studies her friend more closely, before permitting a faint smile, "As you have, I must assume ... but have chosen not to marry."

"We have felt no urgency. Our jobs take us off, here and there. I enjoy meeting people. Marriage will come, at some point, I suspect."

As Belle smiles, she adds, "Still, I wonder if it makes sense for many women ... to expect to live happily together with a man for long periods. Is it even possible? I see few instances of it."

"Some couples manage," Marguerite recalls, narrowing her eyes. "There are no simple answers or prescriptions, as I leaf back through the lives I've known: parents, family, friends, lovers."

Again Belle nods, but she does not want to continue on this subject, and seeing this, Marguerite shifts to describing the magazine in Paris she works for, which requires that she travel, most recently to Provence, where she met Argos, as she laughingly remembers. She sold her boss on Henry's cruise proposal as material for an article. "I've been keeping notes, on the islands, along with the pictures, ignoring Henry and his harem, of which I suppose I was one." And she laughs. "It's funny isn't it? This dance we do, rather than speaking straight out. In some ways, we all might prefer straight talk: I have no interest in you, or I do, or I'm undecided. Women, aware of history and physiology, must be more indirect, I suppose, frequently being less able, historically, to directly exert their wills. " And she shakes her head as an ambiguous smile moves over her face. "The English writer, George Eliot mentioned women's 'indefiniteness' ...But that is changing."

Belle, if she must return to this, now prefers to speak of women. "We are more autonomous now, and in America have become majorities in colleges and med schools. And that changes the conversation." Marguerite is surprised, for there are fewer possibilities in France.

As they talk, gazing out upon the blue waters of the harbor, someone approaches their table and greets them, "Hello, ladies." Even before they look up, they are frozen by the voice, all too familiar. It is Argos, née Henry. The women sit like statues, neither meeting his eye nor speaking. But Argos, feeling no such restraint, asks "May I join you?"

Marguerite looks at Belle, who glances at her then up at him. Inhaling deeply, she forms a reply: "We'd prefer not. You may understand that I, for one, have no interest in spending any time with you."

Argos bows, and acknowledges, "I understand completely. And I apologize with all sincerity."

"Apologies are in no way adequate. I have filed criminal charges with the local police; I've spoken to the American Embassy in Athens, and I have hired a law firm."

Henry digests this, blinking several times. His eyebrows rise; his eyes stare out at the boats turning slowly at anchor, before he responds. "I understand ... I do ... no matter what you may think ... Listen, with regards to all of this, would it be all right, Marguerite, if Artemis and I just walk a little and discuss this. We needn't drag you into it, and again, I admit that I am the culprit, the one who was at fault."

Marguerite looks at Belle who is trying to remain calm. "That is up to Belle."

Argos now peers carefully down at Belle. "I am asking for only five minutes, right here in the harbor, as I think it would behoove both of us to come to some understanding of what each wants."

Belle glances at Marguerite, then back at Argos. "Marguerite knows the story as do the other two. I have explained where I stand, and so I think it would be better to contact my lawyers."

Argos takes this in unblinking, then continues to press his point. "I understand, but I think it would save a lot of time and money, if I could just share a thought or two with you ... Really ... Our lawyers will probably otherwise spend weeks, and fortunes, before arriving at the same understanding. ... In all seriousness, this would benefit you more than me."

Belle weighs this for a moment, expelling a breath. Then looking at Marguerite, she asks, "If I give Argos five minutes, to conclude this, do you want to wait?"

Marguerite says that she will stay and finish her wine.

And so Belle stands and walks with Henry to the water's edge, where they proceed carefully around ropes, cleats, and hooks. Argos repeats his apology, and then tells her that he is willing in some way to make it up to her.

"I think," she says, "that this is something our lawyers could better handle."

"Yes, of course, that is their expertise ... but they are working for us, and as I said, it is likely that they will come eventually to the same juncture we could reach in a few minutes' chat."

"I have no real desire to talk with you, Henry."

"Of course. This is something I have brought upon myself. But you and I are reasonable people ..."

"What you did was not reasonable; it was criminal."

"Yes, and I understand and apologize. I understand that you want justice … and I am prepared to explore what form that could take."

"I don't know if you can begin to understand the affront, the invasion, the assault that you forced on me. And I've learned that I am not the first victim."

"Yes, well, but allow me to say, and I understand that you may not believe me, but I feel some attachment to you, that we are similar in some ways."

"You can't be serious. You expect me to accept that nonsense?"

"… No and yet I feel it is nonetheless true. I am not talking about romance, but about the similarities of our natures."

Belles laughs bitterly, derisively.

"I enjoyed talking with you … and I think you did with me … Clearly I took things horribly wrong, but I do enjoy you."

"I don't see how this is getting us anywhere. I would prefer the lawyers to handle it."

"Have you thought about what form justice might take, emerging from a court case?"

"No."

"Well, to be blunt, as I guess I am too often, it is unlikely I would go to jail. The problem is that we have only our two say-so's, no witnesses. It would be difficult for you to make your case that you were not at *all* responsible."

"My lawyers tell me otherwise. We have your history, for one."

"Okay, well for argument's sake, let's say they are right. What could the outcome be? ... And then, if one factor is the reality that you did not object to me entering your cabin nor sitting on your bunk, what could a judge reasonably conclude? ... And you had given me a kiss earlier ..."

"I was on the way to bed ... and then had been asleep, was still half-asleep. Don't mischaracterize the situation."

"Nonetheless, it is unlikely any sentence will involve jail. So how will you be satisfied?"

"Henry, I'm not going to discuss this with you."

"I understand, but some result is going to come out of all this. In most of these cases, it involves a settlement. There are no objective facts to guide a judge otherwise. So to save a lot of time, anguish, and money, I am willing to offer you compensation, in whatever form you would prefer."

She stops walking and looks at him. "At the very least, I would want to check this with my lawyers. Surely you don't expect me to believe you out of hand."

He looks out over the harbor. "No ... but we might lay out some alternatives that would be acceptable to you ... I *am* sorry for what I did."

"Now that you have to pay."

"... What form of payment would seem most just to you?"

"That is for me to discuss with my attorneys."

"The options, alas, are fairly limited ... and are thus something you and I might easily agree on. I am not here to oppose you, but to seek something that would in part compensate you."

"I understand that you are well acquainted with these discussions."

He looks down as if dismayed by this.

"I will report all of this to my lawyers, and see what they recommend."

"Fine ... but I am willing to make a generous settlement, rather than going through months of all this."

She seems to take little heed. "They will get back to your representatives." But another idea occurs to her, concerning the three other women. "As for our cruise on the Poseidon, what are your intentions?"

He looks at her. "Well, that is up to the four of you."

"All of us have been promised a cruise. I think it would be unfair to curtail it, because of this. But if you return, I believe we would all leave."

He looks at her closely. "I am flexible ... But are you saying that should be part of a settlement?"

"Not at all. Merely keeping your word to them. Our case is quite separate."

"You would sail with them?"

"As you promised."

"I ... Okay. What if I have Mikos complete our planned tour, and then bring you back to Piraeus?"

"I will want to ask the others."

"Fine. Shall we return and see what Marguerite thinks?"

As they swing about and head back to the café, Argos makes one more attempt. "If, Artemis – may I call still call you Artemis? – if in the next few days, you want to discuss a settlement and get this whole thing over with and into the past, I hope that you will contact me. I will try to more than make it up to you. I do like you."

"I understand that you would rather not have this thing get out, and into the papers. The oil industry has enough transgressions to deal with, without one of its executives seen to be a cavalier, serial rapist, exploiting his position and money to attack women. What would the shareholders say? Good value for your lofty compensation?"

He looks over at her with a mix of irritation and amusement, before he replies, "No one cares about the mistakes of some obscure business person like myself. It's a sad, and rather old-story. But as I said, I like you and would value your friendship. I enjoy being with you. I admire your spirit. If we could repair things, partially through a settlement, then you and I might be friends. You're the only one who I feel is on par with me, temperamentally, and intellectually."

Belle makes no reply as they approach the table where Marguerite sits. To her friend, Belle summarizes the brief conversation, and Marguerite replies that if Belle finds it agreeable, she would accept the proposal to continue the cruise, without him, before returning to Piraeus. Of course they would have to consult with the others, but she assumes they will consent. And so it is left that the women will tell the captain later of their joint decision, and he will communicate that to Argos.

With this he bows to them, wishes them good sailing, and strides quickly away, disappearing into the crowd. They sit there silently for moments, mulling this over, finishing their wines. They decide to order another round. When the waiter has left, Belle asks Marguerite if she has any further thoughts about this arrangement. Are they allowing Henry to get away with his behavior?

Marguerite tries to reason it through, but runs into a difficulty, "It's impossible for me to judge what you feel would be just. Emotionally, I too would like to see him locked up for a time, but from all we've heard and read, that seems unlikely. What then, would you want? ... Money is, in a way, a further insult, that you, that we, can be bought off ... and yet it may be the only substantive compensation, as Angela discovered." She looks at Belle.

With irritation jutting her jaw, Belle feels that she wants to explain something. "I've read about these attacks so often, all over. One fifth of college women are raped; date rape is rampant; it's a problem in our military, a problem all over the world, men forcing themselves, often violently. I can't just shrug this off, although I was able to avoid the worst ..." Their eyes meet; Marguerite indicates that she understands. Yet as Belle's thoughts move on, a mixed smile lightens her face. "At the same time, it occurs to me that, we might demand the Poseidon for a time next summer." Marguerite joins her in envisioning this, also smiling thinly and imagining it could provide the opportunity for another article. "We might sail to Sardinia, Corsica, and the Balearic Islands, or up and down the Italian boot ... start a chartering company, find a different captain, but we'd need money for expenses ..." She laughs briefly, recognizing this whimsical fantasy.

Reading Marguerite's expression, Belle agrees, "We think we are free to pursue these things ... but we aren't, are we? ... Nor are they ultimately important. We must remember to separate mere amusement from real inspiration. Our cruise seemed to be an engaging introduction to the Aegean world, but he had something else in mind – shoving us brutally off course. I hadn't anticipated that, or that he had approached all of us in one way or another. I mean it fleetingly occurred to me, but ... So what then should we all demand? Even as I realize that we are lucky, compared to so many who suffer and struggle. How to see it all, weigh it all?" ... Possibilities for using the Poseidon churn in her mind. Maybe she could win it outright, in court ... but probably not, as it must be worth millions. Yet she will ask one of the attorneys ... Or maybe she could win a villa in France or Italy. This idea too lifts the heavy memories, briefly, and she mentions it to Marguerite, who also smiles faintly. But both reject making plans in any way connected to Argos and his money, even if they hover enticingly.

At this point, Angela and Ileana arrive walking casually along, and spotting the two, join them at the table. When they are seated, Belle and Marguerite tell them of the encounter and the agreement proposed. Is that acceptable? Angela and Ileana are at first stunned that he would appear, although Angela had predicted it. She laughs uncomfortably, then turns to Marguerite and Belle to hear more. The two recount the conversation leading to the proposal. Angela shakes her head thinking of Henry, but agrees that it seems reasonable. Ileana, still held by conflicting views of him, is less sure. On one hand, it seems acceptable, while on the other, she suspects he will try to exact something. "He always expects some payment, of some kind." While Angela agrees, she points out that were he not somewhat chastened, he could have acted more contentiously, kicking them all off the boat, or sailing them directly back to Athens. But as it is, they have the option to continue on, proceeding much as they have, pleased to be alone. As such it should continue to be a unique experience. Indeed the last several days have been in many ways sublime, perhaps even more so looking back.

Ileana now shifts the subject, mentioning that Angela will be visiting her in Barcelona, and inviting the other two to come. But Belle and Marguerite must return home, for work, among other things. "Perhaps next summer," suggests Belle, and Ileana encourages them, "Yes, do come. There is much to explore and experience – excellent restaurants and music. And there are even several engaging gentlemen we might dine with." She smiles and swallows. "You see? I am ever hopeful. My work, my painting, sustains me, leaving me independent yet able to enjoy the companionship of the right man."

Belle swings her eyes over to her smiling and thinking we all harbor hope; indeed it was probably hope that misled her with Henry. She thanks Ileana, "I would love to visit sometime. Thank you. How good that would be. And possibly we might figure out if we want to use the boat, or another one. I may have to revisit several of these islands if I get the book."

Reflection on these possibilities moves over their faces, before conversation turns back to accounts of what they have just found here on the island. As Belle listens, she finds herself disappointed that her anger continues to intrude. She ought to be able to dismiss it, refocus, as they explore this historical world. To a certain extent she has, discovering outlines of a whole new life, which does not mean she should forget. Setbacks and assaults, in one form or another, are part of life, which is both gentle and rough, nurturing and savage. She has been able to respond to the episode with her own first responders – an image which draws amusement into her eyes. In fact she has recovered and is ready to move on. New friends, new life, new book – real possibilities. The sun is emerging, and her mind soars over the Mediterranean. Change everywhere is increasingly a factor; many things are shifting; complexity has become the norm. This could be one of the themes in her book: change and adaptation, over the centuries. Periodically, in societies, and now in her life, new developments alter direction, as happened in the magical 5th and 6th centuries B.C. when the ancient Greeks broke through with new insight and thinking. Among these, they conceived of Athena as possessing a more peaceful, subtle character. We need a woman like her.

IV.

His thoughts rush with the cars around him, all speeding somewhere. Thoughts, bodies, things ... life's triumvirate. But rushing to what end? ... Pursuing, sustaining the necessities? Yet how that list has grown these days, far beyond the basics, leaving us with less time to think, investigate, reflect, or speak to one another, or embrace Nature and life, to join deeply with it and our fellow wanderers. Thoreau saw this in the early 1800s; the ancient Greeks long before, valuing material wealth less than wealth of knowledge, experience, and developing their human abilities – their *aretê*. But in place of *excellence* have things taken over? ... How *should* he be living? What should he be doing with his time? These questions seem to leap at him, pestering for resolution. But this urgency compacts into pressure, into headache. In contrast, the world in which Messena, Iscaria, and George live seems simpler and more connected to the core of living, to nature's pulse, to the range of life we've been given and have created, allowing space for these things, above all time to talk and consider. At home, in contrast, how few friends or clients leave room to imagine, exchange, connect with Nature and each other, to weigh their lives and times ... to grope for understanding, to participate in the shaping of our world ... to try to understand and respond to the astonishing fact that we exist at all.

For him the trip and all that it has evoked, and now this temporary parting from Belle, have together revived these questions that have too often been overlooked or forgotten. Should the two of them try to reconnect, or should they move on? Is the former even possible? ... He has seen that she has changed ... as so probably has he – away from the time when each was most important to the other. Then they shared a view of life, and priorities, much as did some of ancient Athenians he's read about. Those and other Greeks asked questions about why and how things worked and what was important. Belle and he sometimes considered them, but with changes and strains, conversation and caring fell by the wayside. And so it struck him deeply to hear the two women broach these things and hint that it was time for *him* to embrace new effort. Being a visual person, he found it was the memories of their faces, their eyes, their studying him that returned and returned with their messages. No one had done that in a long time.

But now his mind flees to less numinous realms, recalling the art and architecture he saw over there, the sculpture and vases, the statues with ideal faces. He's read that notions of beauty are to a degree universal, embodying harmony and proportion ... Is Messena an avatar of Athena? Or does she simply recognize her gifts and offers most graciously to share? Sunlight flashes off her face, and the sharp cliffs of Delphi, briefly blinding him. He tries to imagine the ancient Greeks speaking in their tongue, exchanging thoughts. Were they as open as she? Some, certainly. But he must blink all that away, shake himself, remember that he's driving.

He turns his thoughts to the boys, picturing the instant when they will first catch sight of each other. His mind wanders to the upcoming project, which may give him an opportunity to contribute, to realize ideas ... imagine new ones – a promise that hurls excitement and hope through him.

Uptown on Tenth, then east to the first parking garage he sees. How different is the simple efficiency of the city's grid than winding Athens. Back downtown, striding hastily to the terminal, Hermes hurrying, nearly running to the gate where other parents wait, moms mostly, standing patiently. The bus arrives on schedule. His eagerness can barely be restrained, to see them, hug them. They are physically, emotionally, intellectually part of him, even their differences. When they converse, he likes to hear, and try to understand, the variations, where their thoughts take them.

They emerge in the line, stepping down and finding him, send shy smiles that light their faces. Pat pushes to him first, for

ATHENA

a brief hug. "Hey, Dad. How are ya?" "Gr-reat!" he growls with a laugh, and turning to Alex, spreading his arms. Alex leans in for a minimal exchange. And yet, in his squinting eyes, he seems pleased.

Questions pour from him as they pull their bags out from under the bus. Grunting and laughing amid their terse replies, they heft their heavy duffles to their shoulders and stagger along, throwing back questions and comments. How's Sherlock? Is Mom working? ... This requires a moment to compose an answer. She's taking another week; she needs it, to cruise around the Aegean with some friends.

Confusion, incomprehension, worry fill their faces. Have things fallen further? But they don't ask, avoiding his eyes, swallowing the news, stowing it away, this dark reality. Wren repeats that she'll be home in a matter of days, but they ask no more. He turns the subject to camp, but sees gray concern steal across their faces.

"Sherlock will be happy to see you," he tries.

"Did Mike and Mary take good care of him?" asks Alex.

"They did, but he was excited to see me, even."

"Come on, Dad. You love him; he knows it."

Yes, dear Sherlock. What does he think when no one's around? Is he as lonely as Wren has been?

He presses them for things they liked up there. They offer different highlights. Alex loved being in nature, camping, canoeing across the northern lakes, while Pat loved the day-to-day activities: the water-skiing, basketball, windsurfing, archery, and swimming races. Wren describes Delphi's stadium, the competitions two and three thousand years ago, and the amphitheater where plays and dance unfolded. But this draws little response. Perhaps they can't imagine it, or grasp that life. He glances at them. Were the ancient Greeks at Delphi more worldly, already soldiers, lovers, men ... or just boys? He's read that our increased complexity has extended our developing years. Melville, he remembers reading, claimed he did not come alive until twenty-five.

He mentions the new project. Alex asks, "They gonna pay you well for this one?"

Wren swallows. Their mother's refrain. "The first meeting is tomorrow." Flashes of George's house and the sea return, before he describes both for them. He mentions the earlier part of their trip, through Provence, which seems almost forgotten, erased by discontent.

Glancing over at Alex next to him, he sees that he stares out the window, his brow grown gray and lined. Wren feels dismay, that he cannot allay their worries. But if he tried to speak of it, they would hear his own despair.

Home, the boys throw themselves at Sherlock, tumbling over on the grass with him as he barks and yips. Inside, all head to the kitchen hungry. He helps them put together a snack. Soon all four are gobbling and emoting. Once fed, the boys run upstairs to their rooms and close the doors, to reclaim lives and friends.

He looks down at Sherlock, into his Bassett eyes, both wondering, what now? Sherlock wags his tail, pumping little squeaks of happiness from his throat. Together they wander through the rooms, silent again. How much of his life has this house become? ... Could he leave it, for a time? If he had the money, he would tear much down and replace it with something new ... despite the years of work he's put into it. Could he leave it all ... for her? And the life she brought?

Pulled in opposing directions, he walks outside, looks at his trees and shrubs, contrasting them with memories of dry, rocky

Delphi ... of Iscaria disappearing behind the Laurel trees. Drifting back inside, with Sherlock, he goes to his office, sits down at his computer, draws in a long breath, fingers poised, like columns of the Parthenon.

Dearest Messena, Parthenos: I've just now picked up my sons, each younger, less-formed than Telemachus. We exchanged stories of our wanderings. I thought of, but then held off, describing you, my brief Calypso ... No, Athena ... They wouldn't understand or believe me. I barely do, though I replay our moments together over and over. In time I will tell them ...

Walking through my yard, I noticed that all the trees and shrubs I've planted and pruned, lowered their eyes, their leaves, as I passed by. Do they worry I will abandon them, not attend to them, when I keep my promise to you? How deeply embedded you have become in me, already. You have shown me what I was missing. Living without you is like holding my breath, waiting.

I found these lines in the *Odyssey*, when the wanderer and the goddess met. *"At this the grey-eyed goddess, Athena, smiled and gave him a caress, her looks being changed now, so she seemed a woman tall and beautiful and no doubt skilled at weaving splendid things."*

As the later Athenians saw their Athena, I see you: an embodiment of goodness, reason, wisdom, and beauty. I need not imagine, merely remember. No one whom I have ever met has sustained with me a conversation of such unflinching directness, honesty, and caring. I yearn for it again, yearn in my very center. To share that communication, and love, seems to me the highest, most sublime experience that we can have. It took me out of myself enabling me to see things with more clarity than ever before, all wrapped in an atmosphere of – what can I call it but "love"? Even when our views did not coincide, we were able to hear the other and look anew at our own. For me, for someone who is far from perfect, is that not a gift? I pray that you found something here, in this one, as deeply moving and fulfilling.

And so, with you in my heart, I turn back to my practical, quotidian life. My projects await. My sons have grown, becoming, piece by piece, men, as your daughter someday will become a woman, like you. I can only hope that all our children will find someone with your grace and caring, alive to so much, with whom to talk. It is a supreme joy. Your voice lives within me, and your goodness too ... from our brief time together. I see your eyes watching mine. While our evening and lunch sometimes seem imagined, they have become woven into me. I do not understand why I was so fortunate, yet I must ask you to thank Iscaria, as I kneel before you.

And your book? What women's lives are you discovering? Your predecessors? I hope that you are beginning to find the history that you need in the ancient writings. How wonderful for you to join those stories and lives with what we have arrived at today. How rich and rewarding, and maybe sad, to uncover those hidden lives most women lived so long ago.

Yet even as I gaze back, all rushes on. Tomorrow my promising house project starts, while my wife remains in Greece, sailing the islands. I cannot imagine what we will say to each other when she returns, in contrast to all that you and I have exchanged. Sadly, but undeniably, she and I are strangers now, unable to share conversation or caring – a sad tale, though not unique, as you well know.

In thinking of you, I repeat that what I can offer is the deep appreciation and love which you have reawakened in me. I hope that it will please you, for it will not die, and I will come

With all love, Wren

He sends it off, picturing her that evening and lunch, her different looks ... wondering if he will see her again. An all-too-common dream, or need in us that even Sherlock shares? As Sherlock and he look at one another, Sherlock howls long and mournful. A cry follows resounding through the room.

Naxos is next. The wind blows her dark hair sensually, as Greek women and maenads in those early times must have experienced. The Poseidon heels in the breeze; the spray moistens her face. Her brow and cheek glisten as if ancient bronze, pleasing her, drawing her back through the ages. Feeling free, able to ride the wind, she imagines returning to these islands, researching the book, descending into their histories ... encountering a hero ... the lord of Ithaca.

Knowing that Henry will not suddenly appear again releases her, enabling her to more fully enjoy the sailing and the Aegean. Aeolus is abroad and breathing, around her neck. This is what Henry should be named, the puffing god of wind.

Last night on Mykonos, at one of the clubs, a Frenchman had approached their table and asked Marguerite to dance. She had accepted, happy to speak French with an attractive, youngish partner. They danced for a good while, before she took leave of her shipmates, disappearing, not to be seen again until morning, returning in time to sail. Though evidently pleased, she said little to Belle, perhaps not wanting to explain how this fit in with her fiancé. But Belle reminded herself that the fiancé is likely to be no less adventurous in those foreign lands.

The largest of the Cyclades, Naxos again requires a taxi to take them over its rocky hills, past green farms and vineyards, stone villages and ruins. Stopping at one farm they taste the popular lemon liqueur, Kitron, and, warmed by it, continue on gaily talking, finding the views dramatic and their expectations heightened. Angela reads from her guide book that the island's highest point is Mount Zeus. All laugh, indeed howl, as they scour the passing landscape, bouncing past a tall Greek farmer harvesting melons in his field. Their cries of gaiety summon his eyes, yanking his head around, seeking the source. But in the instant their eyes meet, his stature and long face recall Argos. The women cry out again, incredulous, twisting away. His eyes narrow; his mouth stretches with irritation at the glimpse of florid faces startled, aghast, fleeing his.

Once past, the women search each other. Is it possible? ... No! ... Mere resemblance. Slowly, grimaces reconfigure into smiles; relief expands into full and hearty laughter. Perhaps it is the Kitron that fills the island with sorcery.

Their driver interrupts to ask if they would like him to arrange something of a social evening. Silence falls over them once more for seconds; then gaiety returns in flashing eyes, followed by uncertain, widening glances among themselves. Finally Belle tells him that they would be happy to meet a few at a harbor restaurant for a drink, provided that they have some English. The driver says he will see what he can arrange, and he mentions a good restaurant – the only one – in the harbor. But this will take time and effort on his part, he explains, implying he will need some compensation. Belle allows, "At the restaurant, we will be happy to contribute, when you introduce us to our evening companions."

At first the driver seems disappointed, ready to dismiss his offer, but then he accepts, suggesting an eight o'clock rendezvous. With this tugging at their imaginations, the women gaze out at the passing farms and hills, speculating discreetly as to what may develop.

Back in the village of Naxos, they explore its neighborhoods, which while largely typical, are interspersed with buildings of a more ornate and colorful, Venetian style, from the island's time as part of that empire. And like Rhodes, there is a hilltop castle above the homes rising from the harbor. As they wander, they feel light and lifted, familiar now with the island cultures, aware that the liqueur still magnifies detail and anticipation. A sea breeze whispers in their ears, Aeolus returned. They imagine this journey continuing on, timeless, unimpeded, offering adventure and who knows what.

On a sheltered beach at the edge of the village, they swim and float on the light blue sea, or read on their towels in the sand, or talk and reflect. The afternoon is ideal. All are relaxed and pleased, putting their everyday lives out of mind. Ileana finds that the quiet and space recall painted seventeenth or eighteenth century landscapes, sparsely populated, faintly run-down. And to a degree the others share this. But all agree an ideal vacation includes more: culture, music, cuisine, social opportunities, and beauty, only partly fulfilled here. Marguerite alone seems pleased to imagine returning here or to Patmos – with her beau. The others smile at her fortune, happy for her, before turning their thoughts ahead to the evening, and beyond.

While the boys are sleeping in, he breakfasts alone before driving to his office, arriving before Margaux who has left a pile of mail along with a list of phone and email messages, and a note confirming the time for today's meeting.

She arrives soon after, happily expressing her appreciation for the opportunity to run the business. A quick hug follows, shorter than the parting one, he remembers.

For a moment, she studies him, as if he has changed, as indeed he feels he has. She asks about the trip. He finds that he can hardly turn his mind to the sight-seeing, gripped as he is by that one … Flushing, he turns away a little, but she sees that something stirs him. Her eyes shift uncomfortably. Redirecting their conversation, he asks about the two ongoing projects. She reports that the clients have also been on vacation, but should be back this week, and a few new inquiries and requests for proposals came in, small jobs, renovations. She spoke to them briefly, expressing interest and proposing meetings. The parties will call back over the next few days. Imparting this news, she looks upbeat once more.

Relieved, he now describes George's house and the Parthenon. Smiling, she pictures both, saying she wants to go there with her fiancé. Wren remarks that he's heard the islands are wonderful also. She nods, but with a strange look. Did he not go?

Later he collects copies of prior designs, a sketch pad, tape measure, and camera, for the meeting out in the country beyond the edge of town.

Driving through the deep shade of a rural road, he is nearly blinded by intermittent beams of sunlight streaming down, obliterating detail. He slows and leans left and right to see. The radiance carries him back to Delphi, under the beating sun, climbing to the temple and amphitheatre. Squinting ahead, he glimpses figures and faces of gods streaking above the trees, delivering messages, intervening. The displaced air of passing cars puffs in over his face, breaths of unseen beings. Where is he? Which existence? Iscaria's long body floats along a distant hill, and Messena is suddenly seated next to him, seeking his thoughts. He looks into her eyes, is drawn there ... then remembers the road. Has he, like Pygmalion, fallen in love with she who may be his own creation? He slows again, straining to see, pinching his cheek.

He was chosen, he reminds himself, for this project because his designs pleased the owner. He needs to run with that, take it as permission to stretch, expand, soar. George's smiling face comes back, reflecting the joy he felt in realizing his nautilus. The owner here, Yan Zaraclovic, sounded pleasant, if hurried. A high-level financial type in the city, he said that the house would be a weekend retreat, for his friend and himself. "I want something secluded, interesting, novel. I don't like those traditional, old ... you know, plunked down in a field ... Which is why I picked you. I want something new; I wanta hear what you think can be done."

Pleased, excited, Wren whispers to himself: Yes! I will be thrilled to show you ... An ideal. Another. They come in pairs.

The cost of the house, implied Yan, so long as it stays within reasonable limits, is not of great concern. "No need for the place to be huge. You know, maybe four bedrooms, office, deck, big kitchen, dining and living rooms, media theatre ... the usual drill ... But I want it interesting. That's your job. Don't fail me."

"I hear you, and I, too, want it interesting," he replied with energy. "That's why I do this." That conversation rocketed Wren into orbit.

He finds the driveway, an unmarked dirt track through a field, in toward a rising, wooded ridge. Arriving before Yan, parking in the un-mowed grass, he has the opportunity to get out and walk around. A stream, varying in width, runs along the base of the ridge, in and out of the edge of trees, at one point spreading out 30 feet or so. He follows it, gazing down into it, spying reflections of the house-to-be.

Veering away from the banks, he zigzags back into the field, inhaling the dry smell of sun-baked grass, pausing, gazing round, noting the quiet, gauging where the house may sit, and where trees and shrubs may be added or removed. He turns and studies the hill. Haloes of deciduous trees soften the view, hiding all but a few of the rock outcroppings and steep rises. Darker cedars and pines punctuate the light green hillside, strikingly more verdant than Delphi ... Does he spy a centaur gliding through the shadows?

Ideas, too, come gliding on the backs of those creatures: the house should follow the winding stream, bridging the two environments, field and woods, a foot in both, a side reflecting each. Simplicity, layered with ideas – like her ... emerging from the field, curving with the stream, a prelude to the woods and ridge ... blending in, but also distinct, surprising ... pleasing. He studies the patterns of gray trunks, topped by the soft clouds of light green. He will consider discreet, curving walls of reflecting glass to mirror the landscape, soften the lines, reduce the mass of the house ... Nature surrounding man's making ... a partnership. Much will be modular, under a rising array of round roofs or trellis, sweeping up, an ascending hill of tiled roofs, as in a hilltop village. A wall will follow the stream, twisting left and right, providing mystery. The elevated deck will extend along the edge of Nature, house-length. A bridge might cross the stream, leading to the ridge. He will find places for hints of the ancient ruins he saw. The textures will be varied: cement, stucco, stone, glass, wood, a variety, as in Nature ... No basement; all on stilts, above the flood plain. He recalls the temples clustering the walk to Apollo's temple, from which he may add arches, porticos, columns ... the rhythm of amphitheatre seating ... reaching through time. The mix of ideas fills him with excitement, joy, which the sun bakes into him, as it did over there. He recalls their lunch, his gazing down over the bright city neighborhood ... her face so close.

His mind moves on: solar heating, maybe geothermal ... even a wind turbine – the future. Yes, with luck and perseverance he will make something remarkable, pleasing the owner, and himself.

Hearing a car approach, he emerges from his reverie and turns to wait for Yan, who climbs out of his black Mercedes SUV, stretches, gazes around, before finding Wren. He's slightly shorter than the architect, gray-haired, tanned, somewhere in his fifties. None of his possessions are cheap.

They greet. Yan asks what he thinks. Wren exclaims the property is ideal! With three landscapes, the field, stream, and wooded rise, it offers visual variety, to be reflected in the house. In the Fall, the rise will transform into a great canvas of orange, yellow, and red. Though Yan nods, the idea does not seem to excite him, and so Wren asks what are the directions he'd like to take.

"I thought several of the ideas in your proposal were good. I think what I want you to do is give me two or three options, sketches – those that you think are the best. Then I'll decide. That's not a problem for you, is it?"

"Not at all. I'd be happy to do just that."

"My girlfriend, Kirce, is into this. She's the artist ... has her own ideas. But she'll love this; she liked your proposals. So, give us three, different designs, rough – just the overall look, and we'll choose."

Wren nods, understanding, familiar with, this approach. "Do you want to walk around a little. I can point out some things."

"I'm afraid I don't have time. Got a phone conference coming up. But ... oh hey, Kirce showed me pictures of a house called Falling Water, by somebody ..."

"Frank Lloyd Wright."

"Of course. The Guggenheim, right? Still designing?"

"Long gone."

"Oh ... well, something of that ... You know? Levels, planes, decks, and working the water into it. You can do that, right?"

"Yes ... I don't think you'd want a replica, a knock-off. But something new, exciting, intriguing."

"Of course. Good... and she wants to save the trees."

"Certainly. In fact we would probably add some, in the field and around the house."

"Excellent. That will sell her. I don't know how she could *not* go for this."

Wren hears the hint of something, but there's not enough to puzzle out what it might be. Yet he is pleased with Yan's reliance on him.

Yan asks Wren when he can have the drawings. Wren explains that he'll need to return to make the sketches, take measurements, test the soil along the stream – eventually he'll need an engineer's input. But he could have something preliminary by the end of the week. Site plan and views.

"Good. Uh, because I'm in the city during the week; we both are much of the time, but I'll ask her to take charge, on our end. For the weekends, we're renting a place here in town. So good, let's take a look, say Saturday."

"I'll begin today, come back tomorrow."

Yan studies him for a second, before dismissing whatever question he had. Then he remembers, "Oh, one thing. I'll need a garage. I have a few cars. I see it as a separate building, almost a barn, you know?"

"Certainly. How many cars?"

"I have six ... she has two."

Wren's eyebrows ripple as he smiles. "That should be fun, a second structure. An out-building. Could go in an entirely different direction."

"Yes, that's what we were thinking; I like that. But don't hold back, use that imagination. I want something fun, interesting to look at. For both buildings. And again, something that she'll be engaged by, proud of, you know?"

Wren nods, thinking he does, more or less, and indeed his mind has begun paging through ideas. A barn with off angles, big planes, not squared off, but roundish, seen through trees. A carousel, with skylights, high windows, maybe a dome of some sort. At first glance another mystery ... A different aesthetic.

"So? End of the week?"

Wren nods.

"I say we go ahead."

"I have a contract in my car, for this first stage, including preliminary payment. Then if you're happy with the drawings, when you select one, we can do the full agreement."

"Sounds good." And Yan turns to head over to their cars. There Wren retrieves and hands him the contract. Yan scans it, signs, and hands back his copy. "Done. My secretary will send you a check."

He extends his hand; they shake, and Yan repeats that he's pleased. "Some of the architects I've dealt with want to talk and talk, tell me about every idea and theory they've ever had. Go off in directions I don't want. To me, the drawings say it all. The people who sent me to you spoke highly of your design sense. I look forward to seeing what you can come up with."

And with that he turns, and heads to his car. Wren moves slowly to his, not quite believing that all has gone so well. Great site, no apparent limits or haggling over costs. With Ideas clicking through his mind at increasing speed, he begins jotting them down, making rough sketches of the lot and possible designs, the sections and options. Taking a larger pad from his car, he roughs out the woods and ridge and then the stream, working fast, driven by excitement. He does the same for the garage, and then photographs the site for reference back at the office. Finally he takes preliminary measurements of the overall layout, trotting as he goes, wondering if a deity smiles on him, once again. He laughs, laughs to himself, searching the sky.

Sensually, visually the day has filled them. Now, after returning to the boat to prepare, they walk to the restaurant early and settle around a table overlooking the water, nursing cocktails. Each speaks of the day's delights. Ileana loved the fishermen and women along the water front selling their fish and wares, and she wishes she'd brought her paints. She describes her style, with a wavering grin, as being inspired by Goya ...Van Gogh ... Picasso. Her eyes flash, a laugh erupts. "Of course I bring a bit of myself as well." And she closes her eyes happily. Watching, the other three find pleasure in her humor and enthusiasm, which nudges them to replay their memories of the day.

Turning then to future explorations, Ileana describes the cultures of Andalusia, while Marguerite lists the delights of Aix and Arles along with towns and cities of the Italian coasts, reminding them also that Italian men are famously friendly and attractive. "Speaking of men," Belle recalls, "I read that Naxos was the birthplace of Zeus. Up on Mount Zeus, of course."

"Where else?" exults Angela amid their laughter, and Marguerite imagines, "He must have been the original *enfant terrible.* Was he nursed and diapered, or did he emerge full-blown from Cronos, as Athena did from him?"

Smiles and gleaming eyes convey their shared amusement, before Ileana ponders, "From where did the gods gain their personalities? Did the poets fashion them from living kings and queens?"

"Or heroes of tales passed down through generations," supposes Belle. "We forget the richness of the Bronze Age, when there was culture, trade, and writing across the Eastern Mediterranean, before most disappeared for centuries, until the Greeks led the revival into a new era."

Angela recalls that her favorite myth was the Judgment of Paris, when Hera, Athena, and Aphrodite asked Zeus to judge which of the three was the fairest. Rather than incur jealousy, he directed them to find exiled Paris and solicit his opinion. But all of this grew out of a plot by Eris," she recounts, "the goddess of discord ... Why do we not read of her more, with all the discord sewn into the ages?"

"Perhaps it was simply accepted as part of life," offers Marguerite, and the others agree that discord has certainly been one of mankind's prevailing characteristics. But Belle reminds them that this tale led to the Trojan war, lasting ten years, which possibly symbolized, for Homer, the destruction of cities and cultures that ended the Bronze Age. Many factors may have contributed, besides war. Drought, famine, conquest by the Sea People and the Dorians, earthquakes ... "Or was it the gods, Aphrodite promising Helen, and the others allowing it, leading to the tragic war ... Did Homer see it as the pattern of history, or the inevitability of human nature? ... All flawed, all fragile, all fell."

Somberly she looks around at her friends. "A lesson about how short-sighted we are? Neither gods nor women and men saw clearly enough. Cassandra did, but no one listened. That happened in our country: warnings were ignored; people over-leveraged and brought on the great recession, which still binds us ... And now the same with climate change, an even greater threat. What to make of mankind, lurching ahead, then crashing. And sadly, despite my years of studying man's story, I too lost my way in my marriage ... Scales, it seems, grow over our eyes."

Surprised, the others throw brief glances her way. But she, seeing she has their attention, continues, "Perhaps it is the unusual individual who can consistently see clearly. Perhaps that is what friends are for: to help us see, help put things, anger, in perspective – as some tried to help Achilles and Agamemnon ... It's dispiriting to see no hope ahead ... " Her voice trails off. Marguerite reaches out to touch her hand, as does Angela her shoulder, while Ileana murmurs, "I'm sorry ..."

For some moments all are silent. Eventually Angela consoles, "It is both surprising and sad to hear your story, Belle. If you cannot find a way, who among us can?" And their eyes move carefully among each other, until Angela adds, "It seems we've all experienced deep disappointments in love. Indeed it may be the nature of it. And yet, as I think we all know, there comes rebirth, in nature and in history ... In our time, we cannot deny there has been progress. Women and many in poverty have gained choices and freedom; their lives are no longer as deprived and dependent. Existence is no longer simply to be endured."

Smiling and nodding to Angela, Belle agrees but nonetheless suggests, "But still our expectations may reach beyond what reality can deliver. Our Western civilization, and others, have advanced, but still things threaten, at all levels ... It seems our education and understanding are spread unevenly throughout. Corruption and greed unbalance good governance."

Nodding, Angela reports, "I've read that many of our beliefs or opinions are emotionally based, even as we think them rational. We see it in marriage. Maybe we need to rethink that particular concept."

Eyebrows rise as Marguerite remembers, "People have been thinking about this since Homer and before. Men, and women in power, with freedom, have not been constrained. In France, Scandinavia, and elsewhere, many have given up the traditional structure of marriage. They see relationships as more flexible partnerships."

"I hope they don't abandon romance altogether, "breathes Ileana. "It fills the heart."

Smiling Marguerite reassures her, "They have not given it up, only changed the arrangements that flow from it."

But Belle, reflecting generally, notes: "I agree that women and men can find satisfaction, even love, in sharing and collaboration. Indeed I sometimes think that Plato's aristocracy of the brightest, regardless of gender, is still an ideal to reach for, although history reminds us even the brightest, Pericles, Napoleon, and others erred fatally. But in changing social conditions, we should expect relationships to also change."

"D'accord," breathes Marguerite, adding, "The patterns of life have long been ebb and flow, summer and winter, death and rebirth. Expectations for marriage have long run against that grain."

"But Homer had Athena help re-unite Odysseus and Penelope," Angela recalls. "Does that suggest back then marriage was considered the best arrangement?"

"That was an ideal, an exception, "Belle reflects, before Ileana speaks of her own experience, "In my country, when I was young, life was more communal, with all ages within families sharing. There one could not wander out of the family without facing the disapproval of many. Of course there were problems, but they mostly made it work. They sacrificed for the family. I think we have lost something in moving away from that life."

"I would agree," sighs Angela, "because while we in the West, and in the British Isles in particular, seem to have found the right structures for democracy and personal freedom, we too often place individual happiness above the community. It is my feeling that we need better social education, to teach us about ourselves and how we are interdependent."

"As we have helped each other with Henry," notes Marguerite with a brief smile.

"For which I thank you all," adds Belle, also with a fleeting smile, before Angela acknowledges, "And yet we didn't really come together until he went too far with Belle. I should have spoken up. I knew what he wanted. I wasn't thinking …"

The four look among each other as they weigh these thoughts. After some moments, Ileana confides, "Henry, outside of his unforgiveable presumption, is in many ways not significantly worse than many men I've met, and loved, if you will."

"But Ileana," Belle objects, "it is more than presumption; it is predation ... which fortunately is not characteristic of all men."

"No, not of all," agrees Angela, "but of many in power. Perhaps they have no other Troy to burn." And she smiles through grim features as uneasy laughter moves among them.

At length Belle offers, "Maybe, as Angela implied, we too often allow ourselves to become dependent on men like him. We all came on his boat. Was that a mistake? Must we be ever wary of men? ... Should they be no more than friends, to be enjoyed when it is mutually agreeable?"

"But was that not the case?" asks Marguerite sharply. "When we responded to his invitation, there was no bargaining for our bodies."

"Were we being naïve?" wonders Ileana. "I too should have said something, as I knew his ... needs."

"It is seldom simple," sighs Angela. "Both sexes come with hopes and expectations."

"But how much," asks Belle, "should women assume responsibility for smoothing over the differences and difficulties?"

"Clearly one sex is more adept," asserts Angela. "Look at Athena. Could any of the other gods, the males, match her?"

"Apollo, her brother, and Artemis," suggests Marguerite slightly smiling, before Belle recalls, "The Greeks understood that men and women are different. Men are not always looking to smooth things out, but to prevail, win, attain glory. We shouldn't assume they always have our best interests in mind."

"No, but we understand that we can sometimes illuminate things for them," answers Angela wryly, with which Ileana concurs, "Think how we might open their eyes, if they could but listen to us now." Yet she and the others crease their brows imagining this unlikely occurrence, before she adds, "But we here have not, and probably cannot offer to each other quite the profound connection and feeling that we sometimes find."

"How much of that is in our imaginations?" ponders Belle. And Marguerite notes, "Some women have found love and companionship with each other. Perhaps we don't allow ourselves that option ... Perhaps we should?"

"You enjoyed your Mykonos evening," Angela reminds her gently.

Nonetheless all reflect on this for some moments, until Belle speaks of her own view of their boat owner, "With Henry, I misjudged him, and his motives. I thought him happy to have our company; I was pleased to have his friendship, and thought him more constrained by convention, and by his position. But now I understand that he saw it all quite differently, feeling emboldened by our eagerness. I saw him through my own eyes, though I should have been alert enough not to. I would have thought that my marriage and my life had prepared me."

Softly Marguerite replies, "And yet there must be some men ... worthy of our lofty ideals."

"Your fiancé?" reminds Belle. "No?"

"Il est pas mal," allows Marguerite, eyes briefly shining.

But Ileana, with pale sorrow, now confides, "I do not want to turn cynical toward all men ... even if many give us reason to. To believe that all deserve mistrust seems so sad. They are half the world, our fathers, uncles, brothers, sons ...There must be other ways, to reach between; there must be some who are good."

While the others to an extent agree, they also wonder if it doesn't veer willfully toward amnesia, or romantic fantasy. Angela murmurs, "But where are they? And who starts the wars, or beats and rapes women?"

With heads and eyes still, all consider this.

After some moments, Belle reaches for explanation, "When young, we are driven by nature to want the other sex. But inevitably, for many, or even most, that changes with time. We see more clearly. Things diverge"

"And yet," Ileana repeats, "not all are bad. Periodically, the unexpected, some surprise, springs forth."

"Lasting how long?" asks Marguerite. But no answer is offered by any. And so, silently reflecting, reaching for and sipping their drinks, they notice that the eight o'clock hour has come and gone. No driver or his friends have appeared. Instead the women shrug and smile away vague disappointment, and order dinner and more drinks, mixing indistinct memories and emotions with the relaxed pleasure of talking amongst themselves, revisiting tales and plans, personal histories and myths immemorial.

Rested and eager, the boys roll out of bed early, to make plans, contact friends, bike away to meet in town, and later swim at the town pool. Wren, too, is up and excited, into the office by eight, reviewing existing projects, refining proposals, and beginning to sketch out ideas for Yan's house. Together the projects energize him as he organizes their needs, but it is the house which most deeply engages him. He roughs three approaches, making changes as he thinks of them, lists components, calls the town permit office, and talks with an engineer. When Margaux comes in, they go over all the projects, deciding on priorities and what she will handle.

Just before noon he returns to the site, remembering only as he drives that he has never heard from Messena. Rising like a vapor, a stillness expands around him, cloaking, stifling his energy. He slows, just able to follow the curving road which now seems a tunnel through the underworld, dark, inert, without life ... until cries call him back ... He has work to do ... But what does her silence mean? ... Some purely technical problem? He will resend his email, write a letter ... give her time ... and if all fails, he will call ... will call ... It repeats and repeats, until he realizes that he is turning into the field, proceeding slowly through the grass. Eventually he stops where he did yesterday, but sits without energy or plan. A breeze breathing through the windows tries to rouse him, but his mind has emptied, his body's slumped ... no reason to move ... and yet, he knows somewhere he must ... shake himself ... push out ... get on ...

In stages, he manages, standing, gathering, walking off through the grass under a frown of disbelief. Reaching the location of the nearest corner, he begins measuring where the rooms will extend and rise, where the deck will run with the stream. But emptiness, like a shroud, returns. He kicks the earth. But feels no response, hears no answer. He is but a grain, a spore, in a field. He stares at the stream meandering along the edge of the woods. The house will follow it. He beings sketching the outline and where trees and shrubs will be eliminated or added. The more he imagines, the more vivid it grows, and the more he excludes other thoughts.

Yet periodically he must stop, head down, wondering, what point? Again a breeze nudges him; he re-awakens. Gripping his shovel, he digs down a few feet to find the water table and see what kind of soil and rock underlie this part of the property. But he finds her eyes in the tiny puddles, in the grasses ... Away ... away ... Now he photographs the stream and banks, and records the arc of the Sun on this summer's day, the Sun that warmed him at Delphi, and at their lunch. His chest tightens; he must inhale to breathe.

Mechanically he moves on, marches into the woods, up the hill ... as he did over there ... Vines and branches claw at him as he climbs toward the ridge, until he reaches a shelf from which he gazes back. He may want to stake out a path, suggest a gazebo. He pictures the design of the house from here: a graceful, cluster of circular roofs – a curving clump of mushrooms, tied together by the wandering stream and mirroring deck, all taking on the form, he sees, of a snail on its side, body, shell, head, horns, and tail, sliding along the bank.

He rubs his neck, gazes down into the field. The driveway will describe a graceful arc curling in from the road, before dividing into an oval leading to the front door and a spur bending away to the barn ... Why the silence? ... They have everything to share ... A groan erupts from his chest; he twists away ... What is he doing? ... The barn could be oddly pentagonal, with skylights, a dome, old and new, like his life. Models of the huddling temples on the Acropolis and at Delphi slide through his mind's eye, filling it. ... Iscaria's blue eyes are watching him ... What did she see? ... That he needed love, as she did, as we all do. His heart reaches for the other; he stumbles, catches himself. Where is she? Will he ever see her? ... He swipes the moisture from his eyes. Not now. Put her away ... Concentrate, think. He needs to start pulling ideas out of this landscape. Curving walls ... The first alternative could be long rectangles, balconied rooms, a modern Italian feel ... The second might suggest a hill-top village, or fortress, Florentine, squared, rising ramparts, walkways, sharp, distinct, supporting a tower ... He sees her waving, smiling goodbye ... The master bedroom will offer views in all directions ... a deck facing west from which to watch the setting sun and the stream flowing away. To the side, through the trees, he glimpses a caped female figure disappearing. He almost calls, but catches himself, blinking with incomprehension.

Turning and gazing down at the field, he breathes, searches for other ideas, then hears a car arriving. A black Mercedes convertible winds slowly through the grass and parks next to his. He hurries back down, zigzagging past boulders, bushes, trees, running, leaping. He sees a woman getting out, searching the field. He calls out. The woman turns. Hopping across the stream, staying mostly dry, he lands on the soft earth and slows, striding through the grass to greet her, affixing an artificial smile.

She's a city person, dressed chicly in black tights, black boots, and lavender suede jacket – not the usual local, suburban look.

He greets, "Good morning. Nice to meet you, Kirce."

"And you, Wren."

"So what do you think? The property offers some real possibilities."

"It's why we bought it!" she exclaims, her eyes sweeping the field and woods. Under her dark hair, her squinting scrutiny conveys an intensity evaluating and caring about what she sees. Her Mediterranean features are sharp and attractive ... like Luisa, but softer, more open. He refocuses on her, and when her attention returns, asks, "Shall we take a look? I have some thoughts, and sketches, and I'd like to hear yours." His mind is being pulled in several directions; he hears himself growling inside.

"Absolutely," she replies, sweeping the landscape once more. And so, he leads her toward the stream, where he begins to describe the designs – the familiar drill. The house, curving with the stream, will have its modular segments connected inside by short halls and outside by the deck. Each room will have access to the outside. Seen from the field, as one drives in, the roofs, softly round in this preferred design, will rise in a half circle to the second floor bedroom, presaging the ridge behind. He mentions the snail; she smiles, exclaims she likes it, beginning to imagine.

She seems to approve of much, but is not hesitant to ask questions, or insert a number of her own ideas. She has, he finds, both a design sense and taste, so that they go back and forth on a number of choices. He gets into it, drawn by her enthusiasm. She wants to think about his overall proposal, for house and garage. Unexpectedly she confides, "Yan is a wonderful man ... but he has little aesthetic sense, or taste, or interest. He's consumed with his business, his hedge fund." She stops there, but clearly she has set out boundaries between their areas of interest and responsibility.

Now he leads her along the stream, pointing out the dimensions of the house and where the elevated deck would follow the stream, eight to ten feet above. And he shows her where the small pool might be enlarged.

"A swimming hole! Rustic. I love it."

And he lists a number of other details to consider: a curving stairway down to a landing from which to dive into a deepened pool, a stepped entry into and out of the water, an arcing bridge and gazebo up the hill. Her sharply-defined eyes dance here and there as she pictures it all. He closes his, dismissing the wish to see the other.

He moves on, describing the rooms they may want, with views of the woods or field toward the road, and he explains that because the stream will occasionally overflow its banks, all needs to be elevated, up on pilings – particularly with the changing climate's strong storms and increasing rainfalls.

Following that, he helps her across the stream, then up the hill. There he asks her to imagine the structure, partially hidden and surrounded by evergreen shrubs and trees, making the transition between field and woods. They might consider *a living roof* with sedums, mosses, or other plants. Movement behind the trees steals his attention ...A deer? ... Wiping his eyes, he's glad she has not seen.

He leads her back down and into the field, to visualize the house and barn from the driveway as they walk its path. There, he describes the surrounding landscape: "Three different worlds ever-shifting, through the day, and seasons – a slow-motion movie of changing colors, textures, and shapes."

Squinting, she surveys the field and rise, inserting the house. Finding that his excitement has awakened hers, she exclaims, "Yes! I like it, the place, the ideas, the process. I like the way we can talk about it all. This is important to me, and something, frankly, I haven't found out here, as we're new to the town. Disappointingly I've found that the people Yan knows here, those who I've met so far, are mostly investment types, rather dry and without any real artistic interests. Yan at least recognizes my interests in art, even if he doesn't share them." She gazes back toward the stream and woods. "I look forward to coming up with other ideas. You don't mind, do you? I know some architects can be a little touchy."

"No no, I'm happy to collaborate. I welcome it. It's part of the fun, and I've long found that two minds are more fertile than one." ... Yes, he remembers ... those conversations over there ... But shaking them away, he seeks Kirce's reaction. She is studying him, and seems briefly unsettled by his distracted expression. He tries to smile reassuringly. She looks away, before pulling things together, "So, well ... Yan said that you could have three alternatives by the end of the week. Is that possible?"

"Yes, I've begun, and recorded much of what I need, but I'll probably return once more, tomorrow most likely, as I get into the sketches. You might want to consider some walled gardens or arbors."

Happy with this suggestion, and his full attention, she exclaims, "All of that seems good ... exciting! Let me think where the arbors might go." And moving away, glancing here and there, she pictures the possibilities. Studying her, he's pleased that she shares his enthusiasm. The sun shines down on them, here in the silent field.

When she turns back to him, he summarizes, "I hope that you will give me your responses to the three, and tell me of any other thoughts. Now, however, I should probably head back to my office, to begin including all that we've spoken about." All that was spoken, shared ... he feels briefly unsteady. He resets his feet.

"And you'll return tomorrow?" she checks. Bowing faintly, he confirms. "I can let you know when."

"Yes, I'd like to be in on it. I think this will be half of the fun, choosing and figuring things out."

"I can't say how complete the sketches will be by tomorrow, but they will be a start. New ideas give rise to more ideas; it's an evolving process, so by all means come out. I may try to include some design themes I saw in Delphi, along with something organic arising out of the field. But please tell me your preferences and reactions. Now is the time."

She comes back to him, eyes alight, cheeks reflecting the shining sun. Quickly she steps close, stretching up, to bestow a kiss on his cheek, before falling back, smiling, breathing, "So, tomorrow then."

Surprised, he manages a confused smile as he bow a little, courteously. But her enthusiasm does not waver and pulls forth his own. He feels a smile fill him, as she waves and turns back toward her car.

In still morning air and gentle sunlight, the women breakfast on Poseidon's deck as it slowly swings at anchor in Naxos's port. Having consulted with the captain, they will make the short sail south to Santorini and explore its picturesque villages hugging the rim of the ancient volcano. Angela has heard that though it tends to tourists, it is nonetheless dramatic with several small communities clinging to the caldera.

After coffee and croissants, they watch the crew hoist the mainsail to run south with the light breeze. Gazing back at Naxos, they talk of what will follow over the remainder of the Summer and into the Fall. Belle wonders about the cloud that is her marriage. A decision should be made. And although they have not really spoken of it, the other women have gathered from her comments that she's at a crossroad.

Seeking to brighten Belle's somber face, Marguerite asks her if there is anything comparable to this cruising in the states. Belle describes parts of the New England coast and tells them that though she hasn't sailed there, she's heard the Florida Keys, California, Puget Sound, Alaska ... Hawaii ... all have their attractions and beauty, if not the cultures and history of the Aegean.

"Perhaps a less contentious history is a benefit," speculates Angela. "A gentler, more innocent world, where Nature still presides."

Belle allows that this may be so, in places, "But there is development everywhere, without much culture. With the exception of New England, there is not a lot to interest me."

Her thoughts now slide back, as they often do, to her boys, wondering if they will have opportunities to explore these worlds. And she reflects on the arc of life, its stages. She feels that she has done much and is now approaching a new era, just as her boys will soon join worlds new to them. Life, she reflects, is composed of chapters, often distinct, yet which one must in turn embrace, as she has done. Her marriage had a rich period. They traveled, did things, before the boys arrived, with the perhaps inevitable decline. But now they see things differently. And there is the undermining problem of his assistant. On one hand, men have long done this; on the other, in today's world she needn't put up with it. She hadn't anticipated it, but ... No point in rehashing it. She concedes there is a heartlessness to life's swerves and turns ... Perhaps predictable. But with apology and compromise increasingly unlikely, what else makes sense but to move on? He surprised her ... although early boyfriends had betrayed her, broken her trust, and caring. Maybe it arose out of frustration with his career, but that doesn't excuse it. It's no less irritating and destructive. But of course he's not alone. Look at Argos, at many men ... Maybe Athena got it right.

In the afternoon, in the rim village of Oia, they walk through the narrow alleys and choose a restaurant overlooking the deeply blue sound that fills the caldera. The view is magical, recalling imagined scenes from the mythical world. Indeed Belle wonders if these communities are not a metaphor for man's existence, hanging onto the rocky rim of a volcano, exquisite for a time, but precarious, fragile.

After wine, goat cheese, and kebabs they wander happily, spirits raised, eyes delighted and engaged by carefully decorated shops, homes, and other restaurants, many with views down into the deep blue of the sea, which seems to mirror the cloudless, infinite sky, dizzying them, suspending them ... in Purgatory? For moments, they seem disoriented, until they find reassurance and connection in each other and in the pristine white buildings, some with brightly colored roofs. Does it all not blend the human and the celestial?

Across the tranquil sound, a white cruise ship sits like a toy, disgorging thousands more like them. Without these tourists, would the villages exist in their exquisite, calculated beauty?

While all four enjoy the exploration and views, they agree now that it would be Rhodes, with its greater cultural opportunities and variety, that might call them back, despite the crowds. Belle observes that much of today's world is filled with people able to travel, as they are. Life can still offer incredible variety and interest, to the affluent and fortunate.

These thoughts please her, contrasting this period to the mostly limited ancient eras and their creeping progress. She feels that she stands in the sweep of time, watching empires rising, conquering, passing away. Why should she suppose her existence would be any different? ... And yet she has recovered from the assault and broken marriage, and is ready to start anew, much as many of these islanders did following invasions and changing allegiances, finding new life, new direction and new connection. Life presents an array of experience; history lays out the patterns, the cycles and variations. And she, having studied them, is ready to apply that knowledge, having re-emerged.

He comes into the office early to refine the rough sketches of the three options. Each in turn engrosses him as he moves between them, detailing, filling in, altering. He loses track of time, as he often does, until around ten Margaux calls over from her desk that several emails for him have come in. With his mind held by the drawings, he drifts over to his desk and taps the key board. Several messages from the usual suppliers and existing customers fill the screen, but one from an unrecognized address stops him as he scrolls down. He clicks it open ... It's from her. He checks and checks again, sinking onto his chair, his attention drawn into the screen.

"Hello, Wren. I hope you are well, as I would like to say I am ... but in truth I am overwhelmed, by the project, by all the people I must talk to, all those demanding to be consulted, all the accounts I must read, all the translations and translators I must seek assistance from, and from countless professors each with his own or her own insight and truth. I did not anticipate this. My life before was so quiet mostly, moving at my own pace. Now I can barely manage. I have no time. Everyone pesters and plagues me – with ideas, views, texts. Aarrie is angry at me because I have so little time for her. Moreover I am sick. I caught something – a fever ... I don't know what it is. It's not serious, but it leaves me dragging through the days. I cannot write more now. I don't know what to say about us. You have your life, I understand. I have little time or energy to think. I had hopes, but I wonder if reality has intervened, warning that we are foolish. When I recover and get on top of all of this, perhaps we can talk. Forgive me.

Nomizo o'ti sas.

Messena.

He sits stilled, stabbed, deflated. She is there, real ... but ... what? Is she okay? ... Has she pulled away? Simply exhausted? How to interpret her message, so minimal, un-encouraging ... Perhaps, given her situation, understandable ... Or is she gently expressing second thoughts, letting go? ... He cannot know, not sure he wants to know. If only he could talk to her ... Call her? ... Yes, he will call. He wants to put his arms around her. But what would that solve? Perhaps he could go help her organize her book. The stories, accounts, histories. Should he have offered? Should he now? ... But how can he, with the project, his other jobs, the boys? Should he recognize the impossibilities? With distance, do views so quickly change? He tries to reason it through, several times, but ... each time he reaches an impasse ... a ravine, a canyon – no way across.

He rereads her words over and over, but can squeeze no more out of them ... Has she lost hope? Simply being realistic? Or must he simply be patient? Her project will finish, as will his ... He will call ...

In the meantime, he must complete the sketches. And so he returns to his drawings, doing as much as he can. In the early afternoon he drives back to the site, his mind pulled painfully by her face flashing above the trees. He tries to meet her eyes but they disappear in the light and leaves, a creature of the sky, flashing, fading. He needs to put it away now, but ache fills his chest.

Half blind, he turns into the field, proceeds slowly through the grass. Ahead he sees Kirce's car, parked, top-down, empty. His head pounds; has he done what is needed? Is he ready? His full attention must be directed to the project ... as she has done over there.

Stopping next to her car, he sits for a moment swallowing thoughts, emotion, closing them off, forcing himself to review the points on which he wants to consult. Then pushing out, he gathers the drawings, note pads, and measuring tape, recalling, as he does, Kirce's parting kiss ... A simple, parting gesture, or warning? ... Like Messena, she comes from a different culture. More free to express enthusiasm, passion ... Was Messena's affection as lightly given? ... Was it her job?

From the trunk he takes out his easel, and carries it to what will be the front of the house, there selecting a spot to work. Searching the property, he sees no sign of her, assumes she's up the hill exploring.

And so for a while, he sketches various ground-level views of the three options, altering detail as he progresses. He moves to flesh out the sides, before retreating to address the garage, beginning with a Gheary-like mix of planes at odd angles, enclosing a cavernous structure. It too will need a raised floor with ramps, but how high? Feeling it might look best in natural, weathered wood, soon turning gray, he roughs out the walls, wide doors, and dome, adding vaulting windows. Barn below, windowed athenaeum above. Past and future. Or maybe a Japanese look, more refined, smooth, subtle, in cedar or redwood, if he can get it, or should. Or maybe in white, an apparition floating in the field ... Russian ... Dr. Zhivago ...? At the moment he prefers the first, but again he will sketch the three and see.

Next come measurements of where the oval driveway will deliver one to the front door, and where the modules will curve toward the stream, one after the other. He recalls George's nautilus, its grace, its living walls ... sees Messena watching ... His heart accelerates; he is held ... before, once again, he manages to turn away.

Moving off into the field, he sketches low evergreen shrubs and trees which will partially hide the house, softening its lines, mixing textures – ideas which are anathemas to some architects.

Glancing around periodically, he expects Kirce to emerge from the woods. But no sign yet.

Working quickly he completes the two alternatives. Good at drawing, he finds that his renderings please him, and as new ideas come, he grows more engaged. Many of the rooms will be round and sky-lit, or have high windows, sliding doors, echoing the barn. A few large boulders he's seen at the base of the ridge will be moved near to the house. And he will enlarge the natural pool adjacent to the middle of the house, extending it to the blue Aegean where he swam … remembers holding her … as he tries to embrace his work.

He scribbles notes at the edges of the several drawings. Writing quickly, he becomes aware of footsteps approaching through the grass. Turning he finds Kirce approaching, buttoning her blue blouse over her tanned chest, carrying sandals, yanking her white slacks fully up. Her hair is wet; she has been swimming in the stream and seems excited. Images from another swim briefly overlay his sight as she stops before him. "Hello, Wren … The water is wonderful and refreshing …"

Dark memories slide behind his eyes. He expels an awkward reply, "Water … really? … I can imagine. Already the air is … warm."

Happily she explains, "I climbed up the ridge, to look around … and then I needed to cool off." She gazes past him and around the field, before peering into his eyes. "It is truly an excellent property Yan has bought." Her gaze seems to ask him to read between her lines. But he is uncomfortable lingering there, and so he looks away before seconding her conclusion, "Absolutely. It's beautiful, offering all sorts of possibilities."

And yet he has seen, in the bright sun, with her dark wet hair tightly framing her pale, pretty face, that she is a little too attractive, and dramatic, and that her eyes are investigating him.

Stepping out of the line of her gaze, he tells her that he would like to show her the three design options. A smile moves over her face as she glances at the easel and then back at him, before, with a certain intimacy, she replies softly, "Ohh ... Well yes ... let's see!"

She steps around and leans close to the drawings, as he slides behind where he can explain. Leafing through the pages, she expresses pleasure, and surprise, "I like this first one ... it seems organic, part of the field, and rise." When she has reviewed the three, she tells him, "Yes, it was the first, more than the other two. The second, with its sharp lines, is too geometric, or rectangular for me, maybe even harsh. The third is more Italian, medieval, reminiscent of hill towns, but too martial, a fortress The first is softer, arising out of the field." He waits as she again looks through the pages, until, after studying each, she decides, "Yes, this one ... After our first conversation, this is very much what I pictured. The other two are more ... inserted ..." And she quickly reviews them a third time.. "Yes, I particularly like the rising arc of the roofs, curving up to the crowning room, leading one's eye to the hill behind. I think it would be fun, unique." He feels pleased as she continues, "In fact I love it! I think I will make the field, too, a great circle."

Pleased, he asks, "And Yan? Which do you think he'll prefer?"

"Oh, I think the same ... In fact I'm sure he would ... He relies on me; I've tried to educate him at MOMA and galleries – and in the Hamptons – but ... it doesn't really stick, or interest him. Certainly it doesn't move him."

Now she finds the stream sketches, and exclaims, "Oh yes ... this also ... is very much what I would want ... "And turning to him, she smiles into his eyes. "I think our minds work in similar ways." She gazes intently and happily at him, so that he must again send his gaze away to the drawings.

Swinging around, she leans closely over the pages, studying details. "Yes, but I think the pool could be even larger than you've sketched here, so that I could enjoy a good swim. I love water … and I very much like the deck, broadening here – you could make that too even wider … expand the western extension, for the sunsets."

"Good. I'll re-sketch both ideas, and I'll need to talk further with the engineer," he tells her, "about the stream and hidden pilings on which the house and deck will sit. And you and I should go over the rooms and their sizes and so forth."

Her attention moves from the drawings to the landscape, and then to him, glancing at each with a genuine liveliness. "You don't know how much I enjoy this. I have some ideas for the rooms. But as I mentioned, Yan and I haven't really discussed specifics – a few general themes … Of course he's eager to see which one I like … what you and I come up with. But then his mind will wander off, back to his work … Do you know that, in fact, it was me who really made the decision to go with you? I loved your proposals and sketches. I wonder if you could teach me a little; I can draw only in a rudimentary way … I'd love a few lessons … What do you think? Is that possible?"

This time, when he meets her eyes, he must make an effort not to look away from their intensity. "Certainly … we could do that …"

"Your wife wouldn't mind … Will she come out to see this? Is she interested?"

He isn't sure what to say. "… Well … no … I don't think so … not really."

"…Why? …"

"Well, she's in Europe, for one thing …"

"Oh, where?"

"Greece …"

"Where you were. How was it?"

His first impulse is to express his joy, but then he realizes he'd better temper it. "Interesting of course – so much architecture to look at …" Releasing a breath, he allows his mind to escape up into the sky. But then gathering himself, he finds her watching intently. And so he adds, "In many ways … extraordinary."

She looks at him wondering at the emotion she has seen. She wonders if he is recalling his wife … or someone … She waits. He smiles a shielding smile, and seeing that he is not inclined to explain, she moves on, "And she has stayed on, vacationing by herself?"

"With friends … I had to come home to pick up our boys from summer camp. And meet with Yan."

"Oh … well … this could have waited."

"But not the boys."

"No …" She now seems to grow strangely pre-occupied, until again, she looks up at him with concern. "I'm sorry to hear she's not more interested."

He nods vaguely, glancing away. She surveys the property once more. In the midday sun, it's grown increasingly warm, prompting her to wipe her brow and breathe, "It's hot now, here in the field … What do you think, should we go for a swim in the stream? It was wonderful … the water is so clear and fresh … Will you join me?"

Images from that dark swim snap back behind his eyes. He recalls the chill, and turns away slightly, to avoid her gaze. His mind and tongue suddenly seem thick and slow. Voices whisper; indistinct faces watch soberly. He finds Kirce's eyes, her smile, warm, confiding. He sends a smile back, of appreciation, sympathy, but sees that she is waiting. What to do? Yan, he's sure, would not appreciate it. What would Messena have said? "It would be nice," he tells Kirce, "but I'm not sure I have the time."

"A quick dip?" she urges.

"It would distract us from our work."

"It might inspire new ideas," she breathes.

Not sure what she has in mind – simply a free spirit? ... Not sure that he could control himself, stay away from her, he summons Messena's approach: straight-forward, honest. "You are too attractive ..."

She smiles. "We are adults. It would be a treat, and cool us."

"I don't think Yan would appreciate it," he tries.

"We're not married; we have left each other free."

He turns away, recognizing his own faint temptation. Without looking at her, he blurts, "For me, it would be too tempting, to go beyond." He has not made love in so long. "I would make a fool of myself, and feel I would betray the trust Yan has in me ... and my wife."

Her smile fades. She studies him. And then, with a twitch in her lips, dismisses this concern.

He looks down. "Maybe if we knew each other better. But I just ..." He's not sure where to go – maybe it's innocent, on her part ... but in him ... Best not ... In him also resides she who has completely filled him. How present could he be? And he must hold onto her, lest he shatter. He breathes and meets Kirce's eyes. Lines of annoyance move over her face; she turns away a little, but then pouts ... and seems to release whatever expectation she had. "I appreciate your candor." She studies him for some moments, as he does her, until at length she slowly exhales and concedes, "Perhaps in another time ... another life." A smile flashes across her face, then disappears.

Though he tries to return it, he feels bad that he has disappointed her – a simple swim ... but for him, a temptation. How could he not feel it? And yet he would be torn, ripped apart, trying to reconcile both. Impossible ... Though his impulse is natural ... he must not. Not wise – her words ... He feels faintly sad, that both here are maybe needing something, affection, connection ... What would it impede? Arbitrary convention? ... But it is more, now ... He re-sets his smile. "We might be friends. We enjoy talking ... about this and other things."

Her eyes waver, taking him in, looking closely. She appears to be about to speak, but then presses her lips and allows her thoughts to fall away; she gazes at the grasses.

He reflects on our different views, needs ... modes of talk ... How extraordinary to have found that one to talk with, share, explore ... Kirce is warm, aware; they have interests in common ... But not like that other. He's glad that he was direct with her. A feeling of goodness fills him ... He prays he will see the other again, somehow. But now, here in the field, he must blink all that away. He would like to talk with Kirce at some point ... even embrace her, hold her ... but beyond that ... His hopes for the project pulsate in him; he feels a responsibility to ... all. As these strands of feelings run through him, he feels he is outside, looking in ... Yet he is certain of the love he feels. It is ... a Sun burning in him, a miracle ... after years of emptiness ...

She looks over at the stream, acknowledging to herself that she got carried away, partly by him and the situation, and partly from disappointment with Yan ... She inhales, then redirects her thoughts, "We'll need some shade trees for days like this."

"Yes ..." he replies, relieved. "I've drawn in a few, deciduous and evergreens. You should tell me what varieties you like, or I can suggest a few."

Slowly she scans the field, where the house will sit. "I will ... but it would be helpful if I could draw a bit better ... I wouldn't want to mess up these nice ... renderings."

He smiles as he nods. "A fair amount can be done on computer now ... but drawing, sketching, is not hard; I can show you. Mostly it's observing closely, and recognizing what you're seeing or wanting."

She glances at him, trying to read him, before her eyes again fall away, murmuring assent. He looks at her, feeling kindly toward her. She seems a good person ... maybe frustrated, not quite living as she might want. A member of the club. He sends her a smile when she glances up again. But her mood has shifted; she has moved on. "You know, and I realize that this is none of my business, but there is something sad in your eyes. I can see you are engaged by your work ... but something weighs on you."

He feels his face go blank, at this echo. Images, words, from Delphi fly past ... the valley and hills, the ridge behind ... He breathes. "... No ... Actually I've been hopeful, thrilled ... by this project ... and meeting you two." He wonders if it is Kirce who feels something weighing, disappointing ... He tries to see her, what she is feeling and intending. What he finds are watchful eyes, her lips parted, emotions held within.

Her lips push out briefly, before she pulls them back. A twitch in her cheek allows that she accepts this. "... Well ... for one thing, I'm afraid that you won't see or learn a great deal more about Yan. He's self-contained, a little impatient, and maybe superior, in his views of most people."

Not sure what this means for the project, or if he will hear more, he smiles faintly, acknowledging, then glances away, across the field. She sees his discomfort and apologizes, "I don't mean to get into that ... and yet ... ... I suppose I should mention that things are not ... ideal between Yan and me." Her face grows darker; tiny lines reach out from the corners of her eyes. He waits, feeling a twinge of apprehension. But she veers back to his case, "Is that where you are?"

Is it? He frowns at the difficulty of explaining. He tips his head side to side, not really wanting to convey more. But a spike of apprehension strikes through him. A breeze ruffles their hair. She smoothes hers; he rubs the back of his neck with a single swipe.

"I'm sorry," he hears her say. Their eyes meet again. He recognizes that while they are strangers, and in very different places in their lives, yet they share some unhappiness. She hurries on: "While Yan and I are not married ... he was before ... and I was too, young ... too young ..." This story, too, a familiar chord. She continues, "I want to ask you ... Do you mind? ... I have my doubts about ... this community ... As I believe Yan mentioned, we've rented a house in town, Wescott Road, until this is built ... but ... I really haven't met many people here who have been open and welcoming. Do you find that? Is it a friendly town?"

Relieved, to a degree, at this turn, he studies her, trying to understand her concern, then smiles reassuringly. "It is. It's many towns, or neighborhoods. Some are quite friendly; some are focused on their own networks, be it the university, or their social or sports clubs, or whatever. The sections, the neighborhoods are distinct; many require driving, which makes things a little insular. But the opportunities for contact can be both many ... and limited ..."

"That worries me," she interjects, "about living out here." Her face grows serious and more pale as she confides, "I really wanted to be near the sea. This is so far. And also, unlike in town, there would be no neighbors out here. I already don't see many on Wescott. It's often empty during the day. Except for me. I've been a city person. He too; mostly he's in the city ... but now, recently, I no longer want to be in there as much. So how would that work? How would I meet people?"

"There are all sorts of activities and events in town ... clubs, groups, performances, talks. The library is active. There are a number of theatres, with concerts, plays, lectures; frequent municipal meetings confronting various issues; there are always causes and events that bring people together. I think you could find many friends here."

"So far you're my only one."

He swallows discreetly. "Well I can introduce you."

Smiling wanly at this offer, feeling disappointment, she pauses, looking down and then around at the field, before she resumes, "Although I've lived for years in the city, I've been dreaming of a house by the water ... in the Hamptons, Shelter Island ... I don't know ... but Yan doesn't like it there, says it's too expensive, and too social in ways he doesn't like. Too *chichi*, he says ... And hard to get into the city. Out here at least he has partners, associates ... golf buddies."

He nods quickly, telling her, "There's good variety here, people from all over, Europe, Latin America, Asia, many different types." Yet he feels badly, feels the weight of her disenchantment. How deep a problem? He feels a darkness edging up from the horizon.

She finds him again, less eagerly. "So ... well thank you for the offer ... Maybe ... but I'm afraid ... the conclusion I must draw is ... that ... I'm not sure this place is for me. I'd feel rather isolated; I *would be* isolated out here."

He shakes his head to refute this, but she goes on, "*He* has friends out here, but not really of interest to me ... I mean they're nice ... but I like more artistic people ... alive to the things I like." Her eyes return to him seeking his response.

He tries to smile, as he struggles to understand what this means. Not so different than his own case ... But he feels he needs to repeat, "But there are many artistic types here ... all sorts at the university and other schools ..." Alas he himself knows only a few, several architects, a musician, a writer. He wants to help her; he'll introduce them ...

Trying to calm her discontent, she avoids him, looking around. "I'm sorry to dump all of this on you ... But it's something I have to consider."

Faintly he bows as he searches for other inducements, but none come to mind. He stares down at the grass, brown and green, green and beige, stalks waving in the breeze. An unexpected eddy enters him ... a wraith ... He opens his mouth, blowing it away, then searching for something positive to offer. He's sure he could come up with a number of ideas. He'll throw a party, a summer garden party. "I'll have a get-together ... and maybe get you two invited elsewhere; there are always parties." But is this true? Over the course of a year, yes, but now, many are away in the summer. This realization bunches up, shouldering aside other thoughts. How can he save it?

Her eyes come back, concerned, studying him, stealing his focus. What does she need to hear? He opens his mouth to speak, but inhales instead. She sees this and waits, but he remains unsure what to offer. Finally, in a low voice, without much energy, she says that they, Yan and she, must make a decision. He repeats his party idea, but she seems not to hear, or to have gone past it, away. He finds that her face has dulled; her eyes have lost their shine, no longer catching the sun. "Really, I'll introduce you, throw a party. You two should give it some time ..." But he imagines Belle's reluctance, or outright opposition. "We can go to some performances, events ... readings, talks ... Try things, see what you think. There's a good range here, an active art community ... Lots going on."

She smiles weakly. "Yes ... but now ... I'm ... just not sure it's right for me. I've long wanted to be near the water ..." He pictures her swimming in the stream, the sea ... the sun glinting ... Now as she looks at him, she seems to have found clarity. "I confess that I have wondered if he's doing this on purpose, to drive a wedge between us. He's knows I'd rather be out there."

Wren feels the entire project slipping ... While he indicates that he understands, his eyes avoid hers. Has she pretty much decided? He reaches for something: "Do you want to discuss it with him?"

She nods vaguely. "Yes ... I guess." And she looks at him heavily, with emotion thick in her eyes. "It's too bad that we are not in different places in our lives."

Which 'we'? he wonders. But her eyes are opaque now, unreadable ... What to do? He feels Kirce's parallel neediness, her desire to find something. But her focus is inward. She'd seemed to want some assistance from him, and maybe more, but then changed, turning her thoughts elsewhere ... So, unhappy with Yan ... and now maybe him. If so, this house will be a trap. He cannot know all the intricacies ... He needs to think of something to say, something more. Yet somehow, he feels stuck, inept, unable to find the words.

For some moments they stand there, looking off across the field, into the woods. He senses that her interest in the project is evaporating in the heat, flowing away in the stream, off through the trees.

He makes one last pitch. "Would you two want to give it a try ... build it, see if you like it, see who you meet ... You need the garage ... and if still not happy, sell it? The market here is generally pretty strong."

Sadly, with disappointment, she allows, "I'm not sure I could put the energy into it, that it should receive ... that you deserve."

"Don't worry about me. I'm ready, excited ... It is up to you two."

"I think now ... that this wouldn't work for me ... I should have thought it through more clearly. In a way, you've reminded me of the importance ... of caring ... and place."

This feels cruel ... painful. What closeness does he have? A dream? ... A frown fills his brow; his mind seems bound, frozen, though he reaches for a remedy. "Would you want to give it some time?"

Slowly she breathes. "I appreciate your offers ... It would be nice, but ..."

He swallows and looks out over the grasses stirring in the breeze. It feels, in some ways, as hopeless as his negotiations with Belle. He cannot provide what she needs, neither of them. He tries again, "The town has a lot going on. Interesting people, of all sorts ... My guess is that you would grow to like it. Here you have the woods, field, stream ... Nature, the seasons, the flora and fauna ... the town ... the city and ocean an hour away."

Trying to smile, she looks around, once more, and up at the ridge. "Yes ... on one hand, it's beautiful; I like it ... On the other, it seems wrong for me ... as we may be for each other ... It's tough, as we get older and more aware of who we are, to find the right fit. Sometimes I think I should find someone who's in the arts, is at least artistic, doing something with expression. But the truth is they are not necessarily easier. There can be, in some cases, a goodness underlying it, but also ego ... whereas, in his world ... well, you know ... it's war, cut-throat, few rules ... So, I don't know ... I'll have to figure it out."

A grimace slices his cheek, even as he understands ... perhaps too clearly. He feels a chill working in, filling him, replacing hope ... which is disappearing as easily as it arrived. He inhales, glances around, seeking something, anything ... before he utters, "So ... well ... will you let me know?"

"Of course ..."

He swallows what almost erupts as an ironic laugh. His eyes run over the ground, the trampled grass.

"And you and your wife? What will happen?" she asks in a low voice.

He looks at her, but does not see. Two doors stand before him, leading beyond to two roads, but how he will get through either one he cannot say, nor imagine. Faintly he shakes his head, then blinks and finds her watching, seeing something of this. He wonders who, truly, she is, and what might have been exchanged ... But Messena has drawn all interest and energy.

He hears her shift and turn away a little, then conclude, "So, well ... I will talk to him. But I won't even be able to reach him until late tonight." Looking at him she tries to smile, but cannot quite. "I'll call you, when I have, probably in the morning."

He nods, aware of a fever filling his forehead.

Now she extends her hand in goodbye, and he takes it. They shake once, but hold the other's for some moments. Studying him carefully, she sees again underlying sadness. "May I say something?" He waits. "I would urge you to find love ... as I must too, now. If what was ... has gone, seek anew. It brings life, to those who do." He tries to smile appreciatively, but what he sees are the clouds slowly drifting by ... He imagines segments of the completed house reflected in the flowing stream, its currents rippling over rocks, sliding by the banks. Its perturbed surface reflects portions of the house that most likely now will not be built. The stream flows on, but nothing else moves, except the wind, and his eyes watching the passing clouds. And then she is pulling her hand out of his and turning away, calling out, "I'm sorry ..." He sees her walk quickly to her car, open the door and drop in. He hears the engine start, growl, then watches blankly as she drives off through the field without a glance.

In the early morning, the women come up on deck with coffees and look around at the great walls of the caldera, below which they are anchored. They gaze up at the small white buildings, clinging like barnacles to the rim. The air is fresh and warm, the wind gentle, whispering that they should stay. But they are content to go, and move on with their lives.

As they are finishing breakfast, the captain motors Poseidon out of the sound and into the wind, where the crew raises the sails to begin beating north, back to Piraeus. The four gaze behind, realizing that their odyssey is over. Mostly they agree it was enough. Each island was distinct in its offerings and landscape; each interesting to visit, and yet none of the women fell in love. The islands, they have decided, cannot compete with the cities and towns of the western Mediterranean. For them, these floating worlds, though picturesque and historic, are essentially beach communities for tourists, like them, something they no longer yearn for. While they allow that some of the out-of-the-way islands, such as Patmos, offer peace and charm, they are no longer seeking that. How much of their ambivalence stems from Henry's lingering presence, they cannot be sure, but they admit the last few days have been pleasant and relaxing as they explored, swam, and shared accounts of their lives.

With the Poseidon tacking northwest and northeast, the women look out across the sea, gray now under a fleet of clouds. Chatting, they take in last views, or page through their books seeking where they left off. They realize that as none are sailors, they have not been swept away by the nautical thrill that Henry frequently touted. Belle pronounces it a case of, "boys and boats," eliciting faint smiles from the others as they begin redirecting their thoughts back to the world they briefly escaped, to rejoin the hubbub, as happily as they left it.

They will arrive the next morning, sailing throughout the day and night among the Cyclades, mostly low, dark, somnolent beasts. Stretching out a final time on the deck, they talk of meeting in Barcelona and elsewhere. And they strategize about coaxing Henry to let them take the Poseidon next year, as a means of travel more than an end in itself. Marguerite wonders if she will be married by then. In some ways it seems more appealing now in its offer of a focused life, free of wandering. But who knows? Would she want to bring him along? Would the others feel uncomfortable? She believes he would understand the dynamics and behave in the gentle, tactful manner of the French gentleman that he is.

But is borrowing the boat likely? Each believes that Henry owes her something. Together, they reason, they have leverage. But he leaves a bad taste in their mouths, and probably it would be better to disassociate themselves. There are other means of transportation; he will have induced another harem to join him; probably one voyage is enough. It has provided novelty, a glimpse of the past, each island a partial rendering of that long-ago world.

As evening comes on, Angela asks Belle if she has decided on how to deal with Henry. Belle smiles acceptingly as she replies that she will be guided by the lawyers in Athens, with whom she has an appointment tomorrow morning following their dawn arrival.

Angela's eyes fall, under the weight of her own memories, but then she thrusts them behind her, as she often has. A certain energy returns and she looks ahead, reminding Belle that Henry must be anxious to get it settled; he doesn't like loose ends. In his business, he wants the drilling contracts signed and sealed, as expeditiously as possible. "So, I suspect he will be forthcoming. Don't be shy … Besides, he likes you."

"I won't be shy." But Belle pushes the other observation away, filling her lungs with fresh sea air.

Angela, however, wants to turn this over in her mind, once more, and counsels, "By the same token, he doesn't like paying lawyers to make decisions or arrangements which he can easily do himself. Parasites, as he frequently refers to them, never recognizing that it is precisely people like him who make lawyers necessary, to protect the rest of us, or even the playing field."

Belle smiles and nods patiently before repeating that she is philosophically against allowing Henry to buy his way out of this, despite recognizing there are few other, real-world options. She's curious about the amount that Angela accepted, and nearly asks, but then chooses not to, not wanting money to become the focus. At the same time, the prospect of a large settlement glows strangely in her mind, a fat, golden Buddha. This irks her, that she entertains it, and though she tries to dismiss it, the image keeps returning, until she growls and buries it under other concerns.

As for her marriage, she had initially hoped the trip would improve things, but soon saw it wouldn't. Nor did the disgruntlement she'd felt disappear. Wren was no less preoccupied by his dream world, endlessly investigating the old temples – to what end? – and ever hoping for a breakthrough project, but never landing one, and so limiting the family financially. And ever holding onto his young assistant. For these and various other reasons, they never talk anymore. She can predict pretty much what he will say, and there seems to be little new on his mind … So, what to do? … Separate? … Maybe when the boys go off to college, when Patrick finishes high school. Then it wouldn't matter where she lives. She has friends in the city; maybe she could get a job there, at one of the universities, or over here somewhere. Her book on the islands' histories and cultures may be out by then. It could have relevance for the entire, troubled Mediterranean.

As night slowly settles over them, the crew serves them a light dinner, after which they chat for a time, gazing out over the dark sea and darker islands, before turning in early, to rise one last time with the sun.

When pale, diffident dawn edges into the sky, casting her uniform shawl over them, Belle is just able to distinguish the slightly darker Attic peninsula lying off their starboard bow. Through the lingering haze, a few lights, like pearls, randomly bejewel the slumbering hills. She wonders where exactly George's playfully curled house is and if she can see it. But she soon realizes they are too far off-shore to make out any detail. Somewhere lies the beach where she last saw her husband walking off. Once more it surprises her how infrequently she has thought of him. When love goes, so do most concerns and memories, disappearing like the expended day.

As Athens' suburbs come slowly into view, the women gaze ahead from the deck and smile at each other, pressing hands and sincere embraces, exchanging addresses, numbers, and promises to meet. All that they encountered on the cruise has brought them close: the journey through islands and back in time, dealing with the anachronistic pirate, or keeper of a seraglio. But they have waved him away; his presence drops astern in Poseidon's slowly-churning wake. Belle asks Marguerite about her latest thoughts on marriage. Marguerite smiles as she reports that she now thinks she may delay it for a year or so, freeing her to join them next summer. She glances at Belle for her reaction, and finds Belle studying her warmly, but with curiosity, wondering why she would want to tie herself in any formal way.

But Ileana and Angela, in contrast, laugh and urge Marguerite to go ahead, try it. It needn't be forever. In fact it seldom is. Belle smiles at this. It seems that through all the difficulties, still hope persists. Is it biological impulse, social expectations and pressure, or dreams of romance that push them into these arrangements? She wonders if a different man can be truly different. From the many types she's met, she's found no golden mean, or man.

When they land at the yachting facility, the crew brings their bags up and onto the dock, where the women thank and tip them. And then they gather for their goodbyes. They will stay in touch, meet in Barcelona, and travel again. They look into each other's eyes with openness and caring.

Marguerite says that she will be coming to New York in the Fall and hopes Belle will join her, to which Belle happily agrees, as she leans into a heart-felt embrace. And then they walk up to the street to find cabs. Angela and Ileana are going to one hotel, Marguerite another, while Belle will return to the one she stayed in. Before ducking into their respective rides, they spread their arms once more for a final embrace, the foursome, eyes smiling, catching a last glimpse, while behind, dark islands float in the golden haze.

She hardly notices the white, busy city. In mere minutes, she is there, paying again and then wheeling her bag across the lobby to the front desk to register. She gazes around the familiar, wide atrium, aware of the faint echo of her own footsteps, until suddenly from behind a voice calls, sending a chill through her once again. "Hello, Artemis …"

She stops and half-turns to him.

"I trust your cruise went well."

Stunned by his reappearance, she looks at him, feeling her sight grow dark, her balance waver. But then she swings around and strides on toward the desk.

He follows stepping quickly to her side. "I understand your response. If nothing else, I thought we might come to some agreement. As I said, to save time and wrangling. What do you say, could we talk?"

But she continues, walking more quickly, not replying, reaching the desk where she begins to check-in for the night, before tomorrow's flight home.

Henry waits a few steps behind while she makes her arrangements.

When she turns to head to her room, he approaches. "Listen Belle, I am prepared to make a generous offer. I acknowledge that I strayed far out of bounds. But all of this is going to reach some conclusion, at some point. Why not settle it now, in principle anyway? We're reasonable people, despite what you think of me. Why not agree to a solution?"

She stops and stares at him. "Do you have any idea …?"

He looks chastened, even somewhat crestfallen. "I do … I mean I can't completely, but I have tried to imagine it. It is beyond excusing."

"Until the next one."

"No … I don't think so … It has finally sunk in …"

She scans his features with a skeptical, silent sneer.

"It has, I'm afraid. Honestly. Part of it is you, your influence. Your reaction reached into me, perhaps because in you I had found a woman who interests me, in many ways."

"Please, Henry. Save it for someone else."

"Well, no matter what you may think, it's true. But anyway, I want to make it up to you. My lawyers will counsel me to fight for every Euro, but I want to make a generous offer, to make amends, as far as it is possible, and I understand …"

She looks away, wondering how to put an end to this.

"Belle, it is my hope that we could become friends. Life does not grant infinite opportunities, at least to me. It does not go on forever. I would hope that the affinity we clearly share might find a way … That is my hope … this is my chance."

Annoyed, looking here and there, she nonetheless feels an odd twinge inside, some conflicted contraction.

"I am serious," he adds, and indeed his face is flush with intensity.

She studies him now, trying to gauge this. She wishes she could just blurt out what she might want to say and have it over … go up to her room … So, what to do? … If she waits for the lawyers, this whole thing *will* indeed drag on. She, too, would like to forget it. The temptation to settle looms like a great Sphinx, implacable, edging closer.

He sees her considering things. "This afternoon, I could bring a letter detailing my proposal. A sum could be wired to your bank. And may I say also … that I would hope we might meet again, in New York, London, Barcelona … I hope that at some point you might consider that."

She glances at him. She finds these conflicting ideas deeply irritating. Does he not understand? And yet, he seems contrite, chastened … An act?

"While I understand where you are … and apologize sincerely and completely, I, speaking of course only for myself, don't want to just toss this all away."

With a hiss of frustration, she spins away. Should she just run off, go up to her room, escape this importuning? ... Yet something holds her ... The prospect of settling? ... Her odyssey over, heading home, it might be good to end this too, here and now. Standing there she begins to feel faintly dizzy. She didn't sleep well – the early rise into the gray dawn ... the high clouds above, streaming down from Olympus ... how to escape? Fatigued, her body trembles.

Stepping around to meet her gaze, he sees her waver physically, and reaches for and takes her elbow. "Come. Let's sit a minute." She pulls her elbow free, but then as if in a trance, or called by the prospect of ending it, she does not resist his careful directing her to a couch at the edge of the atrium. There he urges her to sit, which she does, while he slowly lowers himself into an adjacent chair.

"I know this is impossibly rushed. Forgive me, but tomorrow I must fly off. Doesn't it make sense to reach an agreement now? Pretty much whatever you want."

She avoids his face as a welter of thoughts rush through her mind: if this is so distressing, she does not want to carry it home, to the boys and work, where she will be very busy; there will be no time ... And so she says, "I have an appointment with a lawyer, later. I will consult and get back to you. Where can I reach you?"

He reaches into his brief case and finds a card, on which he scribbles his hotel name and number, then hands it to her. She takes it, staring down at it, not seeing.

"Allow me to repeat that I want to offer you a very reasonable sum, as a token of my sincerity. And, by the way, Angela said that she would like to return to the Poseidon next summer. Possibly something can be arranged for all of you, if you'd like."

She looks at him through dimming sight. She cannot calculate everything now. She pushes herself up, telling him, "I will call you after the consultation." She observes, however, that looking up at her, he does appear pale, his features distorted ... which provides some satisfaction, a strange exulting in her chest. She makes an effort to breathe, and then release it, and much more.

He is standing now, facing her, still apparently gripped by the emotion he claimed. But she will respond no more to him. Instead, she sets her mind and mouth firmly, turns, and walks resolutely to the elevators.

Upstairs, in her room, once her bags have been brought in, she sits on the bed, her mind in turmoil. Conflicting desires to be rid of the whole thing, to wash it away, wrestle with that to find justice ... something to sting him. All contend in her mind. She remains ambivalent about a payment; taking-money, for it seems too easy, for him. And tawdry, for her. How many others has he paid? Buying them all off. Ohh! ... That she saw signs of contrition irritates her, for she is sure he was calculating. And his presumption is insulting, again. She vents another cry, then rises and strides into the bathroom, where she wrenches on the hot water for a shower. As she undresses, she notices that the wall tiles depict a god and goddess, without clothes, half-enrapt in love as he leads her up through clouds above some islands. She cries out and spins away.

At the law office, talking with the same attorney to whom she spoke on the phone, she repeats her understanding that a trial is unlikely. The attorney confirms with a dour look, but then, with more sympathy, adds, "Unfortunately, it would be more problematic here than at home." Belle quietly expels exasperation; they both do. "So... a settlement?"

"We should contact his lawyers. I assume, given his position, that he has a firm, a phalanx of them, innumerable hoplites. We will tell them we plan to prosecute. It's the prescribed dance. They will offer some agreement in return, for not entering a complaint. We will say our client was seriously compromised, sustained physical and psychological injury, and she wants justice. They will point out there is little evidence. We will reply that she made a report the morning after to the Heraklion police, with evidence, and that her fellow passengers will also testify that his behavior resulted in similar assaults, and that those same passengers were shown her bruises and contusions. With this, they will suggest that to save everyone time and discomfort, they will offer some unusually generous settlement, and then we will go back and forth on that ... So, what do you think? Will something like that be acceptable, given that nothing entirely satisfactory is likely?"

Belle goes over this now too familiar ground – on and on it goes - then asks, "If that's the only possible outcome, what choice do I have?"

"We can press for prosecution ... but I'm afraid, frankly, that it will entail a certain amount of irritation, pain, and time. I don't suppose that you have a figure in mind, do you?"

"No ... What can one reasonably expect? What should be aimed at, to make an impact? Otherwise it's a mere slap on the wrist." And she rubs hers, still faintly sore.

"Because this person has means, deep pockets, and has a history of doing this, a substantial sum should be expected."

"Meaning?"

"I would say the range should be between three hundred thousand and a million three Euros. Possibly more."

Belle breathes. The figures really mean nothing to her. In fact, because it's blood money, they have little appeal, aside from paying for another trip over here, or her boys' college costs. She shakes her head. "I don't know ... It's only interesting to me because he must pay."

"We could find out his salary, and net worth ... in order to judge whether we're making a dent."

Belle nods unhappily. She tells the lawyer that she doesn't know what she wants to do, but understands that it makes sense to decide something before her flight tomorrow.

"Not necessarily. We have email, phones. No need to rush." And yet Belle is anxious to set some course that puts it all behind.

In her hotel room, she lies down and tries to reason what makes sense. She's been over it so many times. She wants to end it. Maybe just take the money and run. Plan on meeting the three women next summer for a week, then research her book if a contract comes through. Emptying her mind, she lies still. But ideas, on all these subjects, flow behind her eyes, tumbling over each other, and she can find no rest.

At length, she concludes that the only relief to be found is in reaching an agreement, and ending it. She's disappointed that she can imagine nothing else. She closes her eyes and wanders through the dark, endlessly empty sky. Then she reaches for the hotel phone and calls him.

He answers, though he seems to be with another person. Another man's throaty voice can be heard. She tells him she has not decided which option she may choose, but she will listen to his proposal.

He begins by saying that he will give to her a substantial sum, and that he would like to see her again, somewhere.

"Henry, I thought you got it, but you don't seem to. What if someone assaulted you, an even larger male, punched you up, made a homosexual pass, sodomized you, would you just shrug it off, ask for a few dollars and say, Hey, let's be friends? ... Would you go for that?"

There is silence on the other end, until she hears him say something to the other person. A door is closed. He comes back on. "No, of course not ... but Belle, I thought we got along, except for my huge blunder, my insensitivity ..."

"We talked, Henry. We shared a short time on your boat ... all very pleasant, but to imply there was something more, is delusional."

"I'm surprised ... I thought I sensed more."

"You're used to getting your way, as captain of your world."

"You have no idea ... I assure you it's not that simple. It's constant war."

"Well friendship is not war."

"I know ... I thought we had something."

She breathes, not inclined to repeat things.

"Well, okay ... what I propose is that we meet at your hotel at four. I will bring a letter which you can show your lawyers. I will wire a sum to your bank, if you'll provide the phone and account numbers, and we can talk about the Poseidon, for you all, next year ... How does that sound?"

She both wants to ask what sum he has in mind, and doesn't. Indeed she really doesn't want to know. Instead, she agrees to the four o'clock meeting.

Hanging up, she sees it's noon. What until then? A swim in the pool? ... Walk around ... the Parthenon again? Consult Athena? Maybe she'll have something to advise, although she's been strangely silent recently. It's annoying, this dealing with him, but it may soon be over. Perhaps she bears some responsibility, for agreeing to come on the boat, for allowing a goodnight kiss ... but neither was an open invitation ... He took advantage ... Christ! ... How can some of them still think that's okay? Think position and money grant license? Must women be so guarded? One could say that this is Nature, men ... but much has changed, leaving many of them behind. How could he think friendship is now possible? There, too, again, a trust was broken. A spasm of revulsion shakes her.

And so she goes out, taxiing to and walking up the broad pedestrian boulevard to the Parthenon. The visitors are sparse today. By the great columns, she finds herself whispering to Athena, who is at first unresponsive, but then possibly murmurs back. Is it the god, or herself? How can she know? Agitation scrambles her thoughts. Finally she hears her own voice counseling for quiet and calm; her ideas grow more distinct: the real cost to Henry will be a lonely life. For who could he really connect with? Much as will be the case with her husband, pursuing his assistant, a child, and ending up with no one. Athena is more subtle than men are prepared to recognize.

She returns, also, to the museum and looks at the sculptures of her mentor. There is no hint, in her physiognomy, of her fierce competitiveness, or desire for retribution – or her caring, in helping Odysseus reach home and slay the suitors. Instead, Belle reads patience, wisdom, reason, purity. Of course she was sculpted by a man, some dreamer, imagining a powerful but helpful young woman. In place of self-knowledge, equality, respect, men conjure fantasies, helpmates ... and then grow angry when those fantasies don't blossom as they imagined.

Back in the hotel lobby at four he is there, seeming serious yet attempting to smile, be friendly. "Did you have time to enjoy the afternoon?"

"I consulted with Athena."

He's not sure how to take this. "Was she helpful?"

"Of course. She is long experienced in these things, has known men good and bad." She smiles, which comes out more grimace-like. "You have a letter, and will call my bank?"

"Yes." And he reaches into his brief case and takes out an envelope. "If you will give me the phone number of your bank officer, I can call, while you read. There will be someone who can tell me where to wire the money, and then I'll call my bank and have it done. We should be able to get confirmation by this evening."

She feels her cheek quiver as she takes the letter, then hands him the bank officer's information. He moves off a ways, taking out his phone, as she sits to read. The letter is addressed to her and her representatives. It begins by stating that this is first an apology, for going beyond bounds, is secondly a restatement of his wish for friendship, and thirdly is evidence of his earnest hope in the payment described. The amount blurs in her mind; she cannot articulate the sum to herself. Somehow it seems ... obscene. Last, he promises to discuss the use of the Poseidon with all four women and to nail down a date for next summer.

On a second page a statement by her is addressed to him, to be signed by her, that she has accepted the payment, thereby ending any obligations owed by him to her. So ... this will end it, legally ... Is she prepared? She thinks about it, but then recalls the alternatives, the few, the pathetic. She sees that she must affix her signature to the original, and keep the copy for herself.

She looks up and around, once more feeling faint. His letter – the two pages – is more than an apology and compensation; it absolves him of any further responsibility ... It is also an appeal to her ... for, yes, friendship, or something. Her brain seems to pinch, hurt, under his tying these things together. Still pursuing ... She's almost inclined to rip it up. But it does offer closure. She can end it all.

Now on the far side of the atrium, she sees him standing, talking on his phone. She looks down as it suddenly occurs to her that he is alone, stocking his boat with women but not old friends. There may be none; he never mentioned any. Perhaps he is as wanting in this as she had been, until she met the three. But still the issue: Should she sign? There is no complete compensation likely for his crime ... Why does she feel guilty? The money? The breath-stealing sum? ... That she is giving in? ...

She notices that he has finished and is heading back. She rises and waits. Reaching her, he stands silently, attentively, to hear her response. Swallowing, she makes an effort to speak in a steady voice, "I will show this to my lawyers."

Somberly he accepts this. "Your banker said that the money should be in your account by the end of their day. You can confirm it on-line, either late tonight or tomorrow morning."

Avoiding his eyes, she feels her lip twisting.

"May I say something?" he asks. She meets his gaze but holds her mind away.

"As I've said, I enjoy you ... admire you ... I think we get along, if you can forgive me, and I apologize sincerely, deeply ... What I hope is, that in time, and I don't know whether that could be a week, a month, a year ... that we could begin again, in some sort of friendship. I know you have your complicated career and life, your two sons, but I hope that you will understand that we don't find very often another with whom we would like to share life. For me, this is an unexpected reprieve ... and I cannot let it go without doing everything I can ..."

Though their eyes meet, she feels her mind is blank; she can form no thoughts. He tries to read her reaction. "May I ask if you will consider this?"

She turns aside, staring at a table, then shakes her head. "I don't know ... I can hardly begin ..." Why has she not simply answered, no? Is it that she does not want to see his frown again, or begin another argument?

"... Well ... I understand. I do ... but my hope is that you will accept my apology ... and see, maybe, that what we could share might outweigh my misstep, my transgression ... Indeed I implore you to consider it. As I noted, we encounter only a certain number of these chances. It is my sense and my hope that it will become yours. " As he speaks with all sincerity, he becomes unsettled by her resistance. Yet he reminds himself that she is not easy, something he'd found attractive. It may take considerable time and perseverance. But then he hears her, as she hears herself, speaking, "You remember I am married ..."

"Yes, but you seemed unhappy ... as though nothing were left."

She puts the words out of her mind, however close they are to reality. She meets his gaze again. Exactly what to say now, she's not sure. But she is under no obligation to respond. Uncertain what else to add, she extends a hand, and he takes it, holds it for a moment in his. Then she remembers and tries to hand him the letter original before turning away to leave, but he reminds her, "I'm sorry but you must sign ..." and he takes out a pen and holds it for her. She hesitates, then looks down as she reassures herself that this will finally end it, wipe it away. What she sees is the table, the matter-of-fact table, unconcerned with her or her situation. The everyday things, watching disinterestedly through time ... distracting us from the important. She needs to free herself ... find the important: her work, her sons, her friends. Men were, for a period, but that is over. And so, to bring down the curtain on this stage, she reaches blindly for his pen, opens the folded original and bends down to the table ... the table. How many other signatures have been scribbled here? She signs, then straightens and hands it back to him, keeping the copy in one hand. He bows to her, and faintly she acknowledges. Then charged with emotion, feeling freed, released – all of this falling away from her – she turns and walks off, back toward the elevators. He watches hoping that she will look back, but she doesn't, eventually disappearing through the opening doors.

Upstairs, she calls the lawyer, but the woman has left for the day. She asks to be put through to her voicemail, and there leaves a message detailing what occurred. By accepting the money, she has agreed to end any complaint or possibility for legal action. She adds that by everyone's estimation, this is the best she could get. She does not mention how much the payment was for. The figure somersaults through her mind; she can neither stop it nor enunciate its sum. But the lawyer has no particular need to know. Belle says that the firm has her home address, at which to bill her. She thanks the woman for her assistance and support and hangs up.

In her room, she walks slowly between the bedroom and bath, glancing into the several mirrors. Without the lights on, in the late afternoon, she is a dark figure in the reflections, unknown and alone. Somehow the prospect of the money seems to detach her from herself and the life she knows. She needs her boys and her few friends. More immediately she needs to do something, swim in the pool, have a drink at the bar, dine early. She would like to call Marguerite but believes she's already en route home. She will go down to the pool, dive into the tranquil, blue water, as she dived off the Poseidon into the rolling swells ... before all of this. At that moment she had felt such excitement, such promise for the trip. Now it all seems smaller, clouded, shabby ... Glimpses of the islands come back, sunny, white, surrounded by the glimmering, ancient sea ... She pictures the long-ago ships, the sailors, the women... Athena ... the richness ... and yet, limitations too. Today, for people as fortunate as she, there is great potential, a thrilling array of possibilities ... and yet, she notices, or imagines, that on the rising and falling sea swells, something dulls them ... a widening, rainbow-colored slick of oil.

Sitting at his study desk, Wren stares down at the Times, at stories of mayhem and slaughter in the Middle East and Southern Asia, at continuing shootings and a bombing in this country – people frustrated, angry, intolerant ... deranged, exploding everywhere. And recently there was the report of CO_2 in the atmosphere reaching record levels. We know what to do and how to, about many of these issues, but we don't act. Different views and competing interests thwart solutions, as in marriage maybe, where one would think rational discussion would prevail between people who had loved each other. But anger and frustration supplant caring. There are no perfect unions, or people. It's not in us. Even Messena allied herself to poor companions ... husbands ... Maybe it's all we can do, try and move on.

He pictures Yan's house. Maybe he can convince him to go ahead; it's short sighted not to. Somebody can use it; they need a garage ... Kirce may change her mind ...

On another page of the paper, he reads that the changing chemistry of the oceans is killing marine life. Acidification ... And still we don't curtail emissions, enough. And so we may face the next great decline, or extinction. He closes his eyes, sees the image of the house in the field, and the barn beyond, floating in the grasses, fading in the summer heat ...

Eventually other desultory thoughts limp through his mind: Would the project's money have brought Belle and him together? Would it have changed things? He cannot imagine it. She doesn't forget or forgive; she no longer cares. Anger blocks discussion – across the country, around the world. Probably she needs a change; probably they both do. But what did Messena's email reply suggest? What should he do?

He leafs through his drawer, finds her number and calls. The phone rings and rings. Eventually an automated voice responds. He leaves a short message, saying he received her email, and that he will wait until her project becomes more manageable and his house is well under way.. She need not worry about him. He will be patient, until things clear, but then he will come. "I love you." He has spoken from deep within, even as he is aware that this may not be what she wants to hear.

Hanging up, he sits like a statue ... Is work all that he has? ... He hopes that Yan will go ahead. But gray premonitions glide near the ceiling. He looks away. What is he doing? What does his work contribute, what does it bring him or anyone? ... In many ways he is alone in the world, in his marriage; his boys will soon be off ... Only if the house is exciting, unique, will it be of worth ... Yes, she is there, but does she have room in her life, her heart? ... We're here only for a time ... Can she fit him in? Their shared passion? No point in a half-life. He should convey this to his boys: pursue a passion.

The phone rings. A tightness grips him. He almost decides not to answer, but that will only delay things. It's Yan, as he somehow expected. Yan's voice is gruff, husky, abrupt. He begins by saying he understands that Wren met with Kirce today. He wants to know what happened. Wren hears a secondary implication, as he inhales and describes the three alternative designs he showed her. She preferred the one he did. But then she began to express some misgivings about the town, saying she would prefer living near the water, somewhere. She acknowledged that he, Yan, does not enjoy the Hamptons. And so, after expressing her doubts, she said goodbye. He makes no mention of the invitation to swim, indeed doubts that it entered her calculus, as her discomfort with the town was palpable, paramount. Her parting seemed final. She'd lost any desire to build or be out here. And yet she left it to Yan to find his way to that decision.

For some seconds there is silence, until Yan emits a suppressed groan. "She said that you supported her ..."

"I told her that yours is a striking, dramatic, beautiful property and that the town is exciting and lively, offering many things ... but the two of you must decide what you want to do."

"But you agreed with her that the town is not for her?"

"Not at all ... To the contrary I told her there is much to enjoy here and that I would introduce you both to people, throw a party if you'd like. She is concerned that she knows no one, that she would be isolated."

"God ... we've been over this. Why can't she get it into her head? ... Did she say anything about my friends?"

"... Only that they were business associates, and that she hadn't grown close to them."

"Of course not. She only just met most of them. It's exasperating."

"I understand."

"It would have been better if you had not allowed that conversation."

"I'm sorry but it flowed unannounced out of our discussion of the drawings and the possibilities. It took me by surprise."

"You should have cut it off."

"I don't see how. You'd said that she was in charge ... I suspect that had I done so, it would only have added to her discontent. I encouraged her to try the town."

"Well, now she sounds disenchanted with you, as well as the town."

"I did what I could ..."

"Don't you know about selling clients? ... Ahh! ... I know she can be a little difficult ... She thinks she can seduce any listener over to her point of view. Did she try that?"

"No."

"Well ... now she doesn't even want to go out to our rental on the weekends. Maybe she embarrassed herself."

"... I didn't see anything of that ..."

"I should have come. I might have quashed or headed-off her objections. She doesn't know the place."

"I hoped that you two would discuss it and reach some understanding that would allow you to go ahead."

"Yeah well, now that she's got her dander up, she won't say yes to anything. It's really screwed up some business arrangements I've made."

"I'm sorry."

"'Sorry' doesn't cut it."

"I urged her to give it time. I would still urge you both to give it time. I think the house and the town would grow on her."

"Well she's thrown all her hair-brained objections into it. She may have pushed me too far. This may be the final straw …"

"Do you want to have the three of us meet and discuss what's available here?"

"She says she's finished. It sounds to me that she's blaming you in part."

"We had two meetings. At the first she seemed excited. Then, halfway through the second one, she voiced her doubts. That was pretty much it. I certainly wasn't looking to scuttle the project."

"Well … whatever the case, you have. It's off, at least for now."

"… Entirely?"

"Yes! Don't you get it? She says she hates the place now. I thought you would help sell her on it. Instead you play the supportive confidant."

"Yan, you're misconstruing things. I told her I would introduce her to people, throw a party to meet people."

"Well ... damn! This really screws things up ... big time."

"... I was looking forward to it."

"Well ... you should have called me."

"She said you were busy, unreachable. I hoped together you would arrive at a different conclusion."

"Yeah well ..."

"What about a meeting? The three of us?"

"... I explained ... the bloody ... Of course I'll go back to her ... but she's stubborn as all hell ... Maybe I have to make it very clear to her ... what's at stake here ... but when she's like this, reason never prevails ... Listen ... Maybe something will happen, but I ... I'll send you a check for the drawings if you'll mail them into my office."

"Do you want to possibly use them elsewhere?"

"Where?! I have no time to go running around searching for some other little town with culture. And I'm certainly not considering the Hamptons. No, for now this is it. Listen ... I've got to run. I guess she screwed it up for both of us. Seems like ... Oh, I don't know ..."

"... What?"

"I should have warned you, but I thought she was sold."

"Me too."

"Well ... I guess that's it. Send me the drawings, and I'll ... Gotta go."

"Yup ..."

Wren hears Yan expel exasperation as he hangs up. When he has put his phone down, he sits in the darkness ... in blank finality ... ... The project has dissolved ... His mind has emptied; he floats in darkness.

Eventually he reaches for something; maybe he will be able to use the ideas in the future, somewhere, another project. Something may come ...

Unfortunately Belle ... and the boys will be disappointed, disillusioned. He stares down at his desk, at the designs. He imagines his head sinking onto them, imagines gliding through the round rooms. He closes his eyes ... Zeus's great face slowly fills his sight, eyes pale, baleful. Wren stares back through the dim light, feels anger growing, sees it contorting that face. He reaches up; it does not move; he punches it, several times, but feels nothing; the image recedes ... Now he glimpses Iscaria running away through trees ... Escaping? ... Had he misunderstood? ... And yet Messena followed ... Will she vanish too?

As she sits in the back seat of the limo speeding toward home, Belle thinks about the boys, imagines their smiles when they meet, their hugs ... Wren's gray face. What will he have to report? She finds that she has no expectations ... and little interest. Somewhere there must be some engaging, capable, thoughtful man. But even Marguerite's fiancé didn't sound all that entrancing. Diplomats can become full of themselves, if they aren't to begin with. And she's had enough of that.

It's dark when the limo pulls into the driveway. The house lights are on, even the outside ones; someone remembered she would be arriving. The driver carries her bag to the door; she signs the charge slip, then turns, faces her home. She knocks and presses the handle, pushing in.

Wren comes quickly up, sees her bag on the walk and slips past to retrieve it, saying, "Hello ... Welcome back ... How was it?"

She breathes, and looks around. When he sets the bag down next to her, neither of them moves for an embrace. He does lean to kiss her cheek, which she allows, looking past him and asking, "The boys here?"

A sense of chill and distance pass through him, but he lets it go, telling her, "In their rooms, doing summer reading, I hope. I'll call them, but I wanted to say hello ... How was it?"

She sifts through replies she had considered. And yet something prevents her. Instead she sends a nod. At first he had seemed pale to her, without excitement or life, but now she sees that he has gotten some sun, seems healthy ... flushed. But it's sadness he's experiencing, constricting his chest. Yet he sees no point in expressing it. Instead he tries again, "Surely it must have been good."

"It was lovely," she pronounces quickly and with finality.

He waits for more, even as he sees that no more is coming . He twists away a little, not sure what to say.

She releases a breath and looks through the house. It feels both good ... and depressing to be home. This is it? Her home, her life? Her spirits fall ...Yes, outlines of a different life pass behind her thoughts; she has options, money; there is no point in enduring the silence that has grown between them – the lack of love ... Already there are plans ... But now she wants to call to the boys ... then remembers, "And how's the project? Did you meet?"

"We did ..."

"And? ..."

He waits for her eyes to come to his, realizing that he need say nothing, that its collapse will not surprise her. Nor will the arrival of a few small projects appease her. All will only affirm her view of him.

They look at each other. She sees the reality, that it has fallen, failed ... She notices darkness crossing his brow. Despite anticipating something of this, she feels a disappointment, a weight, sink through her, dragging her back into the past. Yes, things haven't changed ... nor will they.

But then, uncertain what to say, she circles the hallway, vaguely searching for something brighter – anything ... "How was Athens?"

He watches her closely and nods, that it was good.

"And Delphi too?"

"Yes ... surprisingly ... infinitely ..."

"Infinitely?" she pronounces, unable to interpret it. She waits for an explanation, but then expels that hope too. Instead she remembers she'd been happy to leave that crowded city ... until ... and yet ... she had fought him off ... won contrition, apology ... payment. She feels a sense of triumph ... rising from a distance, across the sea. An unmistakable confidence has been building. She reacted, responded ... found a new way ... means and friends ... with whom she confided, consulted, who revealed their own trials ... Their conversation and revelations brought them together, enabled them to enjoy the cruise, the islands, each other – even love parts of it, travelling back through the centuries ... The memories summon excitement, life; she sees them walking up to the Grand Castle on Rhodes, walking through the Patmos monastery where St. John wrote ... The trip is even more gratifying in retrospect ... And the book may come;

she may return ... a reward ... And her new friends are closer, worldly, humorous, perceptive, open ... eager for adventure ... beyond those here who seem caught in convention. Marguerite, in particular, is stimulating, alive. But she likes them all: individual, resilient ... open to what can come.

She thought Wren might have done something of interest, something to report, but evidently not. So neither will she mention the dark occurrence. She looks around; the place is as it was. She breathes, before she announces softly but without hesitation, "... I may return ... I may have a project to do ... a book ... and friends to meet ... a new approach ..."

A new approach? A book? ... He searches her, but she does not elaborate. Surprise escapes him, "Return?" But he sees that though some vivid thought holds her, she is not about to explain. As she gazes around once more, the book enlarges in her mind; she inhales, and then pronounces, "... I thought of doing a history of the islands, the influences each wave brought, if I can get a publisher, and I think I can. So if I do, I will need to research it over there. And will connect with those friends in the summer. And maybe before." To herself she whispers, 'Everything may change.'

He waits for her to go on, but she does not. And so he turns away a little, wondering if she found a lover. The captain? But then quite unintentionally he murmurs, "And so may I ... return."

From her remove, she feels annoyance. Did he not hear? Is he getting even? She glances at him. His face is smooth; he is dreaming. "I doubt it would interest you," she tells him.

Blankly, locked in glimpses of possible futures, they look at each other. Their brief statements seem to have silenced the other, until suddenly, and unpremeditated, he adds, "Maybe together ... you and I." He does not know from whence this came, and seems as stunned as she, as he waits for her response.

She feels a frown suffuse her brow, darkening it, like the room around. Why has he said this? Did he not understand? ... She turns away a little. Is he trying to limit her, confine her in some way? That ancient male impulse ... She looks around, considering conflicting replies. But she does not want to discuss, or fall back into their former, unhappy way. She finds him again, to read what he is thinking.

Watching her, he sees her irritation, the wrestling, her face growing hard, pinched ... His proposal has stirred something, but not acceptance. That is clear. He feels the emptiness between them.

Now, as she finds his dispirited eyes, she says, with some disembodiment, "I found what I want to do, how I want to live ... maybe eventually moving over there ..."Her eyes stare past him into the dark.

At first he shrinks from this, her assertion and its implications. But then they settle over him, silent, still ... shrouding memories ... ancient structures ... Seconds pass as they look unseeing toward the other. Should he press her, suggest they try to work things out, despite frail hope? But he sees, and feels, no way forward.

Vague versions of the future form in their minds; strange, god-like figures float about them. Life for them has changed. Both may go in new directions. Why would either want the same? he wonders. She offers no encouragement, no interest in exploring together. Should he offer something? ... Yet she has long resisted such overtures. "Males dictating" has been her recurring response, her eternal vexation. She will not be controlled, limited, or imposed upon. And seeing this, he searches elsewhere ... Words from the ancient tale echo through his mind: *"Sing in me muse, and through me tell the story ..."* – *yes*, their story, in which change has arrived, as it does for many. The nature of things ... Individuals drawn together, holding for a time, then wearing away. Perhaps that is what Athena represents: the sides of woman, kindness, intelligence, tenderness, insight ...

independence, tied to no one, free to pursue life as she sees it – her several sides, which the Greeks observed, understood, and immortalized in her.

And so both will seek new life. He must seek connection through his work, his art, or conversation with that one. For though no hero he, still the dreams she awakened fill his heart. And if she is not real, still her ideals have been implanted. New stories are unfolding; their marriage is at its end. But now, through these thoughts, he sees that Belle is shifting, folding her arms in front, bringing hands to elbows. Lips parting, she seems about to speak, but then memories of Athena's words, likewise fill her mind: *"Oh Father of us all, that man is in the dust indeed, and justly."* ... *"Upon Penelope, most worn in love and thought, Athena cast a glance like a grey sea, lifting her."*

Yes, as the goddess offered Penelope and Odysseus help and hope, so for them she suggests new paths, and they will follow. He recognizes the familiar, distant light filling Belle's eyes, pulling at her features. If it there resides, then she is right; there is no point, no prospect. He had attempted to reach out, but she had turned away, spurning his efforts, tentative though they were. What is left? Nothing in her eyes or words, no shared view of what life might be ... Their views have diverged. Change is Nature's and the gods' way. Life is rise, flourish, struggle, decline ...

How was it that Odysseus and Penelope sustained their love? ... By not seeing each other for twenty years? ... Untrammeled by the everyday, the differences? ... While he believes he reached out, he felt no hand, nor can he convince her when she seems so set. The love they had has worn away. Nothing left to reach for. An emptiness, a vague memory ... And what now? ... With luck, rebirth, someone. Belle must want love too. He'd hoped it would be Messena; it may still may be, but she raised doubts. Found another? No, he trusts her. She would tell him. Maybe simply overwhelmed ... Or has she seen the difficulties? ... She mentioned only her project. Is there more? He cannot know ... Patience is what she counseled. Time will tell. And yet clouds of darkness surround his heart. For a brief time he had re-found light, life; ideas, communication, love ... All danced ...

When they joined together years ago, Belle and he brought eagerness, hope ... and much talk. Now none survives. So both must seek once more. Faint outlines of the ancient temples fill his sight, and like the wanderer making his way over the seas, through storms and darkness, toward an uncertain land, each must stroke to find the next shore, both asking a god's help ... Yet once more he wavers ... Beseech her? ... But her cold countenance stares back. There needs be some glimmer to appeal to, to reach for, but none lights her brow. Both have work and dreams; both seek exploration, expression, passion ... but no longer together, for they have drifted apart over the waves.

His mind and heart reach out to that white city where he glimpsed something new. He glides above the temple to fair Parthenos, and over the great statue of Promachus, both built so long ago ... And then he is descending over Lycabettos, circling slowly down to a familiar street, moving along a familiar hall, to her door. She may not be home, may have moved, married ... or returned to Olympus ... or never have existed at all, outside his heart ... and George's ... Yet all hope is now focused there in her echoing the beauty of Nature, the harmony of music. And he must embrace it all, whether she waits for his return or has evaporated in the sun. He glimpses fleeting images of her, hears cries from the centuries, from lives blown past in the blustering, whistling wind. He envisions flooding faces, lives and their dreams, rising into the pantheon, spinning with joy, among them his boys, before lifting away, looking back, wondering what each had. Resilience, belief in the good illumine the land as our robust, fierce, exquisite existence plays out.

So Belle and he must move on, travel, search ... despite uncertainty, acknowledging the incredible richness of which we are part. He may question the wisdom of going, may list the many doubts, and yet his heart is pounding with her memory, her grace, the maiden, high and good, bringing her kindness, embodying the perfection of Nature that has long moved him. He whispers her name, and in doing so, realizes suddenly that without the house in the field, he is free ... free to go ... to put aside all excuses, to go seek her, who awakened his heart, now beating vigorously, filling him with song. He must go, come what may, fail though he might ... to help her possibly with her work, but above all, to meet and talk ... This is where life has brought the two of them, this new connection of intensity – a gift and a risk ... It is what those two women showed him, that he must try, must reach for the life he imagines and they conveyed, reach for the passion of life which has reawakened in him, and Belle, bestowing new and greater awareness, each having been sensitized by, and to, what is and what can be. A new beginning ... And even if he doesn't meet her, or find work over there, the trying may in itself be ... worthy ... For in acknowledging and listening to his heart, in pursuing passion long held, giving his all, after much recent wandering, he will finally and fully join with the life-giving current that those women revealed is Nature's vibrant stream.

THE END